Gawain had kissed his share of maids, and more, but this was different.

Maybe it was because his nerves were raw after nearly losing her, or he was far too lonely, but he was utterly without defence.

The press of her soft lips was warm, filled with the lingering essence of woman and magic. And the spice did not end with her taste—it was in who she was. Her teeth nipped at his lower lip, inviting him to explore. Gawain didn't need prompting. As her lips parted, he made a conquest of her sweet, silky mouth. Tamsin moaned slightly, the note of hunger urging him on.

Once permission had been granted, he pushed forward, savoring everything she gave. The first spark of passion had been physical, the effect of her beauty and the closeness of their bodies for so many hours. But beyond that was her courage, and the sheer will that had made her survive.

Sharon Ashwood is a novelist, desk jockey, and enthusiast for the weird and spooky. She has an English literature degree but works as a finance geek. Interests include growing her to-be-read pile and playing with the toy graveyard on her desk. Sharon is the winner of the 2011 RITA® Award for Paranormal Romance. She lives in the Pacific Northwest and is owned by the Demon Lord of Kitty Badness.

Books by Sharon Ashwood

Harlequin Nocturne

Possessed by a Warrior
Possessed by an Immortal
Possessed by a Wolf
Possessedy by the Fallen
Enchanted Warrior

Harlequin Nocturne Cravings

Lord Dragon's Conquest
Valkyrie's Conquest

ENCHANTED WARRIOR

—

SHARON ASHWOOD

HARLEQUIN® NOCTURNE™

Recycling programs
for this product may
not exist in your area

ISBN-13: 978-0-373-00963-3

Enchanted Warrior

Copyright © 2016 by Naomi Lester

Printed in U.S.A.

www.Harlequin.com

Dear Reader,

Mythic heroes and paranormal romance go together like chocolate and peanut butter. Add equal helpings of history and fairy tale, swaggering brawlers and sweet-talking ladies' men, and behold—we have the men of Camelot.

King Arthur and his knights are endlessly adaptable, the characters appearing in stories dating back to ancient Celtic times. They've lasted because their essential nature speaks to us. Lancelot's nobility, Gawain's deep loyalty, and Arthur's capacity for hope and justice still have plenty of appeal. The once and future king, poised to rescue us all in our hour of need, is the very stuff of romance.

But how to bring Camelot into the modern day? This story first came to me when I was a young girl visiting the great cathedrals in England. The still, silent effigies of the knights and ladies stirred my imagination. What if I had the power to wake them and make them rise from atop their shadowy tombs? All kinds of adventures occurred to me—and apparently waited for the right moment to become a book!

Indeed, what if? What if the dark forces that haunted the Camelot of yore followed the knights here? And who but my favorite, the fiery and intensely loyal Sir Gawain, would be first on the scene?

Happy reading!

Sharon Ashwood

To Jane, Sol, Lee and Shereen, who hold the prize
for reading my typos week after month after year.
You are steadfast and invaluable.

Prologue

Once upon a time—so much begins that way. What we forget is that once upon a time can be an ending, too. This was a little of both.

Long ago there were many races that walked the world: humans, dragons, changelings, fae and countless others. It was the era of King Arthur and his knights of Camelot, a shining time that rode out of dreams and into the pages of well-thumbed books.

Back then the men of the Round Table were the pinnacle of knighthood, both in chivalrous acts and the might of their swords. They numbered one hundred and fifty of the hardest, the most brutal and the most fearless of men. Their purpose was to defend the realms of mortal kind against those with supernatural power.

At the height of Camelot's glory, there came a war against the demons, led by Arthur and his sorcerer, Merlin. All the peoples—mortals, fae and even the witches—banded against the hellspawn under Camelot's flag.

After a mighty battle, the demons fled the earth, but the magic Merlin used was too costly. The witches and fae were badly injured and they fled the mortal realms, swearing vengeance on Arthur and the humans he had promised to protect—even if it took hundreds of years to regain enough strength to fight.

With great sorrow, Arthur turned to his faithful knights, asking who among them would risk everything to protect the mortal world. Every one knelt and swore his loyalty. So Merlin cast a spell, turning the knights to stone statues upon their empty tombs. They would awaken, fierce and in their prime, when evil rose once more.

After that, Camelot vanished like a mist in an unforgiving wind. But in an ending there is always the seed of a new day.

That time is upon us.

Once upon a time is now.

Chapter 1

Tamsin Greene blew out her breath to ease the tension squeezing her ribs. Her sigh made a cloud of mist that floated upward to the shadowy stone ceiling of the Church of the Holy Well. The ancient English structure had been relocated to the Medievaland Theme Park decades ago, but it seemed to hold part of the past inside it, as if time itself had seeped into the stone. Or maybe that was just the frigid temperature. November in the Pacific Northwest wasn't a snowy deep freeze, but the damp air held a savage bite. At first she'd been annoyed at having to wear a costume to her workplace, but now she was glad of the floor-length gown of green wool. She should have sewn herself a cloak, too.

She told herself her shivers were just the result of the cold. What kind of threat could there be at Medievaland Theme Park, anyway? Even in winter, it was a place for family fun, with costumed performers, games, feasts and make-believe. The worst that could happen was a stomach-ache from too many jalapeño Dragon Fries. The only thing remotely serious—or truly medieval—about the park was the church where she stood now, and normally the old stones echoed with the holiday mood.

But today was different. Tamsin rubbed her arms as the feeling of being stalked crept behind her on stealthy paws. Although a glance confirmed she was alone in the church, fresh wariness settled in her belly. Tamsin turned slowly, senses probing.

Nine times out of ten, being a witch meant nothing more than having a knack with cold remedies and some very odd family dinners, but once in a while her sixth sense was useful. She scanned the space, feeling first the layers of history that shimmered in the air, then the small living things that ran and squeaked in the walls. There was ancient magic sleeping there, but it was too old and dormant for her to understand its purpose. And beyond that…

She probed just a little more before she snatched her psychic senses back, all too aware there were creatures that would sniff out spells and come looking. In the past months, victims—witches and humans both—had been turning up dead, their souls ripped from their bodies. Tamsin wasn't a coward, but that was enough to spook anyone who was far away from the protection of her family and coven.

Habit made her rub the delicate vine tattoo that circled her left wrist—the mark of the Shadowring witches. It should have given her comfort, but it only reminded her how isolated she was. An icy chill rippled down her spine. She spun, reacting to a sound she'd felt more than heard. A movement of air. A phantom footfall. No one but a witch would have caught it. Tamsin's senses strained until they ached. *Nothing.*

She stood perfectly still, nervous sweat trickling down the small of her back. Light slanted through the stained glass, creating an otherworldly atmosphere. There were crowds outside, but the thick walls blocked the noise. The echoing silence made her feel incredibly small and alone.

That did it. As much as Tamsin hated to admit it, she was giving herself a case of the jitters. Time to stand on the porch for a while, where she could see plenty of people. She started for the door.

Huge hands grabbed her from behind, pulling her backward until she collided with a rock-hard chest. Tamsin inhaled, about to scream, but a palm clamped over her mouth. A moment later, the man's free arm grasped her middle. Tamsin lunged forward, but his grip was an iron bar. Her next move was to kick back, aiming for the man's knee. She missed, catching only his shin with the soft sole of her boot. He grunted and pulled her against him so tightly she could barely breathe.

"Don't," he said, the word clipped and cold.

Tamsin froze, going utterly still. Whoever this was, his psychic shields were so powerful he'd been completely hidden from her scan. After fretting about evil creatures stalking witches, she was too scared to reach for her magic. Every instinct warned her this stranger would not tolerate further defiance. This was a professional. A predator. A true threat. She knew it on a level so primitive it was coded into her DNA.

Her obedience seemed to work, because the hand clamped over her mouth slowly moved away. He tasted of salt, sweat and man. He hadn't used weapons to overpower her, just brute strength. That show of confidence made him seem all the more deadly.

"You will not cry out." His words had traces of a brogue—

Scottish, perhaps. His deep, masculine voice vibrated through the line where their bodies touched and sank into her bones.

"Please," she said, her voice barely above a whisper. "What do you want?"

"Turn around."

The arm locked about her loosened, allowing her to move but not to escape. Tamsin shrank away as far as she could, the heat of his body a sharp contrast to the cool November air.

"Turn," he repeated. "I want to see your face when I question you."

Tamsin obeyed, sliding within the circle of his arm. It put their faces barely twelve inches apart, and that was only because he was so tall. Her first instinct was to avoid eye contact, to rebel at least in that small way, but curiosity won. She snatched a glance from under her lashes.

She froze all over again as he nailed her in place with a brilliant blue gaze. He was younger than she'd expected—maybe in his late twenties—and handsome enough that she forgot to breathe. His face had strong bones, the features bold and almost sensual. Heat rose to her cheeks as her insides curled into a protective ball. He was far too magnetic, far too *there* for comfort.

He studied her face a moment longer, his gaze filled with bold assessment. It finally broke when the corners of his mouth quirked. "You are the historian who is supposed to explain this place to visitors, Tamsin Greene?"

Tamsin cleared her throat. "Yes. How did you…?"

He gave a pointed look at the name badge pinned to her dress, and she flushed more deeply. He made a noise of amusement. "Historians are meant to be old men in robes and soup-stained beards. A golden-haired sylph is a pleasant surprise."

"Hey, that's sexist—"

"You may call me Gawain," he interrupted, as if he had no time to waste. He had an oddly formal way of speaking, as if English wasn't his mother tongue. "I do not intend to hurt or rob you. I simply want answers. Keep that in mind and we will go our separate ways in peace."

There was enough arrogance in the statement to break the spell of his overpowering presence. Gawain was roughly dressed in jeans and a dark green T-shirt beneath a battered leather jacket. He had a few days' growth of beard and a mass of curling dark hair long enough to brush his collar. In truth, he looked half-wild. She stepped away, putting more distance between them, and felt the press of the wall against her back. The cold stone sent a chill up her spine.

Her neck aching with tension, Tamsin forced herself to nod. None of this made sense. "If you want information, why not just ask? You don't need to scare me half to death."

His eyes narrowed. "I have enemies. I never know what face they wear. Thus far, you have not attacked. Perhaps you are what you seem."

Tamsin felt her pulse jump with alarm as she swallowed against the dryness of her throat. The man was a paranoid lunatic. "What do you want to know?"

"There should be tombs here," he said in that same impatient manner. "Where did they go?"

Gawain's stare penetrated right through her, boring deep into private places she barely admitted to herself. It was too much, especially from an utter stranger. He advanced a step, closing the gap between them again. The movement was almost a glide, showing the perfect balance of someone trained to use his body. Whether he meant it or not, it was intimidating and—she freely admitted this went against all common sense—incredibly sexy.

Tamsin held up her hands in a placating gesture. "Which

tombs are you talking about? There is a lot of statuary in this place, and much of it's been moved to make room for the exhibits."

His eyes flashed with impatience. Without warning, he pulled her into the center of the church, his strides long enough that she was forced to trot. Rough calluses grazed her skin when he finally let her go, and she automatically rubbed the spot where his fingers had been. The guy was clearly used to working with his hands.

He pointed toward the center of the floor. "They were right here. Look around you. The sleeping guardians are absent."

Tamsin hesitated, unwilling to take her eyes off him. Then she complied, viewing the place with a historian's eye. This wasn't a typical church by any stretch, seeming to adhere to no defined period and no typical design. The main area was a large, perfect circle with a ring of black marble slabs set into the floor. Tamsin knew from nineteenth century sketches that each slab had supported a tomb topped with the effigy of a sleeping knight. In the middle was a space for a larger monument guarded by enormous stone lions. The beasts had many symbolic meanings, but the basic message was clear—the knights who slept there were sworn to protect, even beyond the gates of death.

And now the army of knights was missing. Tamsin made a slight noise of understanding. "You're right, there are some pieces gone."

Gawain was silent for a moment, that hot blue gaze considering her from head to toe until it came to settle on her mouth. For a moment, Tamsin's heart pounded with tension, a push-pull of attraction and wariness making her skittish. She'd seen that look on men about to kiss her.

Then, just as suddenly, he turned away. "There were

one hundred and fifty knights buried in the church. Ten here, and the remainder in the crypt."

Tamsin shook her head. "The crypt was filled in when the main structure was moved from England."

He closed those startling blue eyes and ducked his head, almost as if she'd struck him. "By God's bones," he muttered, so low that she barely heard.

Still, the old oath made her catch her breath. "I'm sorry. Did you have ancestors buried there?"

"No." He took a shaking gulp of air, staring again at the empty space. "Where did they go?"

"I think they're on loan to different places. Museums. Universities."

"Scattered." His jaw muscles flexed, as if he clenched his teeth. His dark mood was gathering like a storm. "I need the exact locations."

Tamsin cast a glance toward the door, wondering if she could escape. "I don't know those details."

"Then you will find out." The words were hard, but beneath them there lurked pain and need.

Tamsin froze, still staring at the gray day outside the door. Right then, in that brief moment, he slipped under her emotional guard. She hadn't—not for one instant— forgotten that he had crept up on her, eluding even her magical senses. But now she could feel his grief and desperation, and it was impossible not to respond.

Her power opened again, almost of its own accord. He was no longer trying to hide, and she could touch his words, touch him, with her inner senses. She'd expected a lunatic. What she found instead was enough to raise the hair along her nape. This man was a killer, brutal and steeped in violence. More than that, he was surrounded by danger.

He *was* danger.

"I need your help," he said, making it a quiet demand.

Before she could answer or turn back to him, he reached out, laying rough, warm fingers against her cheek. It was gentle, almost a caress, but he had her rattled. She jumped, gathering her power to defend herself. "Don't touch me!"

The instant her magic rose to strike back, his mouth dropped open and he pulled away as if she'd stung him. He recovered in a heartbeat, though now he was clearly wary.

He grabbed her wrist, glaring at the tattoo as if he hadn't noticed it before. "Witch," he said in a low, threatening growl.

Tamsin turned cold at the word. Most thought witches were extinct, and the covens preferred things that way. But her temper was roused, and she pulled away, heat mounting in her cheeks. "Felt that, did you? I think you've got a touch of the blood yourself. You certainly have impressive shields."

"No." He said it with fierce finality. All trace of softness was gone from his face, reducing it to bloodless, harsh angles. "Now you *will* tell me what I want to know."

"I don't know where the tombs are," she snapped. "I've already tried to locate some of the artifacts that should be in the church, but the old owner died and the information was lost. What paper records they have here are a mess. That's why the new owners have hired me—to figure all this out."

Silence hung heavy between them, and his face darkened again, promising thunder. "Then have answers for me the next time we meet."

"And why would I do that for you?" Her temper was up and the words out before she could stop herself. Her gut knotted, bracing for the backlash.

"Because scholars like riddles, witchling, and there is

a cost if you fail to find the answer." Gawain wheeled and headed for the door.

Alarmed, Tamsin followed only to see him clear the steps in one graceful leap.

"Wait!" What consequences? How did he know about witches, anyway? And what was the big deal about the tombs? But by then, Gawain had disappeared into the throng, gone as fast as he'd burst into her universe.

Urgently needing to sit, Tamsin sank to the cold steps, suddenly shaking. "By Merlin's pointed hat," she muttered, and wondered if historians ever got hazard pay.

Chapter 2

Flushed with temper, Gawain stormed away from the Church of the Holy Well. He rounded the edge of a green-and-gold pavilion and slipped into the stream of foot traffic passing by—or rather, he tried to. Business had picked up in the theme park and crowds filled the pathways, slowing progress to a crawl. Bright tents and fluttering pennons conjured a vision of the past—but it was an image distorted by a fractured mirror. Medievaland was nothing like the world Gawain remembered.

He cursed, shouldering his way through a knot of tourists. He was a knight of the Round Table and friend and relation to the great Arthur of Camelot. He'd sacrificed everything when he'd agreed to this mission—his family, friends, rank and authority—but it had been the right thing to do. The men and women of this present day were innocents who had never seen actual monsters. If he did his job properly, they would stay that way.

However, to use a modern phrase, sometimes his job sucked. Today, it sucked more than usual because his entire quest was in ashes. The tombs were gone, and they were key to stopping Camelot's enemies. Gawain had heard whispers of witches and fae plotting in the shadows. The doomsday that Arthur had foreseen—and that had inspired the entire plan to put the Round Table into the stone sleep—was almost upon them.

Worse, the information he needed to find the tombs was in the hands of a very pretty witch who inspired thoughts of bedchamber revelry. Tamsin Greene—a witch's name if there ever was one—was a fair beauty, long legged and slender with a silver-blond braid that fell to her waist. Most would call her beautiful—exquisitely so—but that description missed the best part of her. The young woman's big brown eyes had been cautious and bold by turns, as challenging as a clever swordsman testing his guard. Everything about her had stirred his blood until he'd felt her power and seen the mark on her wrist. It meant she was a sworn member of a group of witches, bound to them by blood and magic.

The situation could not get more complicated. He half believed her claims of ignorance, although it could not be a coincidence that he'd found a witch on duty at the spot where the huge stone tombs had mysteriously vanished. No, lovely as Tamsin was—and lonely as he was—witches were dangerous. Gawain knew that firsthand. His own mother had been the worst.

Tamsin's words came back to him with the cold chill of a nightmare: *I think you've got a touch of the blood yourself.* That was his horror and his shame. He'd spent a life in service to his king, spilling his witch-tainted blood over and over in an effort to cleanse it. Five minutes in the company of the little historian, and she'd found his flaw. Ten, and he might have been dragged down into the claws of sorcery once more, a corrupted victim of his bloodline unable to control his own intrinsic evil.

Gawain strode with his head down so he didn't have to look around. A juggler passed by, then a foam dragon wearing a sandwich board that advertised a joust. All the employees were in cheap costumes, some even sporting fake crowns, as if they were kings and queens of the hot dog stands. There was a dread fascination to it all, as if history had experienced a terrible accident.

"I can't make up my mind if this is a logical place to see a knight of Camelot, or a peculiar one." The voice was as cool and precise as a honed blade.

Gawain froze, every muscle readying for a fight. Then he saw the speaker, and his alarm turned to a cautious surprise. "Angmar of Corin."

"The same." The figure raised his hands, showing he was unarmed. "I come in peace."

Angmar was dressed in jeans and a thick sweater and leaning against one of the faux-rustic pillars supporting the thatched roof of a concession stand. The modern clothes made Gawain blink. Angmar was one of the faery folk, so tall and thin that he was almost gaunt. His skin was a warm brown that contrasted sharply with bright green eyes and long white hair. Though his face was young, something in his eyes spoke of centuries past.

The fine hairs on Gawain's neck rose. Even in the chaos of the crowded fairground, he could feel Angmar's power. It was as different from the pretty witch's as a broadsword was from a kitchen knife, and the fae—once allies—were now sworn enemies of Camelot.

Angmar narrowed his eyes and tapped his chin with

a long forefinger. "Surely you're not here for the bouncy castle."

Gawain gave a bitter laugh. "Maybe Medievaland suits me."

With a faint smile, Angmar closed the distance between them. "You are a prince of Lothian and the Orkney Isles. You're above all this."

For a moment they studied each other, both outsiders caught in a world utterly different from where they belonged. Gawain had never known Angmar well. Fae lived by different rules and rarely came to Arthur's court, but finding him here created unexpected common ground.

"I thought your kind had gone to the Hollow Hills and left the mortal world behind," said Gawain.

"We came back—and so, apparently, did you." Angmar straightened, pushing his hands into his pockets in a curiously casual gesture. His tone was cordial, as if discussing the weather. "I've been watching the church. The fae know that Merlin bespelled the knights of Camelot into an enchanted sleep. It was a clever spell Merlin wove, and a daring move by your king. Especially daring as he had just ordered Merlin into exile. A bit like arguing with your barber during a shave."

Gawain didn't answer. He remembered the day the spell was cast: lying on the cold tomb, shivering as he waited to be turned to stone. Remembered the crushing weight of his lungs as they froze in place. Remembered the clawing terror of suffocation, of the sudden savage need to escape just as his consciousness winked out. He sucked in a deep breath, barely repressing a shudder.

Angmar watched his expression with open curiosity, looking away only when a pair of roughhousing boys shoved their way past. "It's long past time for the Round Table to awake. Where are your brothers in arms?"

"Why? Are the fae so impatient to take revenge on us that they sent you to make a wake-up call?"

"Merlin's spell injured us more than you know," said Angmar, his voice now tinged with anger. "But I'm not here to discuss that. I have a warning for you. Assemble your fellow knights, because LaFaye and Mordred are on the move. The war Arthur foresaw is here."

Gawain flinched. King Arthur's vile stepsister, Morgan LaFaye, had brought Camelot to its knees. Her chief conspirator had been her son, Mordred. Both were powerful, with witch and fae blood mixed in their veins.

"What is their interest in this fight, besides an opportunity to cause chaos?" Gawain said, tension ruffling the hair at his nape. "How is this war connected to them?"

They fell into step, wandering shoulder to shoulder down the pathway between the booths. The sweet scent of frying dough curled through the air. Gawain's mouth watered, but he ignored the hunger gnawing his gut.

"You *have* been asleep." Angmar cast him a narrow glance. "After you and your companions turned to stone, Morgan LaFaye staged a coup and took the crown of Faery."

"She did what?" Gawain snarled.

"It's not so strange as you may think. Her father was one of us." Angmar frowned. "Afterward, she bided her time for centuries, consolidating her hold on the throne. Ten years ago, she began plotting a campaign against the mortal realms. Then a few months ago, she gave the final order to infiltrate this world. She claims she wants justice, but I say she simply wants more power."

Angmar's tale explained why Gawain had risen when he did—probably it was the same moment when the first of the fae had touched mortal ground. "Those are evil tidings."

"It gets worse. She's put Mordred in charge of the campaign," said Angmar.

Pure fury surged through Gawain, robbing him of sight for an instant. LaFaye was bad, but Mordred was a snake without conscience. He was also Gawain's cousin—proving one could never pick one's relations.

Angmar went on. "Mordred is using stealth, not armies, and his first priority is finding the tombs to stop the Round Table from rising. You need to find your friends and wake them at once."

"By all the saints!" Gawain's vision went red, but he held on to his temper. He needed his wits, not the fury of battle. Then he took a deep breath, turning back to the fae. He had a thousand questions but settled on the most immediate. "Why are you warning me?"

Angmar shrugged, but lines of tension framed his mouth. "Not all the faery kingdom has forgotten who we are. My people love beauty and justice. We are not indiscriminate murderers, and we should not be Mordred's toy soldiers. Those of us who have resisted his power are turning to the Round Table to ensure our freedom. Merlin created this situation. In some measure, Arthur and Camelot bear that responsibility."

"Why trust us? Why not overthrow Mordred and his mother yourselves?"

"The rebel fae are scattered, disorganized, and afraid. We need Camelot's leadership and its might."

The words were barely out of the faery's mouth when a black-feathered arrow whistled past, striking the side of a barrel. It was short and thick, a crossbow bolt rather than a true arrow. Angmar jerked aside, breath hissing between his teeth. A thin line of blood bloomed across the front of his sweater. Gawain grabbed his arm, pulling him behind a Dumpster.

A quick glance told Gawain the shot had gone unnoticed among the hubbub of the crowd—and an archer strolling through Medievaland would hardly be noticed. The assassin had chosen the perfect place to do his work. A second glance at the arrow told him it was faery craftsmanship.

"Was that for dramatic effect?" Gawain asked drily. "A little extra push to make me agree to help you?"

"No." Angmar clutched the front of his sweater, red oozing from between his fingers. "I thought I'd dodged Mordred's lackeys. If they know I've warned you, they will silence us both."

"Let them try." Gawain pulled Angmar's hand away to see the sweater had been sliced by the bolt's passage. Through the gap in the cloth, he could see the injury was long but shallow. As long as the tip wasn't poisoned— and one never knew with faery weapons—Angmar would survive. Gawain shed his jacket, stripped off his shirt and pressed the wadded fabric against the wound. "Hold that. It only grazed you."

Angmar obeyed while Gawain pulled on his jacket again. "One would think you'd done this before," the faery said drily.

"Can you walk?" Gawain asked by way of reply.

"Yes."

"Good. You need cover. I need a word with the archer."

As Gawain peered around the corner of the Dumpster, he could see crowds packed the sidewalks, half of them children. He was more than willing to fight, but not where innocents could be harmed. But as he reached for his sword, his hand closed on empty air. He swore viciously. Of course he wore no sword. Every instinct he possessed was centuries out of date.

Angmar gave him a feral grin, drawing a gun from a

holster beneath his jacket. "This time has different ways to kill, Sir Knight."

"Perhaps," Gawain growled. "But there are laws in this age that will make this awkward. We cannot do honest battle here in the open, where all can see."

"So true." With a graceful flick, Angmar drew a shape in the air that burst in a blaze of rainbow light. The same instant, everything froze, the sound of the fair cutting off as if shears had sliced it. Time itself had stopped. A juggler's clubs hung in the air. Fluttering pennons stilled as if they were painted against the sky. Only Gawain and Angmar still moved. "This should make things easier."

Gawain moved to help Angmar to his feet. The faery shifted awkwardly with the bundle of shirt pressed against his stomach. Despite the shallow cut, it was soaking through. Gawain gave up the effort to move him. "How long can you hold the spell?"

"Longer if you do the chasing." Angmar pressed the Smith & Wesson into Gawain's hand, holster and all. "Leave me here and go quickly."

Gawain buckled it on and turned to go, but the fae caught his sleeve. "One thing more."

Gawain turned. "What?"

Angmar's face went rigid, as if he pushed down an inner storm. "I said Merlin's spell changed the fae. This assassin is no doubt one of us. Do not expect compassion or mercy or any feeling at all. My people are no longer capable of it."

For an instant, Gawain forgot everything but the faery's words. "How did Merlin's spell hurt you? Arthur would never say."

Angmar's face twisted. "The magic tore away our souls. A few of us escaped—I was not at the battle when the spell was cast—but the rest of my people are damaged beyond recognition. The new queen has used that to turn us into monsters for her war. We need Camelot's protection to keep us from becoming the stuff of nightmares."

Gawain stared as he remembered Angmar's words: *My people love beauty and justice. We are not indiscriminate murderers, and we should not be Mordred's toy soldiers.* Horror crept over him as the enormity of their plight became clear.

The faery gave him a gentle push. "Now go, and do what you can to save us. All of us."

Numb with shock, Gawain ran along the strip of grass that wound behind the pavilions, searching the possible vantage points where the archer might be hiding. Concentration cleared his thoughts. The angle of the bolt had been low, suggesting the bowman had been on the ground rather than a rooftop. Moving cautiously, Gawain approached the most likely spot from behind.

Gawain ducked beneath a sparrow that had been caught midflight by Angmar's spell. It was eerie, passing through the still and silent fairground. The packed sidewalks were filled with living statues. A child had been blowing bubbles, and they hung in the air like iridescent jewels. Gawain was struck with wonder, but he had too much experience to let down his guard. The bowman might be frozen like the rest of the crowd, and then again he might not. With every motion, Gawain was making himself an obvious target.

He was right to be cautious. He heard the snap of the crossbow's mechanism just as a black-feathered bolt streaked his way. Split-second reflex made him dive to the side. He rolled to his feet in one smooth motion and began sprinting in the direction from which the arrow had come. It was a dangerous move, but he counted on the fact that crossbows were slow to load.

Gawain should have known in this day and age an assassin would also carry a gun. He was still weaving through a family frozen in place when he heard the shot, loud as a thunderclap in the silence.

The assassin had fired straight into the crowd. All Gawain could do was cover the child beside him and let the bullet pierce his own flesh. It ripped along his arm like a savage claw, tearing through cloth and skin. He hit the ground, the child beneath him. Gawain scrambled to his feet, bringing up his own weapon just as he saw a dark-clad figure slip away.

The enemy was using the crowd as cover. Cursing, Gawain shouldered through the fairgoers. Blood slid between Gawain's fingers as fiery pain washed his vision with a red haze. "Hold, coward!"

The figure's dark head bobbed through the frozen tableau. Gawain followed him down a long alley of merchants—bakers, leatherworkers, calligraphers, and an armorer's booth. As he passed the armorer, Gawain palmed a blade as he went by and holstered Angmar's gun. He needed his injured right arm to shoot straight, but he'd trained since boyhood to use a blade with either hand.

He'd barely gone another dozen yards before he realized they were heading in a circle. The place where Gawain had left Angmar was just ahead. He heard a whisper of movement from the left and another bolt hissed past his ear, missing by a fraction. Gawain smiled, a brief, deadly flash of teeth. The shot had given the enemy's position away. In a fluid motion, Gawain threw the knife. He dove forward, using the side of a hut for cover.

A sharp cry said Gawain had thrown true, but it was followed by the sound of running feet. Gawain sprang into motion again, aiming for the Dumpster where Angmar was hiding. He heard the curses and scrapes of a struggle. A moment later, Gawain glimpsed two figures locked in combat.

He pounced, knocking the attacker backward against the side of the overstuffed Dumpster with a dull thud. An avalanche of garbage slid down around them, sending up a noxious stench. Gawain drew the gun and held it to the enemy's throat. Then he froze.

His adversary's lips drew back, showing sharp canines. "Hello, cousin."

"Mordred." Gawain snarled the name like a curse. Loathing welled up at the sight of his kinsman's pale, narrow face. Lank black hair straggled across a broad forehead, framing pale gray eyes that reminded Gawain of dirty ice. With some disappointment, Gawain realized his knife had only grazed his cousin's cheek.

"It's been too long," Mordred purred. "It was your brother's execution, wasn't it? Poor old Agravaine."

"Be silent," Gawain said between clenched teeth, but he still couldn't stop the wave of regret and fury. He'd found what Agravaine's sword had left of their mother.

"Can't blame old Aggy. He was just avenging your father. Mom poisons Dad—what's a son to do?" Mordred said with a cruel smile. "Trust me, I know about family squabbles."

Rage swirled through Gawain's brain like powerful whisky. Blowing Mordred's skull apart would be far too quick. Gawain curled his free hand around the other man's throat. "You were Agravaine's closest companion. I blame you for his downfall. The serpent in Eden could have taken lessons from your slithering tongue."

Mordred began to gasp, his face turning red, but the time-stopping charm ran out. With an almost physical force, the cacophony of the fair slammed against Gawain's ears as they were plunged back into a sea of motion. Mordred used the distraction to break free and stumble backward to where Angmar was sprawled facedown in the dirt, apparently unconscious.

Gawain crouched, weapon in hand. Mordred mirrored his stance, eyes calculating. Now that Angmar's spell had broken, they had only moments before someone discovered their fight. Gawain had to act now, but public murder would put an end to his freedom.

He hesitated an instant too long. Mordred dropped to his knees beside Angmar, grabbed a fistful of the fallen faery's hair and whispered a single word of power. The air shimmered as if heat were pouring over them in waves—except it was cold conjured by Mordred's magic. Ice flowed like water across the ground, making Gawain slip and fall to one knee. Mordred gestured, and a blast of blinding cold shocked him, stealing the strength from his limbs. Frost suddenly coated Gawain's sleeves, and the gun dropped from his numb fingers.

"Stay where you are!" Gawain roared, already knowing he had lost. "Angmar! I will bring you home! I swear it!"

The two men vanished in an ear-popping rush of magic.

Gawain crawled to his feet, biting back a torrent of curses. He had to find out where Mordred had taken the fae. And once he had, he would require the swords of his fellow knights to take Mordred down.

But to do that, he had to find the tombs. Tamsin Greene had to provide that information, and quickly. Without it, he was lost.

Chapter 3

Ten minutes after Tamsin had watched Gawain vanish, she was still sitting on the steps outside the church, her chin in her hands. A cloud passed over the sun and she looked up, grimacing as she caught sight of the gargoyles perched over the porch staring down at her. The weather was freezing cold, but she couldn't bring herself to go back inside. Gawain had targeted every one of her vulnerabilities. He'd overpowered her, aroused her, challenged her and, in the end, rejected her. The moment he'd detected her talent, he'd shut down and moved her from the box marked "woman" and put her in the one marked "witch." Untouchable. Repulsive. Dangerous.

The memory of it left her shaking with fury.

Her cell phone rang. "Hello?" She snapped as she answered it, not able to keep her mood from leaking into her voice.

"What are you doing in Washington State?" Tamsin's

sister demanded, fear edging the frosty words. "I went away for a week. Just one week and you skipped town like a fugitive."

"I got a research job. It came up unexpectedly and I jumped on the opportunity." Immediately, Tamsin's anger collapsed into homesickness. She pressed the cell phone tight to her ear, as if that would bring her closer to Stacy. "It's at Medievaland Theme Park."

"Are you serious? Fake jousting and wenches with beer?"

"It's better than it sounds. The church has a fabulous collection of early manuscripts. You know old documents are my thing."

"Carlyle is on the other side of the country," Stacy protested. "You're thousands of miles away."

Tamsin leaned against one of the stone pillars of the porch, grateful of its ancient, sturdy support. "I got approval from the Coven Elders to take the job."

"You did?" Stacy sounded shocked.

"I'm not a fool." The old witch families kept their members close, and breaking their rules was a serious mistake. Their punishments had been the same for centuries—loss of a witch's powers and a lifetime of servitude in the Elders' cold gray halls. "They want me here examining the collection. The coven hasn't had a researcher since Dad passed." Her breath hitched at the mention of her father, even after a decade with him gone.

Stacy heard it and paused before continuing. "What about, you know, Mom's plans?"

"What plans?" Tamsin asked, though she knew perfectly well what her sister meant.

"Mom worries you'll end up alone. She says she'll talk to the Elders about a match for you."

Tamsin blew out an exasperated breath, rubbing at the

tattoo on her wrist. Elders arranged marriages when and where they saw fit, but that hardly ever happened in the modern age. Still, Tamsin planned to minimize that risk by proving herself valuable as a loremaster—and staying as far out of the Elders' sight as possible.

"Talk her out of it," she begged. "Please."

"I'll try, but Mom treats me the same way," Stacy said. "It's not just about finding a husband. She worries something bad will happen if I go to the corner store. A witch needs her coven's protection, especially these days. The shadow world is stirring."

Tamsin pulled the cell phone from her ear. A dark cloud of energy shimmered around it, the magical echo of Stacy's unhappiness. Tamsin swallowed hard, shards of emotion caught in her throat. It would be so simple to give in and run home, like a chick diving beneath the coven's protective wing. But then her future would end at the edges of their small, isolated town.

After a deep breath, Tamsin held the phone to her ear again. "Tell Mom I'll come home for Thanksgiving. But only for a few days. I need this job."

"Okay, okay," Stacy said softly. "I'm worried about you."

The cloud of energy around the phone turned to a faint rose color—a sign of her sister's concern. "Call me if you need me," Stacy added. "Anytime, you hear?"

Tamsin smiled through sudden sadness. "I hear you. I know how to keep myself safe."

"Love you."

"Love you, sis." Tamsin ended the call and slipped her phone into the pocket of her costume.

Tamsin rubbed her arms, unable to let go of the heaviness the phone call had left behind. The Elders didn't reveal much about the shadow world, but Tamsin's father had. There were other magic users beside the witches— faeries and ogres and who knew what else just beyond the comforting lights of the modern world. Once there had even been demons.

Not that anyone believed those old tales. It had been surprisingly easy for witches to move from an everyday fact of village life to the local bogeyman and then to no more than a Halloween costume. Humans had lost track of the shadow world, and when they encountered it, they rarely reacted well.

Like Tamsin's last lover, who had also been her first serious relationship. He'd been a teaching assistant, a few years older and an expert in European history of the Middle Ages. It had been like dating a daydream—everything she could wish for, every box checked. She'd laid her heart at Richard's feet, and for a time he'd seemed to do the same. They'd been sleeping together for almost a year when she'd forgotten to hide what she was. The slip had been minor— she'd lit a candle with a word of power.

Richard's reaction had been instant. He'd rolled out of bed and pulled on his pants almost in one move. When he'd looked up, the light from that fateful candle falling across his features, she'd seen real terror. And then he'd uttered the words she'd least expected to hear: "Get away from me, witch."

The episode had happened well over a year ago, but it still stung horribly. All the rage and hurt of that breakup gathered afresh in Tamsin's soul. She curled her hands around her knees, nails digging through the soft fabric of her skirt. She would not be treated that way, ever again. If Gawain did show up demanding answers, she'd tell him what he could do with his wretched monuments.

Tamsin jumped to her feet and hurried back inside, where she retreated to the chapel's vestry. Her tiny office was set up there, although it looked less like an office than a fort made of file boxes. A musty smell drifted from decades of paper records waiting for her attention. Most dated from the seventies, when the crumbling church had been moved over from England. Despite some public objections, the building had been sold to Medievaland's founder, who had promised to restore it once he had moved it to Washington State.

Switching on her computer, Tamsin scrolled through what little information she had on the recent history of the Church of the Holy Well and searched for anything about the tombs. All she found was a mention of the crypt—it had been filled in, but one hundred and fifty grave monuments had been packed and shipped with the rest of the building. The records stopped there.

Tamsin sat back in the chair, mystified. So where were the tombs? Had every single one been sold or loaned out to other places? She didn't particularly want to help Gawain— he hadn't been kind or pleasant to her at all. And yet, he had raised some very interesting questions. She hitched forward on the sagging computer chair, put her fingers on the keyboard and began searching for clues.

By closing time, Tamsin had a headache from staring at the screen. The remainder of the afternoon had flown by, but she'd found no answers. Still pondering the mystery, she crawled into her ancient Camry for the drive home.

This wasn't the first dead end Tamsin had found in the past week. Beneath its colorful, family-friendly surface, Medievaland had hidden depths. She'd heard rumors that its library—purchased along with the rest of the crumbling church—held books of magic so old they were rumored to have been handwritten by Merlin the Wise himself. But no employee she'd talked to had heard anything about this most valuable part of the library's collection. If it existed, it was kept well out of sight.

Tamsin meant to find the truth, and not just because the Elders wanted answers. Her father, Hector Greene, had been the coven's loremaster before her. He'd traveled the world, searching out rare manuscripts about magic until a drunk driver had forced his car off a cliff when Tamsin was thirteen. There had been little left to bury.

Tamsin pulled into the driveway of her apartment building and, a few minutes later, locked the dead bolts to her studio apartment. She collapsed onto her bed, pulling a blanket over her because the heater never quite did the job, and finally began to relax.

She reached over the side of the bed to where she'd dropped her backpack and rummaged for the side pocket where she kept the book her father had given her. This had been his favorite grimoire, an ancient text with a peculiar collection of spells. She untied the leather thong that held it shut and began to turn the worn pages as she did at least once a day, letting the familiar words comfort her. Handling it was like having her father close again.

The yellowed pages crackled as she turned them. She traced the red-brown handwriting with her fingertips, feeling the depression where the nib of a pen had stroked the page. A charm against roaming spirits. A spell to attract a familiar. A chant to protect against pox. She turned the page again and stopped. Although she had looked through the book literally thousands of times, every so often it showed her a new spell. Tonight was one of those occasions. *A Charm to Awaken Those Who Watch.* Tamsin raised a brow. The watchers couldn't be very effective if they were sleeping on the job. She scanned the ancient words, recognizing a language so old it had been all but forgotten in Merlin's time. She wondered why the book had produced the spell now, but it did that sometimes. Old books of magic had minds of their own.

Tamsin read until the light faded and then put the book away. She had started to drowse when she heard the stealthy slide of the balcony door. She bolted upright, nearly falling when the blanket twisted around her ankles. Tamsin kicked it aside and scanned the apartment. There was a kitchen nook and a bathroom, but it was basically one large space with nowhere to hide.

The balcony door was open, the night wind pouring through a two-foot gap. It was possible for a good climber to get from the fire escape to the balcony, which was why she kept the door locked—but no lock was foolproof. Fear was an icy explosion beneath her ribs. There had been burglaries all over the neighborhood, some of them violent.

She cleared her throat. "Take what you want. I don't have much."

"I'm not here for your property."

She sucked in a breath as she recognized the voice. It was Gawain, his words pitched so low she could barely hear him. She searched the room until she found his form, a shadow within shadows by the curtain. Even the blurry outline of his broad shoulders brought a rush of confused emotions—unease and anger mixed with irrational attraction. Her words dropped to a whisper. "You're stalking me!"

A pause followed. "No, you're not my prey. Not that way."

Then in what way was she prey? Her imagination called up a dozen images, some gruesome, some undeniably hot. "Then why are you here?" Her fingers trembled as she reached for the light switch. She yearned for brightness to dispel this insanity.

"Don't," he said, the word louder than before. "Leave it dark."

Tamsin pulled her hand away, wondering just how good his night vision was. "I want light."

"We'll be too easy to see from the street." Shadows stirred, and she heard the glass door slide closed. A moment later, the drapes blocked out the nightscape. "Now turn it on."

She did, and her floor lamp bloomed to life. It wasn't bright, but it was enough to see the tall form of her visitor leaning against the wall, his right arm cradled in his left. He was hurt—he'd found a fight since she'd last seen him. And he was missing his shirt, leaving a well-defined six-pack exposed to view. Tamsin's mouth went dry as ashes. It really was too bad he was crazy.

"What are we hiding from?" she asked. "And what happened to your arm?"

"Both questions have one answer, but it's not the first thing you need to know."

Tamsin drew in a breath but couldn't get any air. "Are you going to hurt me?"

"No." He leaned his head against the wall, seeming weary although his eyes had lost none of their watchfulness. It was obvious that he was still wary of her power. "Not now. Not unless you use your magic."

"Then why don't you sit down?" Tamsin said, just as distrustful.

"I don't need to sit down." He sounded annoyed and stubborn, his hand moving to hide the crude bandage around his arm. She could see the edge of it beneath the cuff of his jacket, and it looked as if he'd tried to bind his wound with his left hand. "I don't have time. Lives depend on getting the answers I need."

That piqued her curiosity, but safety came first—and that meant calming him down. "I'd feel better if you sat. You're rather tall."

His expression hardened another notch. "I can watch you better from here."

"Oh, for pity's sake." Without waiting for him to answer, she stalked to the kitchen nook and grabbed the bottle of red wine she'd opened the night before. It was almost full.

"What are you doing?" Gawain growled, turning to keep her in sight.

She set the wine and two glasses on her tiny table. "I'm offering you a drink because I'll certainly need one if we're going to continue this ridiculous conversation."

It was too dark to see that piercing blue gaze, but she could feel it all the same. He was all predator, all male, and his will was iron. Tamsin braced herself, summoning her courage. She had to take control of the situation. "You seem to know your history. Maybe you understand the old rules of hospitality. If you accept my wine, then we have a pact. We treat each other with respect while you're under my roof."

He made a low sound of surprise. "You're offering me guest rights?"

"I am."

To her relief, he gave a slow nod and pulled out one of her wrought iron chairs. "I accept."

Gawain sat down carefully, as if expecting the chair to collapse beneath his muscular frame. Then he braced his injured arm on the glass tabletop, the tension in his shoulders easing as he studied her. His expression was still guarded, but she caught a glimpse of smug satisfaction, like a cat that had finally got its way.

The very masculine look made Tamsin's cheeks warm. She poured the wine, her fingers trembling slightly. "Why did you come to my home?"

"The church is being watched."

Startled, Tamsin spilled a few drops of wine. She set the bottle down, her mind racing. "Watched?"

He nodded. "I followed you here so we could talk alone."

"About the tombs? I don't know any more than I did three hours ago."

"You have the means to find out, historian." His lips curved down. He had a sensual mouth, the kind that betrayed emotion as easily as the eyes. "Events force me to insist that you hurry."

"Oh?"

He pointedly raised his injured arm. "I'm running out of time."

Gooseflesh ran up her arms. "And out of time means what?"

"Today it meant a bullet." He picked up a wineglass in his good hand. "Tomorrow something worse. Shall we drink to good health?"

Tamsin's whole body tensed. "Someone shot you? Did you call the police?"

"My story would be a bit much for them." He continued to hold the glass midair, pointedly waiting for her to drink first. Witches were adept with poisons.

Tamsin took a sip, but now her hand was unsteady. Crazy was one thing, but guns were another. His eyes held hers across the tiny table. There was so little space between them that she could feel the warmth of his breath.

"I'm not in trouble with your laws," he said. "I'm simply working by rules that have no meaning here."

She didn't even try to make sense of that statement. "And the man who shot you?"

"Trust me, no jail could hold him. He's part of the faery court."

Tamsin sucked in a breath. "Are you telling me the truth?"

The flash of temper in Gawain's gaze answered her question. "Of course."

"Fae?" she asked quietly. "They died out long ago."

"Like witches," he countered. "Like it or not, the fae are as real as you, and they are here to wage war on this world."

Chapter 4

Tamsin took another swallow of wine—a long one this time. "Okay. So where do you fit in all this?"

His eyes didn't shift from hers. "Right in the middle."

"That doesn't answer my question."

"Then be more specific."

Irritation prickled. He wasn't making this easy. Tamsin cleared her throat. "Let's start small. Where did you come from?"

"Recently, California." His mouth quirked at one corner. "I hadn't planned to visit, but I woke up one day in a museum basement. A week later and I would have been inside a display case."

"I don't understand."

That hint of a smile deepened, but it was bitter. "Nor do I."

It was hard to look away from his lips. "What brought you to Medievaland?"

"I believe you call it hitchhiking."

She gave him a scathing look.

He relented. "I was looking for a means to journey to the Church of the Holy Well in Somerset. Then I saw an advertisement for family vacations in Washington State. Behold, there was the church I was looking for, in a theme park on the wrong continent. That was not just happy co-incidence. My fate is bound to the church. Clearly, once it was in my power to travel, any effort to separate me from it failed."

Tamsin hadn't followed a word of what he'd just said, but in part that was because her attention was on his injury. She touched him, just a brush of fingertips over his wrist. His skin was hot, almost feverish, and her powers told her the wound was inflamed. "When were you shot?"

"Shortly after we met."

She gave him a look. "And since then? It's after six o'clock."

"I lay in wait, watching the church. There was a good chance the enemy would return to find me, and I could follow them from there. Besides, if they knew I had been talking to you earlier—well, there was no way I could leave you without protection."

An unfamiliar ache formed in her chest. "You waited hours with a bullet wound in case a bad faery decided to jump me?"

He gave a slight lift of his shoulders, his expression settling into hard lines. "Witch or not, I need your help, Tamsin Greene. I can't afford for you to die quite yet."

"Gee, thanks." She rose. "I'm going to bandage that arm. While I do it, you're going to tell me everything."

Faster than thought, his good hand grabbed her wrist in a bruising grip. "Swear on all you hold sacred you will not use anything but common herbals."

She pulled against him, but he would not budge. Hot anger bubbled up, burning her cheeks, but it was nothing to the hard, stubborn hostility in his eyes.

"No magic," he said, his jaw clenched.

"What do you think I'm going to do to you?" she replied in icy tones.

He released her, his movements jerky. "Swear." His gaze held hers with unbending will—and a touch of fear.

She released her breath in an exasperated sigh. "All right, but it's not my fault if your arm rots and falls off."

He lifted his chin. "Your pride as a healer would never let that happen."

She stalked to the bathroom for her medical supplies. He was right, blast him.

"Take off your jacket," Tamsin said to Gawain as she set a box of medical supplies on the table.

Slowly, still suspicious, Gawain obeyed. The sleeve of the garment was torn and streaked with dried blood, but it was all he had, so he hung it neatly over the back of the chair. He'd packed Angmar's wound with his shirt, so that left him with nothing from the waist up. Tamsin watched him, her gaze taking in the show with barely concealed female interest. He felt a lick of pleasure at her regard, but he pushed it aside. She was a witch, and that marked her as someone he could not trust.

He resumed his seat and held out his bandaged forearm. It unnerved him to require her help like this, but the heat of infection was spreading up his arm. No doubt Mordred's bullets carried sickness. That would be his style.

As Tamsin reached for Gawain, he caught her wrist again, but more gently this time. Her bones were so delicate, the fine tattoo as much artwork as proof of her allegiance. "Remember, no magic."

"No magic. Just medicine."

Tamsin gave him a tight smile and set to work at once, her touch deft as she positioned his arm on the table. He could smell the heat of her skin as she leaned close. Her scent was sunlight and herbs, like clean linens dried in a summer wind. There was comfort in it, and for a moment Gawain forgot what she was. Her profile was beautiful, the clean, graceful lines of her features marred only by an impish tilt to her nose. To his dismay, Gawain discovered he was almost smiling.

Witchery! He snapped to attention with a physical start that earned him a searching glance. His ears burned. "Forgive me. I am weary."

"You've been shot," she said severely. "You're probably still in shock and need rest."

"I've taken worse blows than this," he grumbled. "I've no time to coddle a scratch."

He had work to do and lives to save. Angmar's fate nagged at him like another, deeper wound. He'd combed the theme park, looking for some clue as to where Mordred had taken him, but there had been no sign. He closed his fist tight, imagining Mordred's throat crushing in his grip.

"Tell me what's going on," Tamsin said in a soft voice as she unwrapped his makeshift bandage with warm fingers. Her hands were delicate but practical, the nails cut short and unpainted. They fascinated him as they eased away the torn strips of linen he'd used—a towel stolen from one of the theme park's food trucks. Using warm water, she softened the blood that had cemented the cloth to his arm, taking care not to aggravate his already torn flesh. The action brought her face close to his. Her tantalizing scent engulfed him again.

She gave him the full force of her brown eyes. "Begin at the beginning."

Gawain steeled himself against that gaze, making his words brusque. "Do you know the old tale of the demons and the alliance who cast them back to the darkness?"

Tamsin's expression grew troubled. "Funny you should mention that old story. I was thinking about it today, in fact." She bent her head to inspect the wound. Her hair shone in burnished waves, and he yearned to feel that golden silk against his skin. Gawain raised his other hand to touch and caught himself just in time.

"What have legends of ancient wars to do with you?" she asked.

How was he to answer that? He'd wanted to ease up to a full explanation, but she was a witch and therefore understood magic. Gawain decided to save time. "I was there."

Her hands stilled a moment, then resumed their work. She began swabbing his arm with something that stung and smelled of bitter herbs. "Go on."

He did, and he told her about Merlin's spell that turned the knights of Camelot to stone. She worked silently while he spoke, applying ointments and fresh bandages. Her lovely face went still and smooth, a mask of concentration making it impossible to guess her thoughts—but he noticed she refused to look his way. Tension wound tight in Gawain's chest, but he pushed on with his story, refusing to falter.

"That must be how I came to wake up in a basement," he finished. "If the church was moved to America and the contents scattered, my tomb must have been sent to the museum in Los Angeles."

"You woke up from being a stone statue?" Her voice was utterly neutral.

"There is a rising threat. Mordred's invasion of the human realms must be what triggered the enchantment to wake me."

Tamsin finished knotting the bandage and sat back, a faint crease between her brows. "How long ago did you awaken?"

"I'm not sure. Months."

She shook her head, that glorious fair hair sliding over her shoulders. "Your story makes no sense."

Gawain's gut turned cold. "Why not?"

"After so many centuries, it would take more time to get your bearings and start to function in this day and age. You should still be speaking—well, we would call it Middle English. Your version of the language would be hard for us to understand."

It was a logical objection. A bubble of panic slid through him as he answered. "Making myself understood was all part of the spell. The magic was designed to provide enough factual knowledge to function in whatever time or place we rose again. I understand firearms and subways. How to buy food in a store. It's not perfect, but I can get by."

All the same, the experience of waking had nearly broken him. Merlin's enchantment did not buffer the shock of moving through time. "Still, escaping the museum was just the start of the nightmare. Crowds of people, whole villages' worth of men and women on one street. Strange vehicles. Pictures made of light. I could name what was around me, but I didn't understand it. There was one day when the only thing I recognized was an apple."

Tamsin was clutching the roll of bandages, her knuckles white. Damn and blast, he had frightened her again. "How did you survive?"

"However I had to." Gawain's voice had gone rough with remembered anger. "I disappeared into the shadows, where a warrior of my skill had respect."

Her lips parted, as if she was about to speak, and then she closed her mouth tight. She swallowed.

Gawain watched, trying to assess every nuance of her expression. "You don't believe me."

Her voice shook. "I don't know if you're mad or on drugs."

At least she had returned his honesty with her own. Gawain found himself close to pleading, something he wasn't used to. "You have the means to find out where the rest of the knights have gone. That's all I'm asking."

She drew herself straighter, still clutching the roll of bandages. "Why? Won't your friends wake up if it's the right time? You found your way here. They can, too."

She was humoring him. It stung worse than her medicines. "Something has gone wrong. They should be here, but they're not." Gawain broke off, hearing the heat in his words. Frustration was a physical ache, but he could not afford to lose his temper. "I need my brother knights."

Tamsin's expression declared him moonstruck or a liar. Anger crawled through him, but he hid the emotion behind courtesy. He flexed the fingers of his injured hand. "Thank you for tending my wound."

"You're welcome. I think we're done here." Tamsin kept her eyes lowered as she tidied away her jars of ointment and rolls of bandages in their box. Tension pinched the corners of her mouth.

Gawain stared at the table, too angry and confused to look at her again. Faces flashed through his mind—Arthur's, Mordred's, Angmar's. He needed help, and honesty had clearly failed. "I have very little to my name. My lands and castles are lost to me. But if you aid me in this quest, I will repay you however I can. You have only to name the service you desire."

"You should know better than to make an offer like that. You have no idea what I might ask."

He looked up to see her studying him from under her lashes. He picked up his glass and drained what was left in two swallows. "I need your help. There is very little I won't promise, witch."

She flinched at his final word. "You don't have anything I want and I'd be happiest if you left," she said, her voice barely above a whisper.

Desperate, he glanced around the tiny apartment. It was neat and clean, but hardly luxurious. And, it clearly showed she slept alone. He'd tried simple honesty. He'd offered his sword. He had nothing left but himself to offer. "I'm good company on a cold night."

Tamsin had the box in her hands as if she meant to put it away, but his last words made her freeze in place. Her lips parted in surprise. "I beg your pardon?"

Gawain narrowed his eyes. He'd been called a charmer, but his famed silver tongue had obviously tarnished. He rose from the table, feeling blood loss, hunger and wine swirl to his brain. "No offense meant, Mistress Greene. Most women are glad of a knight at their beck and call, and I've never had any complaints."

Taking charge of the moment, he took the box from Tamsin's hands and set it back on the table. She didn't resist, though her cheeks flushed a delicate pink. Curiosity and caution warred in her eyes. By all the saints, she was beautiful.

Once her hands were empty, he took them in his and pulled her closer. She was still wearing her costume and, for a brief moment, time fell away. Gawain was himself again, a famed warrior and heir to a kingdom of his own. He was a powerful and wealthy man—a man every woman would desire, whether for a husband or a single night of bed play.

He raised Tamsin's hands to his lips. They smelled of her salves, sharp and clean. He kissed them slowly, one fingertip at a time, tasting the mix of bitter herbs and sweet woman.

"What are you doing?" she asked in a tone of horrified fascination. She tugged against his grip, but her strength was no match for his.

"Has no one ever done homage to you, my lady?" He gave her his best smile. "Has no one sung your praises or worshipped your beauty?"

Her brows lifted. "You don't even like me."

"Strange times make unexpected friends."

He drew her yet closer, until he felt the brush of her skirts against his legs, the silk of her hair against his bare chest. Then he lowered his mouth to hers. She leaned away, but Gawain meant to give her nothing but pleasure. Surely she would come to life with his infusion of pure heat.

Gawain wasn't disappointed. Tamsin parted her lips, and her taste was an explosion of honey, as if someone had distilled summer into a kiss. Gawain's blood surged with desire as centuries of cold fled in a single rush. Only bone-deep fire remained, drawing a groan from his throat.

Tamsin shivered beneath his touch, making tiny noises of surprise. His hands cupped her cheeks, stroking the silk of her skin. She was just tall enough to fit him comfortably, her body slender but luscious. Fitting words to thought, he allowed his hand to clasp her waist, then stroked downward over her hip.

"Stop," she said, her voice small but firm.

He pulled her closer, his ability to form thought compromised by the luxurious curves pressed against his chest. He could feel the magic deep inside her, pulling to forgotten pieces of his soul. They called to each other, power to dangerous power, though he told himself it was simply lust. "There's no need to deny yourself. I'm here for your pleasure."

"No!"

This time the word penetrated his overheated brain. Gawain immediately let go, but it was too late to put space between them. Her powers surged, and a blow like a charging bull slammed him hard enough that his feet left the floor. There was a moment of giddiness before his back smashed against the wall. Stars swam in his vision for a sickening second, and then he slid to the floor.

"I said *no*," Tamsin repeated, but there were tears in her voice. "I *hate* that you made me do that!"

Gawain scrambled to his feet, hands loose at his sides and ready to defend his life. Alarm rose inside him, bringing every nerve to alert. "You turn your magic against me?" he growled.

"And why do you think I did that?" Tamsin folded her arms across her chest. Anger sparked in her dark eyes, reminding Gawain of a storm at sea. "I don't know who you really are or what you're really after, but I've patched you up and now it's time for you to leave!"

Beneath the sharp words was pure misery. He'd behaved with the manners of a troll. He swallowed hard, trying to force down the uncomfortable emotions jammed in his throat. No woman had ever turned him down before—and none had ever knocked him on his backside, either.

Dread seeped through his limbs, as if he was turning to stone once more. He had come to ask her for help, and he'd bungled it horribly. First, she'd believed him mad. Now she believed him a scoundrel. "Please allow me to earn your pardon. My honor demands it."

"Honor?" She glared at him. "How about you honor my demand for you to go?"

Gawain had lost. He cursed himself for his stupidity—his search for the tombs was urgent, but now he was forced to fall back and regroup. It was no more than he deserved—he'd approached the witch with all the finesse of the lowest blackguard.

But battles didn't end at the first skirmish. It was time to rethink tactics.

He picked up his jacket. "Then I bid you good night, Mistress Greene."

Mordred dropped a limp form on the carpet. Nimueh, once called the Lady of the Lake, rose from her chair and stared, uncertain at first who was crumpled at the Prince of Faery's feet. All of her people had the same white hair and dark skin, green eyes and long, delicate bones. This male, however, was barely recognizable beneath the swelling bruises on his face.

"Angmar of Corin," she said finally. She felt only a mild shock of recognition, followed by an intellectual curiosity as to how the high-ranking fae had ended up this way. She'd lost all capacity for emotions like pity or anger thanks to Merlin's spell. She remembered them, though, and knew she should have felt horror at the sight of Angmar's pain. Once, he'd been a dear friend.

"Nim-oo-ay," Mordred drawled, stretching out the syllables of her name. "How lovely to see you lurking about the place. Here to report my deeds to my mama?"

She didn't answer. They both knew that was precisely why she was here. He pulled off his gloves and tossed them onto a side table. They were in a Victorian mansion on the outskirts of Carlyle. Mordred had charmed it away from its owners, convincing them to sign over the deed right before throwing them to his hungrier pets. The house had four stories and dozens of rooms, all appointed in velvet and fine crystal chandeliers. Mordred liked the opulence of the place, especially the high-backed armchairs that looked almost like thrones.

Nimueh watched as Mordred moved to a magnificent gilded buffet and sloshed liquor into a balloon-shaped snifter. "Why is Angmar here?" she finally asked. "What happened to your face?"

"Angmar is a present to myself." Mordred swirled the amber liquid, his cold gray eyes almost jubilant. "He was chatting up Gawain of Lothian, who naturally tried to kill me on sight."

That caught Nimueh's interest. "Your cousin? The knights are truly awake, then?"

Mordred nodded. "It's like Gawain to be first out of the gate. Always trying to impress."

"It seems strange to me that you two are kin," she observed, stooping to examine Angmar. He was still breathing, but barely.

"Our mothers were sisters, more or less. Mostly less. I lost track of the family drama ages ago. It's simplest to assume everyone slept with or killed everyone else—or maybe both—and leave it at that."

Nimueh understood what he meant. In truth, the intermarriages of the old families—human, witch and faery—were as intertwined and complex as they were ancient. And that didn't even touch on their tangled relationship with Arthur of Camelot's kin, the Pendragons, and all the bad blood there.

Mordred set down his glass. "Gawain hasn't changed one bit. He's still strutting around like a barnyard cock." Mordred gave a cold grin. "I managed to put a bullet in him."

"Not very subtle."

"I didn't have the time for subtlety. Gawain was throwing knives."

She turned to look up at him. "Did you learn anything about the tombs? Your mother will want to know."

Mordred's cheek twitched, as it often did when the subject of his mother came up. "I can handle this matter." He kicked Angmar, and the fae grunted in pain.

Nimueh felt anger pass by like the shadow of a faraway cloud. Or maybe it was her imagination supplying what might have been, as men felt limbs they had lost in battle. She gave a slow, impassive blink, wondering if this was what it felt like to be dead. "Are you sure that is wise? The queen expressly ordered that she be told at once if there was news of Excalibur."

It was the one weapon that could kill the immortal, indestructible Queen of Faery and her son. King Arthur had taken it with him into the stone sleep, which was one reason why everyone wanted to find the tomb.

Mordred lifted his brows with pretend boredom. "I'm not about to give Mama the opportunity to micromanage. And you're not going to, either."

Mordred grabbed Nimueh's arm, squeezing until a primitive fear swam into her heart. The fae could still feel the desire to survive, and the prince used that without mercy. In fact, the smile playing around his lips said he enjoyed it.

"Stay focused on pleasing me," he said in a pleasant, smooth voice. "Forget my mother. I'm the lord here in the mortal realms."

Nimueh jerked away from his bruising fingers. "Your mother sent me to be your advisor. I advise you don't forget she is your queen."

Mordred's fingers twitched, as if itching to cause more

pain, but she was spared when Angmar rose to his hands and knees. The fae gasped and twisted his neck, straining to look up from beneath the fall of his white hair. Nimueh could see the full extent of his injuries now, one eye swollen shut and the blood staining the front of his clothes. When Angmar saw where he was, his breath hissed inward.

Fear. The one experience Nimueh could still share.

"Welcome to my home," Mordred purred. Then he delivered a sharp kick to Angmar's wound. The fae fell with a moan. "You're going to tell me everything you learned from Gawain. After that, I'll find all kinds of uses for you."

Chapter 5

Gawain seethed as he slipped away from the building, using the shadows to disguise his retreat. Too many needs had been frustrated at once, and all of them by Tamsin Greene. He spun to look back. She was standing on the balcony, arms folded and shoulders hunched against the wind that tugged at her gown. With the light behind her, Tamsin seemed fragile, a slim, barely substantial silhouette. She should have been inside, out of the cold wind and shielded from unfriendly eyes.

A sudden, hot protectiveness burned through him, completely at odds with the empirical fact that she was capable of protecting herself—at least from unwanted suitors. Surely his concern was because he needed her alive to help him. Too much depended on her aid.

Gawain stood gazing at the figure high above him, wondering what ill luck one more witch in his life would ultimately bring him. He wished he could think of another way to find the tombs, but his understanding of data and archives was next to nil and what little he knew of magic he'd done his best to forget. The only skills he could bring to the tomb problem were his powers of persuasion, which had apparently deserted him.

At last, Tamsin shut the balcony door and disappeared from view. Finally stirring, Gawain checked the knife in his boot—he'd found the one he'd used at Medievaland, the blade chipped but otherwise fine. He wished he had a shirt because it was growing colder by the minute. It was time to walk away for the night and come up with a new plan.

The clock glowing in the tower over Carlyle City Hall said it was eight-thirty, and the streets were quiet. Gawain walked the few blocks to the center of town, past a restaurant, a bar and finally the parking lot beside the gas station. He thrust his hands into his coat pockets, slowly scanning the area for anything that wasn't human. The scuff of his boots on the pavement seemed to be the only sound apart from the occasional car rushing down the main drag.

Gawain might have missed the two figures except for the tingling up the nape of his neck. The only time he welcomed the magic he'd inherited from his mother was when he hunted his enemies, and now those instincts demanded he look toward the gas pumps. When he spotted them, a warning shiver worked its way up his shoulder blades. Something about the way they were stalking across the pavement said they weren't there for the jumbo soft drinks.

He ghosted across the parking lot and pressed himself against the wall, disappearing into the darkness. Lights from the gas station stained the greasy parking lot in swaths of lurid color. Gawain watched the tall, graceful pair of fae pause next to the ice machine. They were wearing modern dress, but he recognized their fine-boned faces and moon-pale hair. He thought of Angmar's warning about the fae and wondered what they wanted.

A figure came out of the gas station, the glass door swinging shut with a chime. He bent over his smartphone, texting as he walked.

Gawain waited, watching the two fae. Sure enough, they were already in motion, swift and silent as sharks. Before the man looked up from his phone, one of them had clapped a hand over his mouth and the other had pinned his arms. They dragged him into the alley behind the building before the man had even made a sound.

Gawain drew his knife with a faint whisper of steel and glided to the mouth of the alley. He stopped, peering into a darkness he couldn't penetrate. Somewhere in that narrow dead end, water trickled and garbage stank and—he was sure of it—something vile was happening.

Turning to make himself as narrow a target as he could, Gawain crept sideways, his back to the alley wall and knife clutched loosely in his hand. In these close quarters, any fight would be short and brutal, reaction time counting as much as skill. His right arm throbbed, but he'd learned to push pain aside long ago.

His eyes adjusted enough to make out the shapes of garbage bins and drainpipes. He stopped, letting his senses gather information. Music pounded from the bar down the block like a muffled heartbeat. Beneath it, he heard a low, rasping breath. He immediately swiveled toward the sound.

It took him mere seconds to surprise the first faery, pressing the edge of the blade to his throat. The human he'd seen leaving the gas station was on the ground, struggling as his body convulsed in frantic jerks.

"What are you doing?" Gawain snarled in the faery's ear.

The faery hissed, nothing remotely human in the sound, and struggled despite the knife digging into his neck. Fae

were strong and hard to overpower at the best of times—
and this one seemed to be feral. Gawain took the chance
of pulling the knife away long enough to bring the butt of
its steel handle down hard on his opponent's head.

The fae should have dropped like a stone, but instead
he whirled, shoving Gawain against the wall so hard he
dropped the knife. Blood streamed down the faery's neck
where the blade had cut, glistening in the cold glow of the
streetlights. Gawain's skin crawled. Despite the fury of the
fight, the creature's eyes were wide and staring, devoid of
any emotion. He might have been fighting with a corpse.

The fae reached beneath his jacket, obviously going for
a weapon. Gawain tried to duck sideways, but his opponent moved to block him with eerie speed. Gawain lunged,
knocking them both to the ground. The faery grunted but
rolled, struggling to pin Gawain. They wrestled for a moment, both too strong to surrender, until Gawain hit him
with a savage cross, landing it right on the jaw. This time
the faery collapsed in an unconscious heap. Pain sang up
Gawain's arm, but there was no time to think about it.

The second faery was straddling the human, his hands
wrapped around the man's skull. Their faces nearly touched,
but this was no kiss. The fae's mouth was open in a snarl
that mixed savage pleasure with a grimace of agony. Faint
blue light coursed over his hands and up his arms as if he
was drawing electricity from the man's flesh.

Gawain's stomach twisted in revulsion as the truth came
with the force of a blow. Angmar had said Merlin's spell
had turned the fae to monsters, but he'd assumed that was
a figure of speech. Now he knew better. Robbed of their
souls, the fae were consumed with an unbearable hunger
to fill that empty void. They were hunting the souls of innocents.

The fae was so lost in the ecstasy of feeding he hadn't

noticed his friend had been knocked out cold—or that there was an enemy behind him. Gawain grabbed the attacker's shoulders, attempting to haul him away, but the fae stubbornly clung on.

The human was starting to shudder, froth coating his lips. He would be dead in moments or worse—reduced to an empty husk. Gawain grabbed the fae's head, cupping the chin, and snapped his neck. The spell died with a sizzle of electricity.

Gawain heaved the dead fae aside and stood panting for a moment, his breath a cloud of mist in the cold air. Despite the temperature, sweat stuck his jacket to his skin. He'd heard whispers on the street about human bodies found in alleyways and empty buildings—inexplicable, random deaths. Now he could guess the cause. Fae were strong enough to survive the loss of their souls, but a human or witch was not.

The victim had passed out. Gawain knelt and checked his pulse—strong and steady. Gawain had been in time. The man would probably wake in a minute or two, weak and aching, but alive.

Gawain gathered his knife and thrust it back in his boot. The fae's eyes were clouding with death, but they had already lacked their vital spark. Mordred had found the perfect warriors for his cause. Motivating them to conquer the mortal world would be easy, for there was no shortage of souls to consume where humans were crammed cheek by jowl into massive cities. Gawain's lip curled in disgust.

He bent and slung the unconscious human across his shoulders, intending to carry him far away from the scene of the crime, for the human police would never unravel what had happened here. The victim could well be blamed for murder.

Modern humans had no grasp of what they were facing. They needed protection. And so did the fae, whether they realized it or not.

Gawain had to find the tombs. Souls depended on it.

Tamsin dropped her purse and backpack in her office. Since she wasn't working with the public that day, she was dressed in jeans and a sweater, her hair pulled back into a ponytail. It felt weird to be in the twenty-first century.

Exhaustion hazed her vision, making colors a touch too bright. She hadn't slept much after Gawain had left. Even now, if she closed her eyes, she was back in that last moment before he'd disappeared through the balcony door. He'd shot Tamsin a glance that said he wasn't done with her. She didn't doubt it. The power of that smoky blue gaze had gone straight to her core like a drug. Her heels had actually dug into the floor, as if she'd needed something solid to brace herself.

Now, back in the light of day, Tamsin pressed her fingers to her temples and pushed back a tide of anxiety. Her life didn't feel as if it was hers anymore. Gawain's tales of crazy stalker fae had her eyeing the shadows, although he was the one she should be worried about. Even if his wild stories were true, he had broken into her apartment and violated her privacy—and then tried to possess her in ways he had no right to. He'd forced her to use her magic to defend herself. That was utterly unacceptable.

If this had happened to a friend, she'd advise them to call the police. But, despite all common sense, she'd found herself drawn to Gawain's story. There was no reason to believe him—sure, she was a witch and knew magic was real, but seriously? Fae had vanished from the earth centuries ago. The knights of Camelot were a legend. Even if they were real, what would they be doing in Carlyle, Washington? Swilling craft beer, wearing flannel shirts and cheering on the Seahawks? That image alone had kept her wide-awake.

Nevertheless, there was something important in his tale, something her sixth sense told her to pay attention to. It felt like pieces of a puzzle coming together, but she had no idea what picture it was forming.

The fastest way to find out was to locate those tombs, and that meant getting down to work. She sipped black coffee from her travel mug and switched on the aging computer. Stacks of paper boxes filled with old, uncataloged records reached halfway up the wall beside her desk. Most of the papers had to do with the study and restoration of the many architectural features of the church, but a few concerned the sale and loan of items. It was completely possible her answers were buried in those old papers. Tamsin opened a box at random, grabbed a handful of files and started searching. The papers were at least thirty years old and smelled of mildew, and many were routine office records—like a bill for a typewriter repairman. Not quite ancient history, but as close as Tamsin could get to the day-to-day operations of Medievaland's first owner, an eccentric millionaire who'd lost interest in the project the moment it was up and running.

She looked up at the clock a few minutes later, only to discover that hours had passed. A rumble from her stomach confirmed it was noon. Tamsin was unzipping her backpack to rummage for her lunch when her cell phone rang.

"Hey," said Stacy. "What's going on?"

"What do you mean?" Tamsin replied.

"Something happened after I talked to you yesterday."

Tamsin immediately thought of Gawain and shivered at the remembered brush of his rough hands. She wasn't ready to talk about that yet. "I'm in a medieval church, remember? No one here but us history buffs. What could possibly go wrong?"

Stacy sighed. "There are disturbances in the aether all over the West Coast. They were particularly strong near Carlyle all afternoon and last night."

Tamsin frowned. "How do you know that?"

"Mom. She had her crystal ball out and was scrying the energy fields in your area."

"Scrying? You mean spying." Tamsin wanted to smack her head against the wall. "I hate it when she does that. It's like having a drone on my tail at all times."

"Maybe, but she's always right. She says there have been significant spikes in magical activity right in your area." Stacy listed off a handful of times, and then her voice dropped to a whisper. "Mom even thinks someone or something stopped time for a moment. No one's used that kind of magic in centuries. What, by Merlin's magic wand, is going on in Carlyle?"

Tamsin sat back in her chair, skin prickling with alarm. "I don't know. I'm a healer. Sensing the aether was never my talent. I don't notice an anomaly unless I'm looking for it."

"Surely you have some idea. Mom might be obsessive and paranoid, but she can read energy from a distance better than any other witch in the eastern covens."

Which meant—what? That Gawain was right, and there were evil fae romping through the streets? "I honestly don't know."

Stacy's tone grew impatient. "You know Dad always thought Carlyle had a significant archive of magical materials. There have to be some serious practitioners out there, and they're up to something."

Tamsin cleared her throat. "There are supposed to be some very special books here, ones I know Dad was interested in, but I haven't found them. They seem to have disappeared along with…"

"What?"

"Other things." Tamsin put a hand to her forehead. She was hot, possibly because her head was exploding. "There are items that should be in the church but seem to have gone missing. I'm trying to find them."

"Magical items?"

"I dunno. Maybe. I'll let you know if I find anything."

"Oh, Tamsin," Stacy groaned, sounding pushed to her limits, "hurry up and come home where it's safe."

Tamsin sighed. "I'd better get to work. I'll call you later."

"Be careful." Stacy hung up.

Tamsin thumbed the End button and sat staring at her phone for a moment as the dark cloud of Stacy's anxiety faded. Her mother's observations bothered Tamsin. Something was definitely going on.

Tamsin needed a break. She grabbed her coat and strode through the cool dimness of the church. Outside, it was bright and sunny, and Tamsin breathed in the air and cheerful, gaudy colors of the theme park. She waited on the porch as an actor rode by in the full armor of a knight, the feathered hooves of his horse clop-clopping on the pavement. Children milled about the beast, who bore the noise and commotion with gentle patience. Tamsin couldn't help but smile.

And then she thought of Gawain, which wiped away every trace of lightness. She jumped down from the porch and began to walk briskly through the grounds, using the exercise to take the edge off her nerves.

The morning's work had made one thing clear. As a historian, she'd been trained to value meticulous research, but in this case the fae army might overrun the mortal world before she made it through all those boxes of paper. There had to be a way to fast-track a solution to this problem.

Tamsin was pondering the question when she reached the booth where brown-robed friars sold paper cups of hot chocolate. She bought the largest size and walked back into the church, ready to resume work.

Except Gawain was sprawled in her desk chair, feet stretched out and arms folded across his massive chest. She started at the sight of him, releasing a sticky dribble through the hole in the lid of the cup. Knuckles smarting from the burn, she set the drink on top of her filing cabinet and licked the sweetness from her fingers.

"What are you doing here?" she asked, trying to keep her tone light despite her suddenly pounding heart. Emotion from last night flooded back—trepidation, anger and, illogically, desire. Somehow the taste of dark chocolate merged with the sight of his big body, sending a burst of need through her synapses. She wanted to touch the stubble on his cheeks to see if it was as rough as it looked— which was utterly ridiculous.

He looked up slowly, eyes traveling from her feet to her face as if committing her to memory all over again. With a quick shove, he spun the chair to face her. The lines of his face were harsh with fatigue. By the rumpled state of his clothes, he'd been up all night.

"I told you I'd come back for answers." His voice was rough, almost a rasp.

"You lost the right to answers." Tamsin shed her coat, hanging it on the hook behind the door.

His jaw went tight. "For your own sake, for everyone's, I beg you to reconsider."

"Right," she muttered. "Evil fae, wicked queen, stone knights."

"I promise you, I will not touch you again. You have

nothing to fear from me." Gawain rose from the chair, stepping aside as best he could in the tiny, cramped office. The movement was graceful, reminding her he was more than he appeared. A knight. A prince. Or perhaps a very good actor.

Tamsin folded her arms, protecting herself but determined to stand her ground. She wasn't prey, and she wasn't about to run—although her knees were trembling a bit. He might say he was harmless, but she didn't buy it. His presence filled the room like a physical force. He gestured to her empty chair with courtly grace.

Refusing to show how much he spooked her, she retrieved her chocolate and sat down. Only then did she notice a newspaper folded and positioned in the middle of her desk. "What's this?"

"Proof of what I've told you."

She picked up the paper and glanced at the headline. "It says there was a mugging. What does that prove?"

In a single, lightning-fast movement, he snatched the paper and slammed it down on the desk. "This happened last night. I was there. Read it carefully."

Suddenly he was too big, too physical. The fury rolling off him pinned Tamsin to the chair. "Look!" He jabbed a finger at the paper. Then he visibly reined himself in. "Please."

At first she couldn't. It was as if her spine had fused with fright. Then, one degree at a time, she managed to move her head. There was a picture of a narrow alley, the outline of a body marked in chalk. The owner of the gas station next door had found the unidentified corpse. "This is awful, but I don't understand the significance."

"The deceased male was a fae. There were two, but apparently the other survived and walked away. Now read the article below."

She did. A man had been found wandering the streets last night. He was hospitalized now, suffering from amnesia.

"The fae attacked him," Gawain said. "I saved his life, but I could do no more. They were consuming his soul."

Tamsin looked up from the paper, bewildered. "They were *what*?"

"The fae were robbed of their souls, so now they devour those of innocent strangers. If I cannot find my king and brother knights, there will be no way to stop their army from taking what they want. I cannot begin to guess how many mortals will die."

The harsh regret in his words shook her. She picked up the paper, studying the eerie scene again before she set it facedown on the desk. The articles weren't exactly proof, but the times coincided with some of the disturbances Stacy had reported. That had to mean something.

He was utterly somber, nothing but pure determination etched on his face. "Will you help me?"

She hesitated, and not because she begrudged him her aid. Even if he were mad, it would be straightforward enough to find one of the tombs and send him on his way. But maybe—just maybe—she was starting to believe him. "What are you going to do if I find your king? Hover over his effigy and wait for him to wake up?"

"If that's what it takes."

Tamsin imagined him sitting by a tomb for days, weeks, even years, waiting for his lord to cheat death. He had that kind of single-minded purpose. "Why spend the time looking for Arthur?" she asked. "Why not lead the attack against the fae yourself?"

"For the same reason you do not hire a blacksmith to etch the head of a pin," he said, matter-of-fact. "We all have strengths. I am the best fighter, but Arthur is the strategist. And there are other reasons." He looked as if he wanted to say more but didn't. He obviously wasn't ready for full disclosure.

Even so, his words made sense to Tamsin. She fiddled with the edge of the newspaper, fraying it between her fingers. "I've tried looking in the files. It's going to take forever to get through them, and if what you say is true, we don't have that kind of time."

She heard his indrawn breath. She hadn't exactly said she would help him, but she'd given him hope. A mix of emotions made her palms go clammy. Agreeing to this meant spending more time in his company, and that was a terrifying prospect. Worse, it had a dark appeal that made her insides grow warm with anticipation. Tamsin wasn't sure how far she trusted herself.

Gawain found a second chair beneath a stack of files and sat. His eyes were on her face, reading her every expression. "Go on."

"There might be another way," Tamsin said slowly. "I came to Carlyle because rumors say there is a collection of ancient books of magic in town. I want to find it and study what's there."

Gawain frowned. "You don't know where it is?"

"No. Strange as it may seem to outsiders, that's common among my people." She took another sip of her chocolate. "Covens guard their archives jealously. Most of the real information on magic was lost after the war against the demons. Merlin's spell compromised our powers and, well, let's just say magic users weren't popular after he was through. Years of persecution followed and most of our books were burned."

Tamsin paused, wondering if she should be telling him her plans. At the same time, an idea was forming as she spoke. "The only books that survived were well hidden.

Scholars like my father, and now me, have to talk our way into collections to study the materials. There is no coven in Carlyle, which makes me think the books I'm looking for might be in a private library."

"And what does this have to do with the tombs?" Gawain asked, the tension around his eyes reminding her of how little he liked magic.

She set the cup down. "I'm getting there. The rumors say the books were originally part of this church's property and came with it when it was moved. They might have belonged to Merlin the Wise himself."

That got Gawain's attention. "You seek Merlin's books?"

"I do. Since Merlin enchanted your tombs, the books may help us find your knights. I could try locating them by magic. One seeking spell might even find both at once."

Gawain didn't speak, but leaned forward in his chair, waiting for her next words.

"So that is how I can help you," Tamsin concluded. "Now I'll tell you how you can help me."

His response was clipped. "Name it."

Tamsin took a deep breath, bracing herself. "A seeking spell requires an object connected to the thing or person you're looking for. You're the closest thing I've got to those tombs."

"You want to use me?" Gawain bolted from the chair, blue eyes wide with wrath—or maybe it was alarm. "I am to take part in your witch's spell?"

"It's up to you," Tamsin said, her throat so tight it hurt. "How badly do you want to find your king?"

Chapter 6

It was dark when Gawain arrived at Tamsin's apartment building a few hours later. His steps slowed as he approached the front walk, for he did not want to be there—not at all. Not when the reason for the visit was to cast a spell. He would rather have faced an enraged ogre than be in the same room with a witch at work—and yet somehow he had agreed to it. That had to be proof of his desperation.

Gawain knew well enough that magic could heal as well as harm. If the stakes were high enough, he could and would endure its presence for the greater good. After all, he had allowed Merlin to turn him to stone so he could follow his king into the future. It was just…

Memories of his childhood crowded in. His mother, Queen Morgause, had been as beautiful as a night-blooming flower—or at least that's what the poets had said. All the recollections Gawain could dredge up were of nightmares. The nameless, many-legged things she kept in her workroom and called her pets. Her deadly potions. The sight of her strangling his hound so she could use the unborn pups for a curse. And then there was the way she had died—slain by her own son, Agravaine. Gawain's younger brother's mind had not survived the twisted evil in their home.

And Gawain, alone of all his brothers, had inherited the potential to create that darkness anew. That was not a future he was willing to accept. As soon as he was old enough, he'd picked up a sword and ridden off to serve the young king, believing an honorable death would cleanse his soul. He'd survived, but never allowed himself to use the least hint of his inherited magic. Not after—well, he refused to think about certain events.

Which begged the question of why he was knocking on a witch's door, about to help her with a spell. If Gawain had thought of any other way to find the Round Table in time to destroy their enemies—anything at all—he'd have leaped on it like a wildcat upon a hare.

Gawain reached the front door of Tamsin's building and found it locked. He knew enough about modern times to search the panel beside the door for Tamsin's name. He pressed the button next to it and waited.

"Hello?" Her voice crackled out of the speaker, making him jump.

He cast a glance around, hoping no one had noticed his less-than-manly surprise. "It is Gawain."

"Come on up."

The door clicked, and he tugged on the handle. This time it opened, and he stepped into the lobby. Fortunately, he'd already learned about elevators and made his way to her floor.

The door to Tamsin's suite was open, letting out the scent of herbs and good food. His stomach rumbled, reminding him that he was hungry. He lingered on the threshold a moment, savoring the aroma.

A moment later, Tamsin put her head out of the tiny galley kitchen and gave him a bright smile. "Make yourself comfortable. Dinner's just about done."

"Dinner?" he asked suspiciously. "I did not expect this."

"I hope you don't mind. I can't perform a ritual on an empty stomach."

Gawain approached the tiny table where just last night Tamsin had bound his wound. There were place settings already laid out, and he studied them carefully. He'd been thoroughly trained to take his place at Camelot's high table, but he was well aware that modes and manners had changed. Gawain felt an unaccustomed flicker of stage fright.

Tamsin bustled out of the kitchen with a bowl of greens. "It's just pasta and salad, nothing much. My mother would tell me I'm a terrible homemaker."

He almost smiled then, a rueful turn of lips. "You realize, of course, that I have not been invited to dine in someone's home for nearly a thousand years."

Tamsin raised her brows. "In that case, you'll be excited to learn about this new thing called a fork."

Gawain looked away from her pretty, open face. "You're mocking me."

"Are you sure about that?"

"You assume I have the manners of a mad hermit."

"Have you used a fork before?"

"Why should I?" His tone grew icy.

"Maybe I should have ordered pizza." She disappeared back into the kitchen.

Gawain watched her retreating form, appreciating the sway of her hips. He knew she was just as wary of him as he was of her—and with more cause—but she refused to let it show. Whatever else she was, Tamsin Greene was not a coward. She was taking a risk, inviting him here. He would show her better courtesy tonight.

"I'm a little behind," she said. "My sister keeps phoning me about one thing or another. Today it was my mother's plans."

"For what?"

Tamsin's shoulders hunched, as if the subject irritated her. "She's threatening to have the Elders find a husband for me."

"Is she?" Gawain's eyes narrowed. Every level of his being rejected the idea like poison.

Tamsin gave Gawain a weary look, but there was a touch of anger deep in her eyes. "It's just my mother. The Elders have better things to do with their time."

"What does your sister believe?" The knot in his chest tightened. He had never condoned forcing a maid to marry, whatever the reason.

"She's older and thinks she knows best."

He could hear the affection in her voice, but also deep exasperation. "I understand. I was the eldest of four brothers."

"No wonder you're bossy." Tamsin set plates of food on the table. "Sit. Eat. I promise it is entirely magic-free."

He flushed slightly at her words, but sat and sniffed at the meal. It wasn't food he'd tried before, but he had seen it in pictures. There were spirals of pasta drenched in a thick and meaty sauce that made his mouth water. Hesitantly, he picked up a piece of crusty bread and soaked it in the sauce. It was hot and savory, and all at once dinner seemed like an excellent idea.

They dug in. He watched the way Tamsin handled the food to make sure he got the rituals of the table just right. Although he tried not to admit it, he enjoyed watching her delicate fingers hold the silverware and the way her lips closed around each bite. It made him think of other, more interesting things her lips might do.

"You realize," Tamsin began, breaking the silence, "that as a medieval historian, I'm fascinated to actually meet someone from the past." She cast him a glance that was almost shy.

"I expect that is true." Gawain shifted in his seat, feeling uncomfortably ancient. It prompted him to change the subject. "You say you are in search of Merlin's books at the behest of your coven Elders. Why did you take on this task?"

She looked down, her face carefully schooled. "To prove myself. Loremasters can travel and conduct business on our own authority in a way other witches can't. I am the first woman to take this position, even on a temporary basis. I want the job permanently. It's the best chance I have for a position with so much responsibility."

No doubt it also ensured escape from a marriage she didn't want. Gawain studied her face, now grown slightly flushed, as if she wasn't used to speaking her mind to strangers. "Ambition in the right measure is an attractive quality. It shows independence."

Her eyes grew wide and she leaned closer. "Tell me about Merlin the Wise."

She'd changed the subject, just as he had. Fencing. Protecting herself. Not quite sure of him. It piqued his interest. "What do you want to know?"

"He was the greatest sorcerer that ever lived. Of course I'm curious. What was he like as a person?"

"I never liked him," Gawain said bluntly, and forked up some more pasta.

Tamsin looked momentarily crestfallen. "Why not?"

Gawain chewed and swallowed. He recognized hero worship when he saw it. He struggled between the truth and sparing her feelings. "Merlin was a mighty spell caster.

Unfortunately, he always believed he knew what was best. There were those who warned him against a war with the demons, but he would not listen and so broke the world as we knew it."

"He was flawed," Tamsin said.

"Then why do the witches honor his memory so deeply?"

Tamsin lowered her eyes until all he could see was the crescent of her lashes. Her voice grew quiet. "Because he reminds us to be humble. If even the best of us can fail, we must cherish obedience. The Elders govern how we live now."

Gawain barely resisted the impulse to reach across and raise her chin. She had beautiful dark eyes but also a way of hiding them.

"I don't think Merlin himself would have approved of your Elders. He never valued obedience."

She gave a lopsided smile. "I think that's the point."

This time Gawain laughed. "Serves him right."

"But you trusted Merlin to put you to sleep for nearly a thousand years."

"I did that for Arthur. He is my friend. I would not let him wake alone in a strange land with no one to guard his back."

Now she did look up, turning the full force of her dark eyes on him. They were the deep brown of rich forest loam. The color made him think of new life and deep mysteries. Tamsin had immense power, even if she did not fully realize it; despite himself, he could feel it like the warmth of sun against his skin. Too much to be thrown away on a man she didn't like or caged by Elders who thought they knew best. With sudden clarity Gawain understood how much she wanted her freedom—and how much he wanted her to have it.

As he looked, her gaze grew clouded with emotion.

"You are a very loyal friend to risk so much. Your king is a lucky man."

"He deserves no less." Gawain cleared his throat, thrown off balance by her reaction.

A brief silence fell. He realized he'd cleaned his plate, eating every delicious bite. "Thank you for dinner. It was very good."

"Would you like another helping?" Tamsin asked. She'd finished, too, but her portion had been much daintier.

He did want more but wasn't sure what was considered polite these days. It seemed better to exercise restraint. "No, thank you."

And yet Gawain wasn't ready for the meal to end. He rose and walked to the balcony, looking out at the city lights. She'd left the curtains open again, instead of shutting them against prying eyes. He should scold her for being careless but had lost the heart to chide her. He'd walked into her home guarded against seduction and, instead, found simple hospitality. He hadn't been prepared for that.

"I'll tell you a story about my king," he said. "When I first came to Camelot, I knew no one. Arthur was my kinsman, but we had not met. My father, King Lot, was a great and wealthy lord and much was expected of me. I was eager to prove my worth and nobility as a knight, and as the Prince of Lothian."

He remembered Camelot with jewellike clarity—the fine clothes and rich food. It had seemed exotic to a lad from the north. "I entered every tourney, accepted every quest and fought every battle that came my way. Eventually, Arthur gave me the task of rescuing three maidens held for ransom by the Black Knight. Of course, I set off at once."

He turned from the window to see Tamsin leaning on

one hand, her elbow on the table. Her attention was entirely fixed on him, and Gawain felt like himself again—a rare thing since awakening in this strange and disheartening century. "The Black Knight's castle was in the Forest Sauvage, a place fraught with magic and treachery. I lost two of my companions along the way, but in the end we laid siege to the castle and brought the women home. When I knelt once more before Arthur, I bore many wounds."

"What did he say?" Tamsin asked.

Gawain had to smile at that. "Arthur picked that moment to tell me that five other knights had tried to storm the castle before me. None had come back alive."

"And he still asked you to go?" She sounded horrified.

"Of course. I rejoiced at the news. Proving that I could succeed where all others had failed was exactly what I'd desired. He knew that, and he knew I would prevail."

Tamsin knit her brows together. "How?"

"Because I wanted it more. Arthur's strength is that he sees passion in the hearts of others. He helps them use it to achieve greatness."

Tamsin folded her napkin, then clutched it, betraying her nerves. "What are you going to do about Mordred?"

"That depends on what he does." Gawain folded his arms. "Mordred and I despise each other, but we were both shaped by our kin and their dark legacy. I understand him better than most."

Tamsin nodded, her lashes lowered. They were a dark gold against her creamy skin. "You'd save him if you could?"

She raised her eyes and did it again—breaking him open with a mere look. Her expression said more than her words, and Gawain's throat grew tight. "He is my cousin, but no. He is consumed by darkness."

He might have said more, but he'd talked about himself

far more than was natural. He wasn't sure why. Perhaps it was because she was far from home, alone with her books. Lost as he was, her solitude gave him an unexpected feeling of kinship.

She looked away first, ending the moment. "Then we should get to work and find your fellow knights. I'll set up the ritual."

Gawain's mood darkened immediately. Once again he saw the two fae in the alley, sucking out the soul of an innocent man. Magic had the power to corrupt in horrific ways. He had known as much since he was a boy. So why was he participating in this?

He knew the answer. For Arthur. For Angmar. For all the knights and fae and mortals who needed the Round Table. He had no choice but to trust Tamsin Greene.

Still, Gawain's skin crawled, filling him with the urge to leap from the balcony and bolt into the night—far, far away from whatever they were about to do.

"Tell me about the ritual," he said softly. "How bad is it going to be?"

Chapter 7

Rather than answer, Tamsin cleared the dishes from the table. Something had shifted during the meal, leaving her shaken. Gawain had dropped his guard for an instant, letting her glimpse the man behind his iron facade. Not that he had intentionally revealed much—they had talked mostly about other people—but she had been able to piece together the shape of his character. Something in his background had driven him to Arthur. She guessed Gawain didn't bestow his loyalty lightly, but it was unshakable once he had. Tamsin found herself envying his king.

She finished her task and turned back to him, a flutter of nerves in her stomach. "This is going to be dangerous. If I do a spell, others will notice. Witches, the fae, and who knows what else."

She'd said it briskly but still felt the prickle of nerves skitter over her skin.

"No one gets past me," he said. "Now, how do we do this?"

"The setup is simple." She spread a fresh white cloth on the table. Although she hadn't said as much, the ritual had begun the moment he'd sat down to break bread with her. Eating together formed a bond that would strengthen their connection. "Sit where you were before."

But Gawain remained standing, drawing the curtains while she went to her backpack and retrieved her father's spell book. Then she opened the chest at the foot of her bed and removed candles, incense, a knife and a bowl of deep blue glass. She looked up to see that Gawain had turned chalky pale.

Tamsin tensed. "What's wrong?"

"My mother had things just like that." He swallowed hard. Whatever he was thinking, it didn't look like happy memories.

Tamsin folded her hands to hide their shaking. "She was a witch?"

He nodded, retreating to a scowl. "She was Morgan LaFaye's sister."

That explained a lot. Tamsin rose, closing the chest and picking up her supplies. If he was spooked, she wasn't doing much better. "Are you sure you're okay with this?"

"Of course." His gaze slid away. "I have seen magic performed before."

Not willingly, from the sound of it. Tamsin shivered, grateful when he stepped back as she deposited the materials on the table. But then he picked up the spell book and carefully examined its cover as if handling something poisonous. The way he was frowning made Tamsin angry. The book was precious to her, and she barely resisted the urge to snatch it from his hand.

Unfortunately, she couldn't afford a show of temper. The Elders had ordered her to find Merlin's grimoires and Gawain was the only link she had to make this seeking spell work. If it hadn't been for that, she would have sent him on his way. They didn't trust each other, and that would make the ritual difficult to pull off.

Gawain was reading the yellowed pages of the grimoire, his brow furrowed. Even from a distance, Tamsin knew the book well enough to recognize the charm for removing rust. Maybe he was planning to clean his armor.

"Does the spell Merlin cast give you the ability to read the old languages in that book?" she asked.

"I had a tutor," he said defensively, glancing up. "I learned Latin and some Greek. I can make out some of it."

He'd been lucky. A good education had been far from universal in his day, even among the nobility. He bent his head over the pages again, dark hair falling in his eyes. For an instant, Tamsin forgot to do anything but stare. Something about seeing him still for once made her notice more details. His nose wasn't quite straight, as if he'd broken it and set it by hand. His long legs bent awkwardly as he sat down in the chair, reminding her of how tall he was. There was a common belief that people were smaller in past centuries, but that wasn't altogether true. No average man had Gawain's bearing, much less such heavily muscled shoulders.

Swallowing hard, Tamsin arranged the candles, finding it nearly impossible to concentrate. Gawain radiated a wild, dark energy, as if his very presence sliced through rational thought. Maybe it did, but it also tasted to Tamsin like passionate emotion—all that anger and desperate loyalty straining at the leash in response to danger.

Tamsin finally took the book from him. She turned from the rust removal charm, past the new page that had appeared last night and found the spell she wanted. A moment's rereading reminded her of the words she needed to speak. Then she filled the bowl with water she'd infused with fresh herbs and set it in the middle of the table. Finally, she lit the candles with a word. Gawain did not flinch at the small display of power. Not like Richard had. Judging by his set jaw, Gawain was braced for something far more dramatic.

He would get it. She dropped a small, red crystal in the center of the bowl. It fell with a splash, sending ripples outward. They shone silvery in the candlelight, ring upon ring. The circle of the spell closed around them, drawing the shadows inward like a cloak. The noise from the street faded, leaving behind a muted hush. Tamsin let her vision lose focus and rode the silvery tides as she set her power free. It prickled through her tattoo, amplified by the magic woven into the intricate lines. "Give me your hands," she said.

Gawain obeyed, his grip warm and strong. Immediately, she sensed his presence on the psychic plane. Like most of mixed human and witch parentage, his power was uneven and, in his case, only partly developed. She guessed he had buried that side of himself long ago. Still, his aura was stronger than an ordinary human's and different from any she'd sensed before.

Careful to keep her touch light, Tamsin searched for traces of Merlin's spell for the stone sleep. When she found it, she opened her second sight and let her mind coast on the rippling water. "Where are you?" she whispered to Merlin's magic. "Show me where you've been."

Images flickered past too quickly to grasp, like a video on fast-forward. She saw impressions of dank, cold stone and wild coastline. Scenes of an ancient past. And then her mind slipped down another path, this time with more coherence. There was a face, gone before she saw it clearly, though a name lingered behind: Angmar. Wasn't that the name of Gawain's friend?

And then she was standing in a library, a solid being in a solid place—or so it seemed. It might have been real, or just a reflection out of time. It was hard to know when walking the web between worlds. Rarely was anything what it seemed there, and that made it all too dangerous.

Nevertheless, Tamsin's pulse quickened as her mind-self hurried to the shelves. There were many ancient books in a dozen languages—history, philosophy, books of music, and books of architecture. But then she saw what she was after—tomes of magic so old she could smell the sorcery like an exotic spice wafting from the pages. These were the books Merlin had left behind.

Tamsin whirled around, seeking any clue about the library's location. By the fancy carving and ornate plaster ceiling, it was a building from the last century. The stained glass window was dark, but she could still make out the design of a peacock with its tail spread out in panes of azure glass.

"What are you doing here?" demanded a voice that was not a voice but a whisper from inside her own mind.

Tamsin spun in the direction of where the sound ought to have been, but she was too slow. Every instinct shrieked trouble as the temperature around her mind-self plummeted. She'd barely finished turning her head—hair flying in slow motion—when she glimpsed the dark shape of a man, his features obscure. He seemed to move as if he was under water, the light bending so that he slid from one distortion to another, but he had locked his sights on her. She felt his gaze like the point of a knife.

"Why are you in my house?" he asked.

Instinct warned her to be careful, but it was impossible to lie in this place. "I came for answers, not as a thief."

"Try again."

Ice frosted over the peacock window, hiding the bird

under a carpet of sparkling white. Tamsin's breath ghosted before her, the air so cold it seemed to shimmer and burn as she filled her lungs. She clutched her chest, suffocating with the pain. "You don't need to do this."

But the ice spilled down the walls to cover the shelves and the books. "But I do," he said. "You're my cousin's spy. You came to find his fae snitch."

Tamsin wasn't about to point out that wasn't the whole truth. Even if she wanted to, there wasn't time. Ice flowed like a sinister carpet toward Tamsin's feet. She stepped away, trying to let go of the vision, to fly back to the safety of the real world, but her power had frozen along with the room. The figure spun, a strange dance of triumph before he braced himself to strike.

Power such as she'd never felt before pounded into her. It wasn't a blow. It was a detonation. With a shriek of unspeakable pain, Tamsin's vision shattered into a thousand pinpoints of light.

Gawain sensed something had gone wrong, though he could not say how. Then, just at the edge of sensation, the magical energy of the spell grew cold against his skin. A moment later, Tamsin shuddered, her nails digging painfully into Gawain's palms.

Alarm shot through him. He knew enough about spells to understand Tamsin's had turned on her. Sometimes witches could lose their way when traveling like this. Sometimes they could be lured away or ambushed. Fighting a crawling sense of panic, he grasped her hands tight, letting her feel his strength. "I am your anchor. Come back to me."

She didn't respond. Instead, she sat like a figure made of wax, her lips parted and her eyes closed. The only sign of life was the straining tendons in her wrists as she clutched at him. Gawain swallowed hard as an old, bad, angry fear clawed him from the inside.

He caught his breath, forcing his mind clear. It had been too long since he'd used magic of any kind, and he wasn't sure what to do. He loosed one hand to reach up and touch Tamsin's cheek. Her skin was cool, and that meant she was losing ground to the spell. He cursed, a fierce rush of protectiveness pushing all other emotions aside. His gaze roved over her still, pale face, lingering on every delicate curve.

"Listen to me, Tamsin Greene," he said, his voice loud in the hushed candlelight. "You have a fierce will. It's up to you to fight your way back."

There was no sign she heard. Not one. He cursed silently—she was growing colder by the second. He rose from the spindly chair, still holding one of her hands. He was afraid of breaking the connection between them, unsure what would happen if he did. Slowly, he moved around the small table and knelt beside her, hoping the closer contact would help. "Come back to the sound of my voice, Tamsin. I'm not going to let you go. As long as you can hear me, you're not lost."

He was drawing on scraps of knowledge he'd tried to forget—stories of lost souls who had to be coaxed back to their bodies like wandering lambs, lured with the promise of safety, warmth and light. Only the strongest made it back. As for the rest...

"This is not so simple as a dragon or a troll. I can't ride to your rescue with sword and spear. This is your fight, but I will stay with you. I am at your side, Tamsin Greene, and I will not leave."

But then he stopped talking because it was doing no good. She was still growing colder. Gawain needed to do more. His buried power stirred like some serpent waking at the bottom of his soul, but neglect and denial had blunted its fangs. He could expect no help there.

Operating on instinct, he gathered Tamsin in his arms and carried her to the bed on the other side of the tiny apartment. Her golden hair spilled over his arm in a cascade of silk, the brush of it firing his every nerve. She was very, very female, soft and slender, and rounded in all the right places. The scent of her called to his blood, a wild, primitive summons so ancient it had no words. Desire rose, clouding his head like strong drink. Keeping his focus was going to be the very devil.

He paused beside the wide bed, taking in the nest of pillows and brightly colored throws. This was her private haven. Feeling like an intruder, Gawain set Tamsin down, arranging her limbs so that she looked comfortable. She lay still, pale and cold, a sleeping nymph in her bower. Unable to stop himself and needing to keep physical contact, he smoothed the hair from her face, deeply aware of the soft perfection of her skin.

Simply putting Tamsin to bed would not be enough. Through the thin fabric of her blouse, he could detect shivers rippling through her, a sign that the unnatural cold went deep inside. He needed to warm her, and quickly. Gawain piled the covers around her, but it had no effect. Finally, he peeled off his jacket and shirt and climbed into the bed beside her. Desire pounded through him with the urgency of a war drum, but this was not the time for conquest. This was the time to protect. He drew her close, cradling her head on his shoulder and heating her with his own warmth, willing his warrior's strength into her soul.

It grew roasting hot beneath the blankets—too much for Gawain's comfort—but Tamsin's teeth stopped chattering only when the temperature reached tropical heights. She curled on her side, head tucked beneath his chin. She was a perfect fit against his side, their position forming a long line of body-to-body contact ideal for counteracting the spell. Temptation goaded Gawain, torturing body and mind, but he spent the time talking nonsense and hoping the sound of his voice would do some good.

The candles were guttering before he detected the slightest change. The heavy feel of the spell dissipated from the air, letting the sounds of traffic and voices drift up from the street below. Tamsin's breathing quickened, fingers fluttering across his chest. Gawain was wide-awake, too worried even to drowse, but her sudden movement still caught him by surprise. Wild relief stormed through him and his hand went to her hair, stroking it before he knew what he was doing.

She raised her head slowly, blinking in surprise. Shock spread over her face as she realized he was half-naked beside her. Gawain bit back a chuckle.

Tamsin threw off the covers, rising to her hands and knees, then looked down at herself, clearly noting that she was still dressed. "You held me." She looked up, her dark eyes somber. "That's all you did."

"I hope from now on you will think better of me," Gawain replied quietly.

She cleared her throat, a small, nervous sound. "Thank you."

"What happened to you?"

"Give me a minute," she said, her expression so vulnerable it made his chest hurt.

The physical pull of her swamped Gawain's reason. He'd lain next to her for hours, and so much contact had wound him to a painful pitch. Still, he read the awkward uncertainty in her eyes. "Do you want me to go?"

She shook her head. "I'm not ready to be alone yet."

"Then I would like to kiss you," he said, drowning in

the heat still trapped between their bodies. He had held himself in iron restraint, but his discipline was spent.

Tamsin gave a startled jerk. "What?"

"I want to kiss you," he repeated.

"Oh." She hesitated so long he was certain she would push away. But then she gave a slow blink that changed the knot in his gut to a liquid heat lower down. "If you're sure you want to." The statement was half a tease, but there was a painful honesty in it, too.

"I am." He brushed her cheek with the backs of his fingers. "I can think of nothing more pleasant right now."

She sank down onto one hip, her mouth curving into a bemused smile. "Really?"

Her expression was shy, but she tilted her mouth up to his, inviting him. It was something Gawain had never expected after she'd thrown him out just last night, and he wasted no time. He had kissed his share of maids, and more, but this was different. Maybe it was because his nerves were raw after nearly losing her, or he was far too lonely, but he was utterly without defense.

The press of her soft lips was warm, filled with the lingering essence of woman and magic. And the spice did not end with her taste—it was in who she was. Her teeth nipped at his lower lip, inviting him to explore. He didn't need prompting. As her lips parted, he made a conquest of her sweet, silky mouth. Tamsin moaned slightly, the note of hunger urging him on.

Once permission had been granted, he pushed forward, savoring everything she gave. The first spark of passion had been physical, the effect of her beauty and the closeness of their bodies for so many hours. But beyond that was her courage, and the sheer will that had made her survive. Few came back from wandering a vision. He had to respect her strength.

Gawain rolled to his knees, pulling her up with him. His fingers tangled in her long, sun-bright hair. He loved the thick, shining wealth of it. Wanted it against every inch of his skin.

The movement had broken their kiss, but still their breath mingled. Tamsin was panting, eyes hazed and lips swollen. Gawain held her gently, not sure of her yet, not certain what pleased her. She was a puzzle he was determined to solve, but he would do it the right way.

"More?" he asked.

"More," she whispered, a bare movement of air shaped by that lovely mouth. At the same time, her hands were stroking the muscles of his abdomen.

Gawain groaned. His body ached with need as he traced the edge of Tamsin's collar with his fingertip. The blouse was prim and tempting at once, and his fingers found their way to the top button that sat at the notch of her collarbone. They were small buttons for his big fingers, but determination was a powerful thing. The softness beneath was a more than adequate reward. There was a delicate undergarment beneath and he bent, pressing his lips to the curve of lace cupping her breast. He slid his hands down, cupping her backside, ready to sink into her.

Ready to give in to an attraction that broke every one of his rules. Tamsin was a witch, and they were all but strangers. The aftermath of magic had them in its thrall.

A flicker of caution broke through the haze of arousal. When he raised his eyes to Tamsin's, he saw the same hesitation in her eyes. They had come a long way toward mutual trust, but they were not there yet. Gawain snapped his mouth shut before he unleashed a dragon of a curse. To take her now would be the act of a wastrel.

He released her, sliding off the bed and grabbing his shirt. Tamsin watched his retreat with startled eyes that quickly darkened to hurt. "Did you suddenly remember I'm a witch?"

That caught him off balance. He wanted her to the point of painful frustration. "That is not my concern at the moment."

"Then what is?" She sank down on the bed, her hands folded between her knees like a child.

Gawain went still, not sure how to frame what he needed to say. "You were in trouble. I held you. If I make love to you now, you will regret it after. Gratitude only goes so far."

Tamsin's cheeks colored. Her jaw set in a way that said he'd struck close to the quick. "Maybe you're right."

"It happens after a battle. Danger makes us crave intimacy." He pulled the shirt over his head, ignoring the pang of disappointment hollowing his chest. "Did you see the tombs?"

She shook her head. "No, I'm sorry."

Gawain ducked his head so she wouldn't see the frustration crushing him. His fist tightened, but there was nothing to punish. She had tried, and nearly lost her life doing it. "I thank you for the attempt."

"Not so fast," she replied. "I saw the books I was after and I think I saw your missing friend. They might be in the same place."

Gawain looked up at her. There was a look of triumph that hadn't been in her eyes a moment ago. He thought he'd ended the dance between them, recalled himself to duty, but she'd just changed the rules. Gawain found himself giving in to a slow smile. Tamsin really was full of the unexpected. "You found Angmar?"

"Maybe." She rose from the bed, moving slowly as if every joint ached. "But getting him back isn't going to be easy. The place is guarded by a heavy-duty magic user with an affinity for frost."

Gawain sobered in an instant. "Mordred. Cold is his trick. By the saints, he was the one who attacked you!"

A shadow of fear crossed her features. "He didn't win, though."

"Maybe." He took her hand, cradling her delicate fingers in his. This time, the warm physical contact was for his benefit. He needed tangible proof that she was safe and well. He wasn't leaving her unguarded, even if that meant sleeping outside her door.

He met her eyes, holding her deep brown gaze. "Mordred never counts a battle over until he is the victor. Victory to him always means death."

Chapter 8

The next afternoon, Tamsin hissed in frustration as a stack of files slithered to the floor of her office. An avalanche of yellowing paper and fading mimeographs fell with a crash. Pages fluttered across the tiles, destroying what little order she'd managed to create. Belatedly, Tamsin grabbed the last of the stack before it toppled off the desk, then wiped her hands on her jeans with a grimace.

She'd found another mildewy box from the 1970s. After handling the papers for an hour, she was dreaming of a hot shower laced with disinfectant. Getting down on her hands and knees, she began scooping the pages into a messy stack. It would have been nice to have a spell that could bring order to the mess, but she'd never heard of such a thing, and after the night before, she had no stomach for more magic.

To be perfectly honest, she didn't feel well after last night's adventure. She'd known the spell was risky—all visioning spells were. She should have had her coven around her, but she'd only had Gawain for support. Gawain, who hated magic and witches. It was just good luck that he knew how to help her when she'd needed it.

And then there was what had come after. Heat, and then pleasure, and then—what? It was as if Gawain had taken off protective armor long enough to drive her wild, and then donned it again the moment things got interesting. He didn't trust her—that much was clear—but his unexpected respect for her feelings said something had changed between them. Gawain had put her needs before his own and Tamsin wasn't sure whether to be glad or wary. Such restraint made her admire him far more than she cared to admit.

Crawling on hands and knees, Tamsin slid the last piece of paper from under the desk and added it to her stack. She sat back on her heels, exhausted by doubt. To be fair, Gawain had stayed with her until she fell asleep. After that, she was certain he didn't stray far. He was watching over her like a scowling guardian angel, afraid because Mordred now knew Tamsin existed. Just like Stacy had warned, using magic had put Tamsin on the bad guys' radar and that had nearly killed her. If Gawain hadn't coaxed her back to her body, she would have died.

Based on that, Tamsin knew two things. One, if Mordred had Merlin's books, as her spell suggested, they were in trouble. In the wrong hands—which Mordred's undoubtedly were—that much knowledge would be an unbeatable weapon. Two, if finding the tombs would stop Mordred in his tracks, she was all over the problem like a terrier determined to find its bone.

Tamsin dumped the stack of paper back onto the desk and resumed her seat in front of the computer screen. She'd been making notes in a spreadsheet, cross-referencing the paper records with a list of artifacts from the original sale of the church. Much of the church's contents—including the famous tombs—had been warehoused, but there the trail went cold and the warehouse had burned down since. She'd been hoping these files—boxed up for forty years, from what she could tell—would give her a hint as to the fate of its contents.

She picked up the top piece of paper. It peeled away from its neighbor with a tacky sound that spoke of damp and ancient photocopier ink. It was an inventory of reliquaries, complete with an assortment of saints' bones. Tamsin wondered what a DNA test would reveal. Most of those old relics turned out to be the bones of pigs or other animals.

The next page was a memo for the purchase of acid-free packing materials, and the next was someone's job application. On the fourth, Tamsin hit pay dirt.

It was a bill for transport, just a few words on a pre-printed invoice form from what looked like a small local company. Tamsin's stomach flipped, a wash of excitement making it hard to concentrate on the words in front of her. It was the second page of a carbon copy form, and the ink had faded to a pale gray. At the bottom was some writing she didn't understand, but the top looked like directions for delivery. All she could make out there was "stone" and "knight" and "Pacific College for" and "History." Pacific College for the Study of European History, she guessed. It had been absorbed by Oceanside University in Seattle back in the nineties, but the campus itself hadn't moved. This was the first real clue she'd found.

Excitement pounded in her chest. She had to tell Gawain. Unfortunately, he was out wandering around Medievaland in search of bad faeries and he didn't have a cell phone.

Without warning, the door opened, letting in a gust of

cool air. Tamsin looked up, shock sliding through her like a slim blade of ice.

There was a fae standing in the doorway. Tamsin had never actually seen one before, but there was no mistaking what species the female belonged to. She was exquisite, her skin a dark honey brown so smooth and fine it look polished. Her hair was frost white and fell in a thick tumble to her hips. In that exotic coloring, her eyes seemed to shimmer like green gems. Tamsin noted with surprise that the fae held a set of car keys in her hand. She'd never thought about such creatures driving, but she supposed they had to get around somehow.

The female took a step into the office, the heels of her boots clicking on the tile. Tamsin's first thought was of the newspaper article Gawain had shown her, and his tale of soul-devouring hunger.

Tamsin jumped slightly as the office door clicked shut. She licked her lips, fighting the urge to panic. The woman was exquisitely lovely, but her eyes were empty as a doll's. A creeping dread began to rise in Tamsin, protesting the presence of such utter wrongness. Forcing an outward calm, Tamsin folded her hands across the invoice, obscuring the fading text.

"May I help you?" she asked, her voice cracking on the last word. Where was Gawain?

"My name is Nimueh, and you are Tamsin Greene, the historian." The woman's voice was low and rich, though spoiled by an odd, flat quality. "Am I correct?"

"Yes."

Tamsin would have expected her visitor to look around for a chair, perch on the desk or make some move to get comfortable. Nimueh stood stiff as a wind-up mannequin, staring at Tamsin with unblinking eyes. It was, in a word, creepy.

"I was sent by Lord Mordred, son of the Queen of Faery," announced Nimueh.

Tamsin scrambled for options as her spine went rigid. "What does Lord Mordred want?"

"He should have destroyed you last night," the fae added without emotion.

"Which begs the question of what else there is to say," Tamsin snapped, her temper rising. "Sorry to disappoint."

"Lord Mordred is curious. He is not accustomed to set-backs."

As if Tamsin had lived just to spite him. She bit back nervous laughter.

The fae regarded her coolly. "Accordingly, he gener-ously offers safe passage to you so that he might learn why you survived his power."

"How thoughtful." All the aches from last night throbbed in reminder of how close Tamsin had been to extinction. "Why didn't he come himself?"

"I am less threatening. You are more likely to respond favorably to me."

"Really?" Tamsin asked, unable to stifle sarcasm. "Are we going to exchange tips on manicures and boyfriends?"

"How you approach this is your decision."

Tamsin sat back, keeping the movement relaxed. She was sure Mordred had the books she wanted, but she wasn't about to walk through his front door. "I think I'll decline your invitation to visit."

Nimueh's eyes glinted dangerously. It was the first sign of emotion Tamsin had seen. "I have been given my or-ders."

Tamsin's mouth filled with the copper taste of fear. Her fingers gripped the arms of the chair, forcing herself not to flinch. "I've heard of you. You're in the old stories, the one they called the Lady of the Lake. You gave the sword Excalibur to the king."

"And?"

"You don't seem like the same person at all."

"I'm not," Nimueh said, almost sounding wistful.

Tamsin's chest felt tight. "Whatever it was Merlin did, surely it can be undone."

"Do you think we have not tried?" The fae's voice sank to a whisper. She leaned forward, bracing her hands on the desk. "Do not waste time seeking our redemption."

Pity wrenched Tamsin, but also fresh fear. "Maybe the Round Table can help you."

"Do you cling to the dashing Sir Gawain?" Nimueh's voice was still soft, but the flicker of sadness was ironed away, as if it had never been. She pushed away, holding her hands out in a gesture of negation. "Do not be fooled. He despises your kind. You would be far wiser to ally yourself with Lord Mordred and tell him what you know of the lost tombs."

Tamsin barely heard Nimueh, because now she was conscious of the fae's power winding around her like a deadly, strangling vine, sapping her will. She could almost see it, a twining tendril of light sliding with a serpent's grace. The touch of it was silken, but it was also hideously strong. When it finally caught her, she would be unable to refuse anything Nimueh asked. For a fleeting, horrible moment, she saw herself handing over the invoice with the clue. Walking into Mordred's lair and becoming his pawn.

The snake of power was a thousand serpents now, tendrils weaving a web that would strangle her will. Nerves finally cracking, Tamsin pushed away from her desk and jumped to her feet. "Stop it!"

Nimueh's elegant brows arched. Her magic still tickled and scraped against Tamsin like tiny crawling feet, straining to pierce down to her soul. Tamsin brushed at her skin, although she knew it did no good. "Get off me before I make you regret it," Tamsin said with more bravado than she felt.

"Really?" Nimueh raised an elegant long-fingered hand, then clenched her fist. The weave of magic drew tight.

Tamsin gasped, instantly suffocated, and felt the power burrowing into her. Rage swept through her like sudden fire. Grabbing that white-hot anger, Tamsin pushed Nimueh away with her power, sending her skittering backward. Then Tamsin followed up with a blast of power. The fae slammed into the door and grabbed the knob for support as her heels skidded on the tiles.

"Well done." Nimueh pushed her long, pale hair away from her face and blinked, her expression almost surprised.

The magic crawling over Tamsin's skin faded. She should have been relieved but knew it was just a change of tactics.

Nimueh raised her hand again, this time to snap her fingers. Tamsin heard the heavy boom of the front doors of the church slamming closed. "Don't worry," said the fae. "The moment I arrived, the visitors and your docent had a sudden desire to go see the tourney. You and I are alone."

Tamsin listened. She could hear no voices, but something rustled outside the office door, making a thin, dry, leathery sound. She sat up slowly, the hair on her nape rising when she heard the scrape of... Was that claws? "You lie. There is someone else in the church."

"Not someone," Nimueh said calmly. "A helper of a different kind. You seem to need persuasion."

Tamsin's palms went clammy. "What have you done?"

By way of reply, Nimueh turned the handle of the door and pulled it open. Almost panting with fear, Tamsin came out from behind her desk. Afraid or not, she wanted space to fight. She gripped the heavy tape dispenser, then released it. Whatever Nimueh had conjured was probably immune to something as mundane as a crack to the head.

The space beyond her office door seemed dark, lit only by the light falling through the stained glass windows. Nevertheless, Tamsin saw something move. She stepped forward, then hesitated. The fae swept an elegant hand toward the door. "By all means. Escape if you can."

Sucking in a breath, Tamsin barged past, reluctant to put Nimueh at her unguarded back. The church echoed with her hurried footsteps, each scuff resounding in the stone ribs of the vaulted ceiling. The fae followed but turned the other way, giving Tamsin a wide berth.

Within seconds, Tamsin knew why. Something flew from her left, diving at a steep angle. She ducked, dropping nearly to the cold stone floor, but her attacker pulled up sharply in a flap of leathery wings. Tamsin glanced up, her jaw dropping when she saw a creature with a wingspan as wide as her office desk circle to land on the edge of the largest window. For a moment it was backlit, a silhouette of pointed ears and clawed bat wings, but it shuffled along a ledge until the light caught its features. It had a face like a demonic lemur, all huge eyes and fangs, with a tufted lion's tail that twitched with impatience. Tamsin gaped, all danger forgotten while she absorbed the strange sight.

"You brought one of the gargoyles to life," Tamsin said, her voice trembling. This was power of a kind she'd never encountered before.

"Indeed I did," said Nimueh. "And it's rather hungry."

The monster hopped off the ledge with a screech like nails on a chalkboard. It swooped toward Tamsin, wings spread and tail flying straight behind it. Tamsin ducked again, using a fat pillar as cover from its slashing claws.

It wheeled in the air, far more agile than Tamsin would have guessed, and came at her again.

Tamsin slipped around the pillar again, but the creature was wise to her now, rolling end over end in the air and using its tail like a rudder. Tamsin bolted for the safety of her office, but it outdistanced her immediately. There was no easy escape.

"You aren't pledged to the Round Table," said Nimueh. "You aren't one of their human subjects—you're a witch. You owe them nothing. Lord Mordred could offer you much."

Tamsin whirled, running for the stone lions now. Her feet were slipping on the floor, her braid bouncing against her shoulders as she ran. Behind her, the gargoyle's wings beat like thunder. It would have been easy to give up and tell the fae about the clue she'd found. Maybe it would buy her some time, give her a chance to plan a defense. But every one of those knights was a man like Gawain. Turning them over, even a single one, would be little better than murder.

Tamsin's lungs burned. She was gasping with fright as she dove between the stone lions, hiding in the space where Arthur's tomb should have been. She crouched under the shelter of the nearest head, making herself as small as possible, as the gargoyle landed close by. It swiped with one claw-tipped hand, but Tamsin jerked out of reach. Up close, the gargoyle's face was something out of a nightmare, with fangs jutting from its lower jaw and slits where there should have been a nose. Its eyes—huge, watery green marbles—were worst of all. For all Nimueh's magic, they held no more life than the stone.

"You're an abomination," Tamsin growled at the creature.

It made a soft chittering noise, crawling on all fours, wings folded tight and hugging the shape of the stones it clung to. The movements were more insect than animal, sending every one of Tamsin's nerves frantic with revulsion.

Tamsin could hear the heels of Nimueh's boots clicking on the stone floor. Tamsin squirmed, trying to see over the lion's back. The fae was coming closer, businesslike but unhurried. Tamsin fell back. The lions were a refuge, but they were also a dead end. She panted, nerves jangling. She was going to have to break cover and try for the side exit before Nimueh cut off her last hope of escape.

The gargoyle suddenly dropped in front of Tamsin's face, gripping the lion's mane with its back paws and grabbing with the front ones. Tamsin shrieked in surprise as needle-sharp claws raked her cheeks. Covering her face with one arm and batting with the other, Tamsin scrambled for freedom, but the gargoyle dropped onto her back, clutching her braid and hanging on with jabbering, squeaking glee. She cried out in pain, reaching around to jerk her hair free, but it chose that moment to bite, sinking its fangs into the flesh of her wrist.

Anger took over. Tamsin gripped the gargoyle and let fly with a pulse of blue energy, sinking it straight into the beast. It flung away with a squeal, arrowing at hideous speed until it hit the wall. The impact was horrific, an ear-splitting crash ending in an almost gentle tinkle like the fall of broken china. The gargoyle was in pieces. Tamsin froze, horrified despite everything that she'd destroyed a piece of art. Then Nimueh was there.

Tamsin felt the stir of fae magic and didn't hesitate. She hit first, hurling a bolt of power. The first caught Nimueh square on the shoulder, sending her off balance. The fae spun in a swirl of pale hair, using the momentum of the blast to catch herself and throw her own pulse of energy. Tamsin dove out of the way, rolling to her feet, and then struck out again. A flash of light strobed through the church, bleaching everything white with its brilliance. By the time Tamsin blinked the world back into focus, Nimueh was gone.

Tamsin swore, furious and relieved at once. Had she hit her?

A moment later, the main door groaned open. It was Gawain, looking around the gloomy cavern of the church. He caught sight of her and bolted to her side. "Are you all right?"

He skidded to a halt and dropped to one knee. After one look at her scratched face, he pulled her closer. Tamsin gulped down the aftermath of panic as she buried her face in his shirt, breathing in the warm scent of him.

"Tamsin?" he asked gently when she didn't speak.

"I had a visit from Nimueh." The words came out slowly, mumbled through a sudden fatigue. She'd fought back, she realized with a giddy lurch. She'd stood her ground well enough that the enemy had withdrawn.

He drew back. "How badly are you hurt?"

Tamsin looked down at her wrist where the creature had bitten her. There was an angry red mark, but it could have been worse. "I'm fine." Then she started to shake, the adrenaline leaving her body in a rush. The world went foggy with tears.

"Hush." Gawain folded her into his chest, comforting her with the warmth and strength of his arms. "I've got you. You're safe."

Tamsin let herself melt against him. Only a few days ago, he'd grabbed her in this same church, scaring her half to death. Now his gesture was one of concern. The rapid, fundamental shift left her shaken.

"Tell me everything," he said, resting his cheek against her hair for a long moment before he helped her to her feet.

She did, leading him back to her office as she described

her encounter in detail. Gawain went quiet with worry. "I was afraid that Mordred would trace you. That makes working here a risk for you."

"I might not be working here long. I'll have to come up with some excuse about the gargoyle." She grimaced. "I can't exactly say it came to life and attacked me. Maybe I could say there was an earth tremor."

Gawain looked dubious. "I wouldn't believe that story."

"Thanks. That's helpful." She stopped, picking up a set of car keys from the floor. She remembered Nimueh holding them. The fae must have dropped them during the fight. Tamsin shoved them in her pocket and went into her office, Gawain on her heels.

Beyond the office door, visitors were drifting in again. Tamsin heard an exclamation of dismay that said the ruined gargoyle had been found. At any moment, she'd have to start answering questions. Tamsin closed her eyes and stifled a groan. Then she remembered what she'd been doing before Nimueh ruined her day.

Tamsin picked up the invoice from her desk. "I might have found one of the tombs."

Gawain snatched the page, his features tight. As he frowned at the faded writing, his nostrils flared, the lines bracketing his mouth growing deeper. He looked like a man afraid to hope.

"I don't understand all of it," she said. "There's writing at the bottom of the page that looks like it might be something out of heraldry, but it's so faded I can't be sure."

"'Purpure, a two-headed eagle displayed or, beaked and membered gules, over all a bendlet gules,'" Gawain said, apparently having no trouble with the strange words. "It's a blazon."

A blazon was the formal description a herald used when recording a coat of arms. This one described a golden two-headed eagle with red beak and talons, wings spread against a purple background and crossed by a red diagonal stripe.

"What's the significance of it?" asked Tamsin.

Gawain lowered the page, swallowing hard. His gaze was guarded, almost terrified. "It means you found my youngest brother, Gareth Beaumains."

Chapter 9

They had a tomb to find.

By the time Tamsin and Gawain escaped Medievaland and gargoyle-related paperwork, it was dark and rush hour traffic had eased. As a result, the drive into Seattle took only about forty minutes. Gawain amused himself with the Camry's car radio, pushing buttons until he found a station that played heavy metal.

"That is proper battle music," he declared with satisfaction. "It sounds of hoofbeats and the clash of weapons."

"I had no idea ancient warfare and retro rockers had so much in common. Maybe it's all the long hair and sweaty leather."

Gawain raised an eyebrow. "You're mocking me."

"Maybe." Tamsin bestowed an innocent smile, though her nerves were still jangling. "It gives me something to do besides worrying about Mordred."

"You surprised him," Gawain cast her an approving glance. "He has forgotten how strong witches can be."

"The covens keep to themselves."

"Will your coven Elders approve of you helping me?" Gawain asked.

"I don't know. As I say, they're not crazy about getting involved with other people's conflicts." Tamsin shrugged. "But if I bring them Merlin's books, the Elders will forgive anything." They wouldn't be able to resist the knowledge—and power—such ancient lore could bring.

"And if you don't bring them the books? Will they forgive an indiscretion then?"

Tamsin bit her lip, anger and determination bubbling up in her. The car sped up, and she had to force herself to relax and slow down. "If I really made the Elders angry, my powers would be stripped for disobedience. I would be made a servant of the Elders so they could watch me. That's a lot like being their live-in secretary, nanny and housekeeper until I find a husband who can afford to pay them enough to let me go. If they never find out what I'm up to but I fail to find the books, I lose this job and go home. There won't be any second chances at a life outside our town."

Gawain watched her carefully. "You don't want to go home. Not like that."

"Everybody prefers choice. The only reason I play by the rules is because I love my family and don't want to leave them forever. This job—and these books—are my one chance to have everything I want. A little risk is worth it if I can get the job done."

Gawain folded his arms. "We made a bargain. You help me, and I help you. We will find your books."

They parked at the edge of the university's campus and walked toward the Humanities Center. It was a sprawling new building, all concrete and glass with little architectural imagination. Tamsin searched the web on her phone as they neared the entrance, the cold wind numbing her fingers.

"What are you looking for?" Gawain asked.

She slowed to a stop, reading the tiny screen. "There's an arts center in the lower level of this building and I'm guessing that's where the tomb is housed."

Tamsin paused again, reconsidering her words. "Gawain, there's no guarantee the tomb is here. That invoice was from decades ago. Anything might have happened since then."

After a moment's pause, he turned and strode for the doors. "A chance to find him is better than nothing."

Tamsin closed her eyes, barely able to imagine what finding his brother as a statue would be like for Gawain. When she recovered, she had to jog to catch up to him.

Gawain pushed open the glass door and held it for her, his gaze already searching for a way to the bottom floor. It was close to eight o'clock and only a few students lounged on the benches near the door. Every one of them looked up as Gawain stormed through the foyer, reminding Tamsin of animals wary of a passing lion.

The stairs to the lower level were to the left. They descended and began searching the corridors, passing drinking fountains and bulletin boards, computer labs and vending machines. "I don't see any art," Gawain said with irritation.

"Let's keep looking. This place is a rabbit warren."

Gawain made a doubtful noise but kept walking. They finally found a set of double doors that opened into a separate section of the building. The first thing Tamsin noticed was a poster for a theater production, and the next was that the decor was much fancier than the area they'd just passed through.

She looked around to realize she was in the lobby of

the art center's theater, complete with wine bar and crystal chandeliers. The main doors were up a flight of marble steps to her left. There must have been nothing on that night, because the place was empty.

"There he is," Gawain said, pointing toward the back wall, where a large block of stone stood against the wall.

They both hesitated. Tamsin sucked in her breath, suddenly nervous. She'd found the clue on the invoice—now she was struck with a sudden sense of responsibility. She'd raised Gawain's hopes, so this had to end well.

He started forward eagerly. Tamsin followed a step behind, casting a quick spell to hide their presence from security cameras and wandering guards.

Gawain reached the tomb first. He gave a faint cry and fell to his knees beside it. Slowly he reached up, touching a hand to the figure's frozen arm. Then he bowed his head, despair in every line of his big frame.

The figure on the tomb was life-size, his feet resting on a crouching lion—a symbol of his bravery in life. His hands were crossed over the sword hilt placed on his chest. The fall of the knight's lashes was so real, the curve of his fingers so natural, that she could believe he would rise and stretch at any moment, yawning himself awake.

"It's beautiful," she whispered, then remembered she was talking about a man, not a sculpture.

Tamsin reached out, her fingertips grazing the cool stone of the figure's youthful face. Her fingers touched rough stone as she reached the cheek. "There's damage here, as if something scraped the stone. Does that matter?"

"Those are scars. His face was burned as a child." Gawain shifted with sudden disquiet. "I don't like seeing him this way. He was never so still. My brother seems truly dead."

Tamsin put a hand on Gawain's shoulder, which felt

fever-hot even through his coat. She squeezed gently as a tremor of emotion passed through his body, but he didn't seem to notice. He leaned his head forward, resting it against the edge of the sarcophagus. Hands fisted, Gawain wrapped his arms around his body, as if he would shatter with grief.

Tamsin had promised to help him, but she had not thought beyond locating the tombs. Now she blinked back tears, aching to ease his pain. Finding the knights was not enough. She had to do more before her heart broke in two.

Sudden inspiration darted through her like an electric shock. Clumsy with excitement, Tamsin dropped her backpack to the floor and fumbled with the zipper. She rummaged until she felt the side pocket inside the pack and withdrew her father's spell book. She cradled it in her hands a moment, feeling the worn leather of the cover against her fingertips. Grimoires had a way of knowing when they'd be needed, sometimes before their keepers did. This was one of those times. She untied the thong that bound it and began turning the pages to find the entry she wanted.

The page crackled as she finally turned to *A Charm to Awaken Those Who Watch*. Unlike some rituals, it didn't call for elaborate preparation. There were no potions or talismans, altars or symbols painted in sacred inks. These instructions had been old before much of that had been invented. This was simply words and will, unadorned and raw.

She began to read, slowly at first, chanting just under her breath. She felt the vine tattoo on her wrist warming, channeling her strength. The words were in the ancient tongue of witches and, while she knew it well, she hadn't spoken it since she had learned it from her father. The language felt strange in her mouth, almost like muscles she hadn't stretched for so long they'd gone to sleep. She felt the mark around her wrist begin to prickle with heat.

Gawain slowly raised his head, turning to look at her. "What are you doing?"

"Hush," she said, and kept reading.

Magic began to collect in the air. It was not like the blue energy most witches used, because this spell didn't stem from the modern school of magic. This was older, warm where the Elders' power was cold. A mist of gold formed above the tomb, the tiny sparks glittering against the gloomy shadows.

Gawain got to his feet, apprehension filling his eyes.

She reached the end of the spell, refusing to stop until the words were done. "I know what I'm doing. Now let me work."

Tamsin began the incantation again. She had to read it three times from beginning to end for the spell to take effect. Gawain grabbed her arm, interrupting her. "This is too dangerous. To you. To Beaumains. What if Mordred senses what you are doing?"

"Then we need to hurry." She stepped back so she could look up into his face. "But we can't walk away and leave your brother here."

A stricken look flashed across his features. Of course he knew that. He was trying to protect her. She could not fault him for that, but she needed his trust.

"I beat the Lady of the Lake and her gargoyle today. Trust that I'm strong enough to do this." Her encounter with Nimueh wasn't quite the same as waking Gareth Beaumains, and she could see the protest gathering in his expression. "If you don't want me to keep going, I will stop. But if you do, I will give your brother everything I have."

Gawain pressed his lips together, clearly struggling, but

he nodded. "Go on. I will keep watch." He stepped aside, giving her room.

She released her breath, his acceptance easing the crushing tension around her ribs. She began the incantation again. The golden mist had begun to fade, but now it flooded back, brighter than before, with tiny sparks like silvery shooting stars. Magic built in an unseen presence, an invisible visitor that ghosted through the room, almost touching her, almost breathing against her skin. Tamsin wasn't the only one who sensed it. Gawain had drawn the knife he kept in his boot and had backed away, looking up and down the room as if he sensed watchful eyes.

He hated magic, but he had chosen to trust her anyway. That meant something, and it gave her strength.

By the third time Tamsin read the words, she felt the magic drawing upon her reserves. She focused her will, concentrating on the stone melting away like ice from a warm and living body. She imagined the beat of a human heart and warm blood coursing through muscle and sinew. She envisioned the heavy yawn of the newly awakened, the first flame of intelligence lighting the sleeping features. The more intensely she projected those thoughts, the harder she felt the magic sucking at her, drawing her vitality up like a milk shake through a straw. Pressure began to build behind her eyes, and she knew she'd have a headache later. Her knees began to quiver.

But all that meant nothing, because the golden mist had steadied into a thick, constant glow. It surrounded the effigy in a dome, the surface catching rainbows like a soap bubble. Through the haze of light, Tamsin began to see the stone figure shimmer. Change began at the feet, where they rested on the lion's back. The supple leather boots deepened in color, shifting from stony gray to brown leather. Tamsin nearly faltered in her reading as her heart pounded with excitement. Colors began seeping upward as if the stone was soaking up life from the surrounding cloud of magic. The hem of Gareth's surcoat changed to deep blue, the mail coat beneath glittering silver. Buckles turned to brass, fur to dark sable, the scabbard of the sword to crimson leather. Finally, the loose curls of hair became auburn. The flush of youthful skin showed the knight was no more than twenty.

Tamsin finished reading and closed the book, slipping it back into her pocket. Her fingers trembled with exhaustion and the knowledge that she'd done all she could. If her magic was true, Beaumains would wake. He had to. Any other outcome was unthinkable.

Gawain was beside her now, his warmth a welcome comfort. He slid an arm around her waist, pulling her close. The affectionate gesture was so unexpected she nearly jumped, but then soon leaned against him, needing his strength.

"What happens now?" he asked.

"We wait," she replied, hoping with every cell of her body that this would work.

The golden dome of magic seemed to harden around Beaumains. Tamsin wasn't sure how long that took, but it felt like months. At that point, it grew dull and opaque. Tamsin imagined it cracking and falling to pieces, but instead it just began to fade in patches. Finally it shredded like mist in the wind, but the effigy remained utterly still.

Tamsin could feel the tension growing in Gawain as he watched his brother's unmoving form. Her own body coiled like a spring under pressure, every muscle cramping with the urge to shake the young knight until he woke up. She could still see Gawain in her mind's eye, kneeling before his brother's tomb. She would do anything to

erase the agony she'd seen in him and prayed her magic
had been enough.

The hope and desire, her need to make it right for Gawain sapped the last of her strength, and she dropped to
one knee.

"Tamsin!" Gawain supported her with one arm around
her middle, making sure she didn't fall. "Are you well?"

The room tilted, and Tamsin braced one hand against
the floor. Gawain wrapped his arms around her, getting
a better grip.

"I'm just tired," she said. A sense of failure crept over
her with a sickly touch, leaving her skin clammy. "I need
to sit down for a moment, that's all."

Gawain gathered her up and helped her to her feet,
speaking no word of reproach. That, too, meant much,
but it left a hollow feeling inside her. She had longed to
do better.

When she lifted her head, her gaze fell on the effigy and
she was forced to blink twice. All the color was gone, but
that wasn't all. Where it had been exquisitely detailed before, now it seemed blurred, worn by time to a crude version of itself. Her first thought was that she'd damaged it.

"Gawain," she said uncertainly. "Something—"

A noise made them both turn. Tamsin's lips parted, but
no words came. Beaumains was standing a few feet away,
wide blue eyes scanning everything around him. When
he spotted Gawain, a profound look of relief flooded his
features.

"Brother, this is a wondrous strange place!" he said in
a voice deeper than Tamsin had expected. Then he caught
sight of Gawain's arm around her waist and one corner of
his mouth quirked upward. "But it seems you have already
found its secrets."

Chapter 10

Nimueh stared out the bay window of the Victorian mansion at the garden beyond. A sky the color of ashes turned the thin light to a silvery wash. The mansion was set on a large lot shielded by trees, which provided privacy Mordred liked and scenery he ignored.

The Prince of Faery lurked by the door, demanding her attention. His presence was a claw hooked into her psychic senses, not quite painful but ready to tear on a whim. It was one of his power games, a way of making her address him first. It would have been more effective if she'd still had the capacity to care.

"I would have called this scene lovely once," Nimueh said softly. "I know it should be. There is a lake and willow trees. Even though it is winter, there are many subtle shades of green and gray. And yet, my soul doesn't feel the loveliness. My mind knows, but my heart does not."

"Does that bother you?" Mordred asked mildly. "I

thought you pureblood fae were no more than walking corpses."

"That is cruel." She said it without rancor. Once, she would have tried to scratch out his eyes for saying such a thing. She missed that capacity for rage.

"I'm asking a legitimate question," he said. "I'm not cruel."

"Yes, you are. It's your reason for breathing." She lifted a shoulder slightly, still staring out the window. "It's not just beauty I miss. I miss hating you. That much anger felt clean."

Once the fae had been the most creative spirits in all the realms. They had danced, laughed, made war and loved like no others. They had been capricious and quarrelsome, generous friends and implacable foes. Now they were dusty shadows bereft of purpose. Worse, they were immortal. There would be no final forgetting to end their loss.

Mordred himself had been spared. His power made him immortal, but with more witch blood than fae, he had escaped Merlin's spell. Rather than sharing the fae's loss, he'd found ways to exploit it.

"You could drink a soul," Mordred suggested. "I'm told that restores all your lost perceptions. We have prisoners to spare."

Nimueh turned to the prince, a faint echo of disgust quickening her pulse. "It hardly seems worth it. A few hours of feeling, and then the grayness begins again." Worse was that brief moment when the fae realized what they'd done. The self-loathing was worse than not caring at all.

"Then have another. There's no shortage of mortal cattle."

"No," she replied with a dismissive flick of fingers. "Those who've taken that road cannot stop. They become the fae version of a drunkard seeking their next bottle. It lacks dignity."

"Suit yourself." He shrugged.

But Nimueh knew she was right. Addiction was Mordred's ticket to controlling her kind. Once the fae were trapped, he had a system of reward and punishment to exploit. She refused to step into that snare.

Again, a faint shudder of distaste passed through her. It wasn't quite an emotion, but the echo of one. Such episodes came and went like the tingling of a lost limb, leaving her with a sense of profound disquiet.

Mordred was pacing, his mind obviously on other things. "You failed against the witch."

"You failed to tell me that she is strong."

"Of course she's strong. She escaped me," Mordred snapped.

Perhaps that was why Nimueh had abandoned the field and let Tamsin Greene go free. The idea of a young witch no one had heard of—one wily enough to escape Mordred—had stirred what remained of her curiosity. In another time, she might even have hoped.

"You should have crushed her," Mordred added.

"Maybe." Nimueh turned back to the window and the greenery beyond. "I'll try harder the next time our paths cross."

Was that why she'd dropped her car keys? To leave a clue the witch and her knight could follow and maybe, just maybe, put an end to the Prince of Faery?

Mordred caught Nimueh's arm, digging his fingers into her flesh as he forced her to face him. "Indeed, you shall try harder. And while you're thinking of all the ways you are going to carry out my orders to the letter, perhaps you can assist me with some housekeeping. There is another mess I need to clean up."

He waved his free hand through the air, describing an arc that shimmered and then darkened into a doorway between place and time. With Nimueh still firmly in his grip, he dragged them through. She felt the kiss of cold, clammy air on her face, and the elegant Victorian parlor disappeared. All at once, she stood in Mordred's dungeon, deep underground beneath the hills of the faery kingdom.

Nimueh looked around, certain here at least it was better to be numb. The dungeon was vast and dark, honeycombed with tiny caves that served as cells. Roots crawled through the dirt walls and ceiling of the caves and twined around the limbs of the helpless prisoners, trapping them in damp, black oblivion. Scuttling things rustled in the shadows, the hard shells of their bodies scraping as they passed. Scavengers, Nimueh supposed. There was plenty of dead meat down here in Mordred's playrooms.

"You have been keeping busy," she observed.

"Housekeeping." Mordred smiled, but there was nothing pleasant in the expression. "A few of your people still had opinions about my mother taking the throne."

The rebels who had escaped Merlin's spell. "I see."

"Do you?" There was threat in the two words. "I wonder if you understand the brilliance of my plans. Conquering the mortal realms is a question of stealth. I could bring an army, thousands of fae warriors, but there is an easier way. The modern world is different from old Camelot. For all their fancy weapons, humans are even less prepared now than they were in the so-called Dark Ages."

He was right there. In the old days, every peasant knew monsters were real and most had a few charms around the house for basic protection. "So you do not plan on a full-scale invasion?"

"No. A handful of fae here and there, strategically placed where the power brokers can fall prey to their beauty and influence. I'm thinking corporate boardrooms, political functions, cocktail parties for the rich and famous. No one will notice the soulless among them."

"And then what?"

"Once the right people are under fae power, numbers won't matter. Armies and weapons won't matter. The human realms will be mine for the taking."

As plans went, it wasn't bad. Still, Mordred had forgotten his mother. The mortal realms would ultimately be hers. Unless he meant to fight her for them? That could get interesting.

They'd reached a long row of cells. Nimueh noticed a spider the size of a dinner plate webbing one of the entrances shut. She turned away. "Why are we here? You said there was a mess to clean up?"

Mordred waved her forward. She went, although her feet refused to hurry toward whatever he had to show her.

"I thought, after your unsuccessful venture to capture the witch, that perhaps it was time to review our plans," Mordred said smoothly. "I find it useful to clarify priorities from time to time."

Nimueh stopped when she came to the end of the tunnel. There was a figure huddled in the last cave in the row of cells.

"I find explanations go better with visual aids." Mordred nodded toward the bound form.

"Angmar," she said softly. The fae was bound to the earth with so many pale, twining roots that he was immobilized. Even so, he'd been in a recent fight because there were savage bruises wherever his clothing was torn away.

"Angmar is an example of what does not work in my regime. You, at least on days where you do not fail me, are an example of what does. The difference is a spirit of obedience." Mordred pushed ahead into the cell and grabbed

Angmar's tangled hair, lifting the fae's head so that Nimueh stared right into his broken face. "Those with souls have difficulty following my orders."

Mordred made a gesture before Angmar's face. The fae's eyes cracked open beneath swollen, bruised lids and he began to struggle against the roots that pinned him tight. It was useless. A trickle of light escaped through his clenched teeth. Mordred bent down, inhaling it with a connoisseur's pleasure. Angmar began to howl, the sound rising to a scream of protest and despair.

His soul. Nimueh's heart hammered with desperate hunger. It did not matter that Angmar had once been her friend. She yearned to fill the aching void within her. Through the haze of numbness, she was aware that she should be disgusted, horrified, revolted. Merlin had damaged the fae, but Mordred made them monsters by tempting their hunger.

Nimueh had refused Mordred's offer to feed her craving, and now he was dangling the bait again. If she took it, she would be his slave. She drew herself up, setting her jaw in refusal, but she couldn't look away from the spectacle of Mordred tearing out Angmar's soul.

"My lord, you don't need to feed," she said with cool precision. "Merlin's spell never touched you."

"That's part of the joy in stealing it," he retorted. "Excess is its own delight."

Nimueh made no response, giving him nothing. With a loud sigh, Mordred stopped, letting Angmar's head drop. The fae collapsed, sobbing in pain.

"There's quite a bit left if you want it," Mordred said, sulking. His flat expression said that he knew he'd failed to seduce her.

Nimueh stared at a spot just above Mordred's head. The urge to wipe him from existence welled up in her

like a madness. There were so few things that could kill
the faery prince or his mother, and she'd possessed the
greatest of them all—the sword, Excalibur. She'd given it
to Arthur Pendragon to bring peace to the mortal realms,
and now the sword was lost along with the king's effigy.
If only she still had it so that she could skewer Mordred's
slimy carcass!

That was anger! Nimueh schooled her face, hiding
the fact that she'd just had a bout of genuine rage. Sweat
slipped down her spine, a symptom of her episode. Mordred could never find out she had a scrap of individuality
left or she would end up like Angmar. Mordred's smile
speared her as her gaze slowly, painfully crept toward her
old friend's shuddering form.

"There is a disturbance in the aether that tells me the
witch has awakened another knight," said Mordred. "That
would be the witch you failed to destroy. I suggest you rec-
tify that situation."

Nimueh struggled to find her tongue. "Yes, my Lord
Mordred."

Chapter 11

Tamsin gaped as Gawain and Beaumains embraced with back-thumping, shoulder-pounding affection. Her astonishment wasn't at watching two time-travelers from the Middle Ages overcome incredible odds and arcane magic. It was because Gawain was actually smiling, a big grin that lit up his eyes with real joy as he ruffled his little brother's hair. He almost looked friendly.

For his part, Beaumains tugged at his brother's shirt. "These are strange garments, but I see you're still wearing green. You never change, brother. Stubborn as an ox."

"So I have noticed," Tamsin put in with a smile. "I am Tamsin."

She put out a hand to shake, but Beaumains bowed over it instead, the picture of chivalric grace. "Madam, I owe you many thanks for reviving me."

"Think nothing of it," Tamsin replied. If she hadn't already met Gawain, she'd be tempted to swoon. Beaumains was utterly charming, the scar on his cheek giving him a rakish air.

"Nevertheless, I am entirely at your service." He gave her a wicked grin.

"We'd best go," said Gawain, clapping his brother on the shoulder hard enough to make him stumble.

Beaumains cast him a wry look and released Tamsin's hand.

It wasn't hard to get Beaumains out of a building filled with theater majors. His chain mail and surcoat might have been explained away as a better-than-average costume, and his bright-eyed good looks could have belonged to any undergraduate. He obeyed Gawain's command to remain silent until they were in the car, but the questions started once they were on the road back to Carlyle.

"I don't understand," Beaumains said, his accent a touch thicker than Gawain's. "Are you telling me that we have all been asleep for hundreds and hundreds of years?"

"Yes," Gawain replied. "There is much you must learn."

"Well, I would say that's obvious," Beaumains said drily, looking around the interior of the car. "What did I miss? Have they sorted the Vikings out yet?"

"They have their own television show," Gawain said, disgruntled.

"A what?"

"I'll explain another time."

"Very well." The young man's tone was tense, but he sounded more excited than afraid. Tamsin spared a glimpse in the rearview mirror. He had his face all but pressed to the passenger window, watching the world speed by. He reminded her of a cat with its ears pricked, alert to every sight and sound.

"There are so many lights," Beaumains murmured. "Are

we at war? Are the torches built that high up to convey a signal to the enemy?"

"Those are streetlights," she offered. "I thought Merlin's spell helped you understand the modern world."

"Not all at once," Gawain said. "It takes days. I still do not understand the words to most popular songs, and mathematical reasoning behind cellular plans still eludes me."

Tamsin laughed. "That's probably because the phone companies are run by dragons looking to increase their treasure hoard from your pocket."

Beaumains gave her a look of alarm.

She took the ramp onto the highway and turned the car toward Carlyle. She wasn't sure what to do with Beaumains. Gawain had been acclimatized by the time he'd arrived on her doorstep, but his brother was another matter. She hadn't thought about the consequences of acquiring a mob of knights in need of housebreaking. She sincerely hoped Gawain had a plan.

"I am hungry," Beaumains said, breaking into her thoughts a moment later. "Is there a place to hunt? Or a tavern?"

They were all hungry, Tamsin especially. Spells took huge amounts of energy. She settled on a drive-through and they pulled into a parking lot to devour the greasy, salty food. Beaumains approved of the fries but gave the burger patty a suspicious look. "I am not sure what beast this was."

"A common question," Tamsin replied. "It's better not to think about it too hard."

Beaumains smiled, showing a slight gap between his front teeth. "It has always been that way, Mistress Greene, with hostels upon the road."

"I can imagine," Tamsin said. She'd read about pilgrimages and the booming medieval tourist trade.

The young man chewed and swallowed. "Your kindness and hospitality is beyond question. I am yours to command."

"I am hers to command," Gawain frowned. "Find your own lady."

"Don't be so sure of yourself," Beaumains retorted. "You are the only knight of Camelot in her acquaintance. Soon she will see the error of her ways and make a better choice."

"Hold your tongue, devil," Gawain growled.

"I am no devil." Beaumains laughed from the safety of the backseat. "I am younger and far more sweet-tempered than you. Besides, I can cook."

"That's a bonus," Tamsin said, mostly to annoy Gawain.

"Indeed. I spent my first months at Camelot as a kitchen boy."

"Why did you do that?" Tamsin asked.

"Because all my brothers had left home to become knights and I refused to be left behind. Unfortunately, I had to keep my identity a secret if I did not wish to be sent home. With no noble name behind me, the only position I could get was in the kitchens. I was willing to work, but the other kitchen boys teased me mercilessly, for they could tell I was no peasant's son. That is how I earned the name Beaumains—pretty hands—unused to hard labor. Then one day Lancelot found me out and made me his squire. By then I could bake a good loaf of bread and roast a chicken to perfection." Beaumains popped a fry into his mouth. "So you see, mistress, I could be of far more use than this loutish brute."

Deep in his throat, Gawain made a noise that sounded like an angry wolf. "I said hold your tongue, or I shall see that it ceases to flap so freely."

"Boys," Tamsin said in a warning tone.

Beaumains sucked on the straw of his milk shake, already having figured out how to make a rude bubbling noise. However mighty a swordsman he might have become, he was still a little brother.

A wave of nostalgia washed over Tamsin. She missed Stacy, and their little sister, Clary. As they finished their meals, she absently rubbed the tattoo on her wrist and listened to the two brothers argue.

As she'd told Gawain, she needed Merlin's books to please the Elders if she was going to return home on her own terms. Unfortunately, if Tamsin's vision was correct, she was going to have to steal the tomes from Mordred, and that put everything in a different light. The mission wasn't just personal anymore. Even if her own freedom hadn't been at stake, Merlin's spells were far too powerful to be left in the Prince of Faery's hands.

As she gripped the steering wheel again, her fingers trembled. She was afraid, but she was in the company of knights. If she was going to keep up, she was going to have to pick her weapons and show she could fight.

"You worked a spell strong enough that Mordred will certainly have felt it. You can't remain alone tonight," Gawain declared in a tone that brooked no argument. "You need protection, and we shall stand guard outside your door."

They had arrived home a little after midnight. Though the food had done her good, Tamsin was exhausted. So was Beaumains, judging by his yawn. Apparently waking from a centuries-long sleep was hard work.

"I think two big guys loitering in the halls would upset the neighbors," Tamsin replied, envisioning the cops showing up and trying to arrest the knights, one of whom was still in armor and carrying an enormous sword. Yeah, that would go well. "I have an idea."

The apartment next door was empty, and locks were no match for her magic. Under ordinary circumstances she'd never commandeer the landlord's property, but tonight was far from normal. She gathered extra blankets and pillows and put her knights to bed on the carpet of the empty suite. Or at least she managed to settle Beaumains.

"I am forever in your debt," Gawain said softly as he came through the door to Tamsin's apartment a few minutes later, closing it behind him. "I cannot tell you what it means to have my brother safely returned to me."

Tamsin was lying on her bed, the lamp shining on a book she was too weary to read. She'd showered and changed into an oversize T-shirt, letting fatigue creep over her. But now she sat up, Gawain's presence alarming and enticing. All at once, she wasn't tired. "Is Beaumains asleep?"

"As sweetly as a babe."

Tamsin smiled at the image. "Good."

"If his experience is like mine, he will rest until late tomorrow morning. After being trapped by magic, the body craves a normal rest above all else." Gawain stopped in the middle of the room, a shadowed figure just outside the pool of light. "You are a special woman, Tamsin."

The tone of his voice struck a spark inside her. Suddenly she was too awake to remain in bed. She rose and crossed the floor between them in a few steps. Hesitantly, she placed her palms against his chest. "I know that spell probably pinged on Mordred's radar, but I'm glad I did it."

His blue eyes danced with a happiness she hadn't seen in him before. Gently, he pressed a kiss to her forehead. Tamsin released a sigh and leaned closer, resting her cheek against his chest. The fabric of his T-shirt was comfortably soft, but the muscles beneath spoke of hard strength. "Is that why you came back to my room tonight? To tell me your brother is asleep?"

"No." He curled one hand around her nape, cradling her head against him. "I came to ask if you want me to stay here for a while."

"Aren't you forgetting what I am?"

"No." He held her gaze, his fingers tracing the tattoo about her wrist. "I know your powers. I do not trust them or your kind. But I am coming to trust you."

She could have argued, but it was a giant step for him. "Then stay."

He pulled her close. Tamsin closed her eyes, listening to the strong beat of his heart. She could still smell the ozone scent of magic clinging to his clothes, but beneath that was the warm musk of his skin. She liked the way he held her, gently but with the confidence of a man who knows his strength. It opened a well of longing inside Tamsin that had never been filled. She wanted to be loved without reservation, but more than that she wanted to be accepted for what she was—not just a witch but a woman with a mind of her own. Gawain had seen both and was still at her side. How long that would last was uncertain. Maybe only for as long as he needed her. At least until his king was found.

At least for tonight.

That would have to do.

She tilted her head up, finding his mouth. Gawain's kiss began as a soft, caressing thing, but a wave of desire rose in Tamsin. All at once, tenderness wasn't enough. Her hands slid upward to lace behind his neck. Gawain made a soft grunt of pleasure.

Slowly, she drew him down until their lips met again. She opened to him, inviting him to deepen the kiss. The invitation drew an instant response. His hands tightened on her, pulling Tamsin into the embrace until she was on tiptoe. Gawain's kiss was no mere meeting of lips. It was a deep, plundering exploration that went on and on until her core began to glow red-hot with need.

"Did you like that?" he murmured, rich amusement shading his words.

"What do you think?" she replied, so close that their breath mingled, the ghost of another kiss.

His hands circled her waist, finding the hem of her shirt. And then he was touching her skin to skin, the rough heat of his hands stroking upward over her ribs. Tamsin arched into the sensation, craving it, finding it not quite enough. She grasped the T-shirt and began to pull it over her head. Gawain, ever the quick study, slid it off her, letting the cascade of her long hair sweep over her shoulders. With a slow gesture, he pushed her hair behind her shoulders, his touch lingering on her collarbone. Then he stepped back enough to admire the view. His expression was all male pleasure, but there was reverence in it, too.

Tamsin felt the sweep of his gaze like a physical thing. It left her vulnerable but bold, as if he'd granted her some of his warrior's spirit. She moved to step into his arms again, but he raised his fingers to the lace of her bra, the light caress stopping her. He ran his fingers over the arch of her breast, his eyes intent with fascination. "I have seen pictures of these garments, but they do not do justice to reality."

It would have been easy to deflect the compliment with a smart remark, but for once Tamsin held her tongue. There was nothing mocking in Gawain's manner. He made her feel worthy of being adored in a way no man had done ever before.

"But how do you remove this infernal temptation?" he

muttered. Tamsin unhooked the front. Gawain caught her hands. "Please allow me."

She did, and he unwrapped her like a present. The bra hit the floor with the barest whisper of fabric, and Gawain's hands instantly caressed her. Tamsin's breath hissed inward, her mind briefly short-circuited with sensation.

"Not fair," she complained. "You're still dressed."

Gawain pulled off his shirt. The low light showed every dip and valley of his torso and softened the silver tracery of long-healed wounds. Tamsin stroked her hands over his muscles, unable to resist petting him as she might a cat. Everything about Gawain's body demanded to be touched. He gave a growl that might have been a purr.

"Come here," he commanded, lifting her as if she were no more than a child.

She wrapped her legs around his waist, gasping as he caught one nipple in his teeth. It was the lightest nip, but her body was so aroused that the sudden flame it created struck all the way to her core. Gawain chuckled, a low, male sound that had her squirming against him. In three strides, they were at the bed and she slipped from him, taking her time as she slid her body down the front of his jeans. It was his turn to make a quick, hissing inhalation.

Tamsin pressed her lips to his chest, kissing slowly down and down, lingering on a jagged white scar that cut across his abdomen. Gawain's muscles tensed beneath her lips, but he made no move to stop her. When she finally reached the button of his jeans, she unfastened it with care, leaving a kiss on the warm flesh of his stomach. Then she grasped the tab of his zipper.

"Be careful," he said in a voice so low and husky it was nearly a growl. "Your touch will finish this before we begin."

Gawain's gaze locked with hers, a warning and a dare

simmering in its blue depths. Tamsin caught her breath as he closed his fingers around hers and drew the zipper slowly downward. The briefs he wore barely contained the fullness of his erection. He said something, but she didn't hear it through the pounding of her pulse. She ignored the bed and slowly sank to her knees, peeling his briefs and jeans down inch by inch and pressing her lips to the skin she unveiled. She caressed the taut flesh of his thighs, enjoying the curve and play of thick muscle.

"What are you doing?" he demanded.

"Taking my time," she said primly, now scraping her nails lightly over his most sensitive flesh. "Playing."

"Shredding my sanity."

"Pleasure is a journey, not a destination," Tamsin replied, blowing lightly on his heated skin. An impish impulse pushed her to tease him. "You should learn to relax."

Gawain cursed and pulled away, the movement so sudden Tamsin jumped. "I'm not a tiger whose tail you can tweak."

"No?" The imp was still in charge, refusing to let her give in.

Silent, Gawain stripped off the rest of his clothes as Tamsin got to her feet. When she next looked up, he was entirely naked. Her first thought was that he was shockingly beautiful, a sculpture come to life. Then she saw the hungry look in his eyes and nearly quailed.

"Tigers aren't careful," he said.

Tamsin sat on the bed, her knees too weak for anything else. There was rather a lot of Gawain, the sheer virility of him leaving her solemn. Every witch knew spells for moments like this, magic that protected both partners in every physical way—but there was more at stake here than just her body. Gawain would not be a pleasant tumble that she could fit into the rest of her life. This was going to be a game changer, demanding body and spirit both. Maybe she had rushed things.

"Come here," he commanded, putting an end to her doubts.

He pushed her down onto the quilt, crawling after her with flowing grace until his arms and legs trapped her in a cage of hard, eager flesh. Tamsin's heart was pounding, desire mixed with apprehension. He kissed her then, chasing her thoughts away like startled birds. Tamsin surrendered to the heat of it, riding a wave of lust that threatened to reduce her to ash. He smelled so good, so male she wanted to drink him in through her pores. She ran her hands down his ribs, reveling in the feel of bone and skin and sinew. Scars chased each other like lightning across his flesh, some pink and new, some white with long healing. His was a body that had been well used, and judging by the hard ridge pressed against her stomach, he wanted to use her.

Gawain fisted his hands in her hair as he licked and sucked at her breasts. Tamsin arched into it, hot breath and wetness sparking a blaze deep in her belly. He wasn't tentative or particularly gentle, the demands of his lips and teeth one step away from pain. She traced her fingers over the bunched muscles of his shoulders, down his back.

Nothing had prepared her for this experience. Her last remaining particle of reason said she was looking for a landmark, a handhold, something to anchor herself in this storm. But Gawain never gave her a chance. She had invited him inside her walls, and now he was laying siege against her every defense.

He released her nipple, leaving it erect, aching, and glistening from his suckling kiss. Tamsin shivered as he turned his attention to her collarbone, his lips transforming it into an erogenous zone she didn't know existed.

She reached down, finding the thickness of his shaft. He shifted so that she could get a better grip, let her stoke the smooth length of him.

"Are you pleased with me?" he asked in a low, husky voice.

Tamsin groaned as his teeth grazed her throat. "Are you fishing for compliments?"

"I want to dictate the terms of your surrender, my lady."

"You want a white flag?"

"I want utter mastery. I give no quarter."

Despite her protest, he moved out of her reach. His fingers slid into the slickness of her cleft, massaging her in slow, tight circles. Tamsin sucked in her breath, catching her lip between her teeth to stifle any noise he might take as a sign of her defeat. She wasn't giving up that quickly, not when she had barely mounted an assault of her own. But her traitorous body rose and angled itself to meet Gawain, giving him entry as he stroked and probed, finding her point of pleasure. A wild spiral of sensation coursed through her, making her forget anything but her need for more and more of Gawain's expert touch. He took her to the abyss, led her right up to the edge, and then pulled her back from the brink. Tamsin cried out, but from abject frustration.

"What are you doing?" She twisted under him, desperate for resistance, for something to ease her ache.

"Taking you." Angling his hips, he slid into her.

Tamsin all but came at that single, hard thrust. Places she'd almost forgotten stretched wide, welcoming the invasion. Her vision went black, her mind a kaleidoscope of sensation. Gawain pulled back with exquisite slowness, making it feel as if she was turning inside out in the most delicious way possible, and then drove home again. Tamsin arched, hips rising to meet him. Tears slid from beneath her lids, her emotions roiling from sheer sensory overload.

She crushed the quilt in her fingers, digging for purchase, but that wasn't enough. She grabbed his shoulders, sinking her nails into flesh. He laughed as she raked him, leaving pink furrows behind. He pushed, and pushed again. Tamsin moaned.

"Surrender, witch," he whispered, grabbing her hips and driving home to find her point of pleasure.

Tamsin's entire body tightened, throbs of pleasure radiating through her. At that moment, Gawain's control slipped and he abandoned his slow, deliberate rhythm for a wild, hard claiming. She cried out, a wordless sound of release and defiance. He took her mouth, silencing her cry as he gave one last, shuddering thrust. He came, hot and wet as the burst of sensation inside Tamsin overwhelmed every other thought. The world ceased.

Tamsin came back to herself some moments after Gawain rolled onto his back, pulling her onto his chest. He was breathing deeply, the steady thunder of his heart echoing the aftershocks of desire in Tamsin's core. She feathered her finger over his lips, studying his face. Even now, lines of tension etched his features. Gawain never quite let go of his wariness. Tamsin suddenly wanted to wrest that away from him. She would stand guard for once, so he could rest.

I might have surrendered this time, Tamsin whispered inside her own mind, *but that was only the first skirmish.*

Chapter 12

If any woman was worth waiting centuries for, it was Tamsin.

Gawain lay with her head tucked under his chin, her breath fanning across his bare chest. Sunlight crept around the blinds to leave stripes on the carpet. The scent of baking drifted from another apartment, reminding him it was time to eat. Gawain ignored his stomach. Their nest under the quilt was too snug to move. Instead, he let his eyes drift shut, feeling the light beat of Tamsin's heart. Her warm, soft weight was delicious and sweet, an armful he refused to surrender. And why would he? This morning he felt as if, for the second time, he'd been awakened from that cold death of stone.

He shifted, careful not to disturb Tamsin. She was draped across him, her hair scattered over the sheets like skeins of golden silk. Her face was soft with sleep, the rounded curve of her cheek almost girlish. He longed to run a finger over the arch of her brow, the upturned tip of her nose, but was reluctant to disturb her.

Laughter rang from the street below, followed by a puppy's yap. The noise made Tamsin stir, her nose wrinkling as her eyes squeezed shut. It was adorable. Gawain willed her back to sleep, and it seemed to work.

He didn't use magic—never that. By the time Gawain had grown tall enough to ride a horse, he'd discovered his mother's spell cupboard and learned which potions could rot the flesh of a living man or destroy a village with a plague of boils. He'd seen her strike down a serving maid who'd dared to steal a ham from the castle pantry. The memory of the poor girl's crippling illness still made his skin crawl.

And yet here he was, his heart reaching for Tamsin as if she were the sun. Little by little she had been slipping past his defenses, until last night she'd broken through. And why not? She'd given him back his brother. To him, that act shone like a beacon on the dark sea of terrible deeds he had witnessed. It did not chase back all the darkness, but neither could it be ignored.

Tamsin woke with a lazy stretch, reminding him of a contented cat. She lifted her head, strands of golden hair falling into her eyes. Gawain brushed them back, letting himself sink into the warm brown of her gaze. "Good morning," he said.

She squirmed delightfully until her mouth reached his. "Good morning, my good knight."

Her kiss was the brush of apple blossoms against his skin. Sudden hunger surged in him, demanding more bed play. "Come here."

"No, you come here." Tamsin straddled him, her hair falling around them like a curtain of gold. She kissed his eyes, his nose, his chin, taking her time to find his mouth again. When she did, it was to nip and suck, drawing out the simple act of kissing into an epic poem. Gawain cupped her breasts, their velvety smooth weight enticing. He brushed his thumbs over her nipples, bringing them to straining peaks. She gasped and squirmed, sparking a flood of heat to his nether regions.

He chuckled, earning a searing glance that spoke of exquisite torments. Tamsin was an instinctive seductress.

"Are you ready to surrender?" she said in grave tones.

With little effort, Gawain rolled her over, tangling them both in the soft mounds of covers. He highly approved of these luxurious modern beds. "You have much to learn of warfare, Mistress Greene."

"Are you going to lay siege to me again?"

"Indeed." He dug her out of the billows of the comforter, appreciating her slender, smooth form anew. Her legs were long and lean, delicate as a doe's. He positioned himself between them, leaning forward to run his tongue over the graceful planes of her stomach. "I intend to devour you."

With that he bent to her most private entry, breaching the gates with tongue and teeth. Tamsin tasted salty-sweet and pure as April sunshine, and she shivered for him as he found the secrets of her inner chambers. "Are you ready to surrender?" he growled.

"Not so fast," she said, though she was panting by then.

Then Gawain found the exact spot that crumbled her defenses. She came around his fingers, muscles contracting as she cried out. But when she finally stilled, she made it clear they were not done. "I see you have a tower in need of capture and demolition."

Gawain let Tamsin have her way. Hot and slick, she closed around him, let her warm him with her playful teasing and the touch of her ivory skin. The sun seeped through the curtains, lighting her from behind like an angel in a church window, all gold and brightness. By the time her conquest was done, he was drunk on woman and bliss.

She slid down beside him, one slender arm thrown over his chest. "White flag?"

He closed one hand over her bottom. "I reserve the right to initiate an exchange of prisoners."

"I thought you said last night that you didn't take prisoners," she said with a sly glance. "Change your mind?"

The moment was broken by a thump on the apartment stairs and a child's bright laughter. The world was coming to life, however much Gawain wished to deny it. They kissed again, but soon she was sliding from his grasp and reaching for her robe. "We should see how Beaumains is faring."

Gawain caught her hand. "You would leave me so soon? You're my healer."

"So?"

"I'm sure I have a fever that needs tending."

She gave him a withering look. "I hear ice water is good for that."

He sank back into the pillow. "You are a cruel woman."

She knotted the tie of her robe, but sat on the bed beside him. Her fingers trailed along the scar that slashed his ribs. It was an unconscious gesture, but it pleased him. He liked that she was comfortable with his body, content to curl against him for comfort.

"Finding your brother was a victory, but there is so much to do yet." She sighed, breath warm against the skin of his chest.

Gawain understood. "None of this will be easy, but I'll be at your side."

"You are my knight in shining armor," she murmured, tilting her head up to meet his gaze. A smile lurked behind her soft brown eyes.

He couldn't stifle a grin. "In case you hadn't noticed, I'm not in armor. I'm not wearing anything at all."

She gave him a kiss that said she had noticed and approved. Gawain smiled against her lips, feeling like a man reborn.

Tamsin held on to her joy while she dressed and made breakfast, fed her ravenous warriors and then erased any signs of intrusion from the vacant apartment next door. She wasn't sure how to solve the problem of housing extra knights, but at least now she had a whole day to figure out what to do with Beaumains. Meanwhile, Gawain took his brother off to find modern clothes and acquaint him with the basics of the twenty-first century. Gawain had been reluctant to leave Tamsin alone, but she refused to be afraid on a sunny Saturday morning. Besides, she needed some peace and quiet. She had sleuthing to do.

Tamsin began by phoning Stacy.

"What's up?" Stacy asked. "You have that take-charge tone in your voice."

"I'm hot on the trail of those books I'm looking for."

"You found a clue to their location?"

"Better than that. I found a set of car keys." Tamsin fished in her backpack and pulled out the set Nimueh had dropped at the church. "I need a favor."

"Is it legal?" Stacy asked.

"Probably not," Tamsin said with a sigh. "The car keys have one of those tags where you can return lost keys through the mail. The code on the tag doesn't give me the address where the vehicle belongs, but the charity who sells the tags has a registry that does. Can you get our little sister to work her computer magic and find that address?"

"You want Clary to hack into a charity's database?" Stacy asked incredulously.

Although it wasn't common among the coven families, their father had insisted his children receive an education in a human university. Where Stacy had studied law and Tamsin history, Clarissa had gone into computer science.

"It's for a good cause," Tamsin pleaded. "I don't want to do a seeking spell. I think the, uh, person with the library is a wee bit dangerous, and the more I stay off his radar, the better."

Tamsin finished on a grimace. It must have communicated itself, because Stacy made a noise of assent. "I'll ask her. I know the Elders want those books. I'll call you back when we find something."

Tamsin put the phone down and began washing up the breakfast dishes in her tiny sink. She was putting away the last freshly dried plate a half hour later when the phone rang. She picked it up, wondering if Clary could have found an answer already.

"Hello, Ms. Greene. This is Benjamin Waller."

Tamsin nearly dropped the phone The crisp, dry voice belonged to the Chief Elder of the Shadowring Coven. "H-hello, sir. To what do I owe the honor of your call?"

"Your request for information on the owner of a late-model Lexus SUV. Your younger sister alerted me to the fact that you asked for her assistance with this unorthodox search."

Tamsin cursed Clary. She had counted on her little sister's rebel streak to keep this quiet. That had been a mistake.

"Oh, don't blame her," Waller said smoothly, as if reading Tamsin's thoughts. "There have been a few indiscretions on Clarissa's part that convinced me to shorten her leash. She does nothing without keeping me informed."

Tamsin's mouth went dry. "How much trouble is she in?"

"Not enough for you to worry about," Waller replied. His tone all but patted her on the head. "This is just a course correction for the moment. She is still painfully young, after all. Plenty of time for her to settle down and form more acceptable habits."

Tamsin drew in a shaking breath. Waller's words were innocent enough, but she could hear something nasty behind them. With a sick feeling, she realized he was enjoying this.

"Clarissa found the address you asked for, but I wanted to take the opportunity to deliver a warning. When we sent you to Carlyle, we did so with a degree of hesitation. Not because of your credentials, which are impeccable, or your commitment, which is clearly of the highest order."

"Then why, sir?" Tamsin sat down at the table, her legs suddenly unreliable. The air around the phone buzzed with a dark, stormy energy that said Waller was deadly serious.

"Because Carlyle is dangerous, particularly for you. The address you found led to a name that caught our interest. It also ignited our fears for your safety. There is little we can do for you as a coven from this distance, but at the very least we can arm you with what information we have."

Tamsin swallowed. The Elders were strict to the point of repression, but they did take their job of protecting the coven to heart. "What information would that be, sir?"

The coven Elder continued. "The owner of those car keys was an extremely powerful solitary practitioner by the name of Henderson. As far as the human authorities know, he is still alive, but no one has heard from him or his wife in months."

Which was no surprise, since Mordred's lackey was driving his car. Tamsin swallowed. "Do you believe Henderson had Merlin's books?"

"Your father believed the books were there. That was why he made the trip to Carlyle in the last year of his life."

Tamsin's scalp prickled. "He was following the same

trail." She'd known that, but suddenly the fact held fresh significance.

"Yes, he was. And he disappeared in Carlyle, never to be heard from again."

Tamsin rose to her feet, utterly stunned. "My father died in a car crash! He was on his way home when it happened."

"Yes, your father died ten years ago." Waller sounded almost kindly now, all too aware of how their family life had changed. "But there never was a body."

"Pardon me?"

Waller's voice sank low, as if trying not to be overheard. "He is unquestionably dead, make no mistake, but the car accident was a, um, piece of theater created for the benefit of his friends and family. Your father was a man who inspired much loyalty among our people. We were better served by putting a final chapter to his story than by entertaining endless conspiracy theories and romance tales."

Tamsin was stunned. "I don't believe this!" She remembered the funeral with painful clarity—the ritual, the burial, the guests in their living room, with her mother weeping upstairs where no one could see. "We deserved the truth."

"Child, the Elders did what was best. There were a lot of brave Shadowring members who would have tried to find your father if they imagined he still lived. We believed they would die just like he did if they charged off to Carlyle in search of explanations. The same thing would happen now, so think about that before you repeat what I just said. I'm taking you into my confidence and expect you to respect my secrets."

"But…if Carlyle is so dangerous, why did you let me come here?"

He chuckled. "Tamsin, we never expected your inquiries to get far enough to put you in danger. We—the Elders, your mother—we know you're restless. We thought if you tried to find the books and failed you would find it easier to forget being a loremaster and settle down."

Tamsin's mouth dropped open. By letting her take this mission, Waller and the rest had been humoring her!

"You exceeded our expectations." Waller cleared his throat, as if banishing amusement. "Congratulations are in order."

Tamsin tried to say something—she knew she was expected to be grateful for his compliment—but words failed. Instead, unease crept over her. There was something intensely wrong with everything Waller was saying.

After a long moment, she managed the one question that bothered her most. "Why are you telling me the truth now? About Dad? About what I'm doing here?" In other words, what sort of a game was the all-powerful Chief Elder playing?

"Child," Waller said kindly, "never mind all that. You underestimate the danger in Carlyle. Come home and tell us what you've found out. We'll take over from there."

"No," Tamsin said, dragging the word out of her parched throat, aware she ran the risk of Waller's wrath. She'd never live with herself if she gave in. "I'm too close to getting the books, and if I don't act now, they'll slip out of our hands."

"Are you sure?" Greed tinged Waller's voice. He wanted Merlin's grimoires—but was that enough for him to gamble on her? "How close?"

"A whisker," she said. "I just need a bit more time."

"Bring me the books," Waller said, the air around the phone turning the color of blood. "The coven will be forever grateful. You have my personal guarantee you'll be our loremaster. I'll even make you an Elder."

Tamsin silently started to cry tears of fright, absolutely certain the Chief Elder had just lied to her. Again.

Chapter 13

Tamsin ended the call a half hour later, after Waller had told her what else he knew—which wasn't much. She sat on the floor and drew her knees up to her chest, as if that would protect her vulnerable core.

She clasped her fingers around the tattoo that bound her wrist, feeling her coven's presence even though an entire country stretched between her and Shadowring. Had her father, when he had come to Carlyle in search of Merlin's books, felt the same pull to his family and the sleepy town he called home? More to the point, what had happened to him in Carlyle and why had the Elders lied about it?

In a single swift movement, Tamsin was on her feet before she realized that she was trembling with anger. *We were better served by putting a final chapter to his story than by entertaining endless conspiracy theories and romance tales.* Fury swamped Tamsin, making her close her eyes against a rush of weeping. She'd served the coven all her days, believing the Elders were necessary to govern the power of its members. Maybe that meant giving up some freedoms, but they'd taken too much this time. They'd taken the truth. They'd taken away the chance to avenge her father and give his death meaning.

Why? What hostile power had struck down her father? And why was it an automatic death sentence to any Shadowring members who came here? From what she understood, her father had visited before Mordred's arrival in the mortal realms, so it was something other than the Prince of Faery. Did Waller even know the answer? Or had she stumbled into something the Elders didn't want found? That was reason enough to push on.

Tamsin was still sitting at the table, a street map before her, when Gawain returned with his brother. The two men were flushed with high spirits. Obviously, Gawain had enjoyed showing off the new world to Beaumains, who now wore faded jeans and a shirt that looked as if it might be Gawain's. In one hand, Gawain bore a faded sports bag.

"I gathered my possessions from the place I've been staying," said Gawain. "If Mordred is aware we oppose him, it would be wiser for us to remain together."

Tamsin glanced at the bag, not sure what to say. He was moving in, which might have been romantic after last night, but he was right about the threat. The bag was long enough for a sword and clinked like chain mail. That Gawain could fit everything he owned into one bundle said much about the life he lived.

She nodded, unable to bring herself to make conversation yet. She was still reeling from Waller's call. If she started in on that topic, she'd waste precious time ranting.

Gawain immediately picked up on her mood. "What's wrong?"

She pointed to the map, forcing her face into neutral lines. "I have Mordred's address."

"Where?" Gawain and Beaumains gathered around.

"Here." Tamsin pointed to a spot north of Medievaland. "There are some old houses up on the hill. Big places with private woods around them. One of them was owned by Dennis and Marian Henderson. He was from an old witch family but never joined a coven. It's rumored he collected rare books of all kinds, including magic."

Gawain's eyebrows shot up. "You think he has Merlin's grimoires?"

"Henderson was one of the people who invested in Medievaland back in the day. It's no stretch to think his contribution paid for a few books from the church's collection."

Beaumains furrowed his brow, confused. "I thought Mordred had the spell books?"

Tamsin swallowed. This part of her research made her queasy. "I think Mordred killed the Hendersons and moved into their house. The Henderson family built it a century ago on a natural wellspring of magical energy, and Mordred would want to take advantage of that free-flowing power."

"How do you know this?" Gawain asked.

"To make a long story short, I had a call from one of my coven's Elders. He believes the Hendersons are dead. The human authorities just haven't figured it out yet."

There was a moment of stunned silence in the room. Then the two brothers moved as one, Gawain sitting across from Tamsin as Beaumains leaned against the wall, arms folded. "Go on," Gawain prompted her.

"If Mordred did take over this address," she said, "he might not realize he has the books. Not unless he's gone through the library in detail and looked at every title. Unless he's a scholar of magic, he might not recognize what they are even if he has given them a glance."

Gawain and Beaumains exchanged a look. "He's not much of a reader, but it's just a matter of time," Gawain said. "Sooner or later he'll realize there is a vast opportunity for mischief waiting on the shelf."

Beaumains shrugged. "Then I propose we pay Mordred a visit. Why take the chance he'll discover them?"

"Another thing," said Tamsin. "I've been going on and on about the books, but I haven't forgotten that I caught a glimpse of your friend Angmar during my vision. The Henderson house is large and there's a good chance Mordred is holding him prisoner somewhere on the grounds."

Gawain knit his dark brows together. "I would rather have waited until we had a greater number of knights before confronting Mordred in his lair, but there is too much at stake to delay any longer. If we wait, Mordred will have even more advantages."

"What about Excalibur?" said Beaumains, obviously worried.

Gawain shot him a sharp look, as if his younger brother was going to say something he shouldn't. Tamsin shifted, waiting until Gawain finally turned her way, his cheekbones flushed. "What—or who—is Excalibur?" she asked.

"A very useful sword," he said. "We don't have it, so there's no point in talking about it."

Beaumains gave his brother an uncertain look but held his tongue. Tamsin had enough on her mind that she let the exchange pass without comment.

Because the Henderson house was one of the main historical buildings in Carlyle, Tamsin was able to find a house plan on the internet. That led to hours of strategizing before Gawain and his brother settled on a plan. Meanwhile, Tamsin stocked a small belt pouch with a healer's tools and a few magical powders. Her favorite was heal-all, which could cure small hurts or act like a field dressing on a major wound. Her pouch didn't hold enough supplies for a serious emergency, but having a few things made her feel better.

Gawain and Beaumains dressed for battle, an affair that involved a lot of buckling and lacing and glimpses of scarred, muscular flesh. Tamsin had a fleeting worry about getting stopped for a traffic ticket with two armed knights in the car, but that close to Medievaland they had a plausible excuse.

But when she looked up and saw Gawain dressed for battle, all practical thoughts ground to a halt. She'd seen Beaumains in his medieval clothes, but not Gawain. The sight made her catch her breath. He was a large man to begin with, but now he wore a quilted tunic with a shirt of chain mail over it, and then a dark cloak over that. He filled the tiny room, and not just with his physical bulk. In putting on the armor, Gawain had donned his role of warrior. Every gesture, every line of his body spoke of hard strength and harder will.

Gawain drew his sword a few inches. The steel scraped against the scabbard, the sound raising the hairs on Tamsin's arm. It was as if she had an ancestral memory of battle, something so deep in her genes that generations could not erase it. Gawain gave a smile that hovered between bitterness and anticipation. It was the smile of a man who did not shy away from violence but understood the cost. He slid the blade back into place and met Tamsin's eyes. "I am ready."

Beaumains nodded, twirling a dagger in one hand before thrusting it into his belt. "Ready." All at once, with his determined eyes and scarred face, he went from charming to dangerous.

They were on the road soon enough, Gawain riding shotgun. Conversation in the car had died to a brooding silence until he finally spoke. "You are unusually quiet."

"Are you asking if I'm afraid?"

He gave her a frank look. "Yes."

"I am. I'd be crazy not to be."

"But you are thinking of something else?" he guessed.

Tamsin didn't want to talk about it, but decided it was better to unburden herself after all. She would need a clear head once they reached their destination. "I was thinking about my father. Waller told me he didn't actually die in a car crash. He disappeared from Carlyle when he came to find these same grimoires."

Gawain sat back with a huff of surprise. "Interesting that the Elders kept that to themselves."

At his words, a dam burst inside Tamsin, flooding her with hurt. "How can they do that to us?"

Tamsin turned the wheel none too steadily and had to correct her direction. "Waller said we hadn't really buried a body, that they just wanted to give the coven closure so nobody went looking for him."

"Do you think he is alive?" Gawain asked carefully.

"No. If he was, my father would have come home. He loved us." She slammed on the brake just before she ran a red light.

Gawain cast her a sideways look. "If you are upset, we could stop the car for a time."

"I'm fine to drive," she snapped, and then instantly regretted her temper. "I'll be all right in a moment, but I have to tell you I hate the Elders right now. I hate them for lying and never bothering to find out the truth. I'm supposed to be able to trust them, but instead I'm afraid of what else they might do."

He put a comforting hand on her knee, his presence big

and warm and solid as a rock beside her. She took a deep breath, forcing herself to focus on the streets around her. "This is a lot to take in on top of everything else."

"I understand," Gawain replied. "I swear to you, on my honor as a knight, that I will do everything possible to help you find the truth."

"So do I," said Beaumains from behind them. He'd been silent up until now, but he leaned forward with a clink and rustle of gear. "Trust me, that's how the Round Table spends a lot of its time—getting to the bottom of these things. You might say we're the experts."

His confidence made Tamsin smile despite her mood. "Thank you."

The conversation took them to the bottom of the rise that marked the edge of the Henderson property. Tamsin parked several blocks away to avoid attracting attention, and they walked around the perimeter until Beaumains found a track that climbed through the brush to the main part of the grounds. Tamsin found the trek hard going, especially when her feet seemed to find every crackling leaf and snapping twig possible. Despite their size, the two men moved almost in silence, stopping often to listen. At those moments, Tamsin would freeze, her breath misting in the fading light, and spread her senses wide. The information Waller had given her was obviously correct. The house sat on a nexus of natural magical energy such as Tamsin had never felt before. Any spell cast on these grounds would carry a wealth of power, although only an expert could safely harness the full strength flowing from the rocks beneath. There was little wonder why Mordred chose this particular house to make his own.

The path led them to a break in the trees on the west side of the house. Tamsin crouched, making herself small as she viewed the huge Victorian mansion. It was beautiful, a mass of gingerbread and wrought iron that rose up three stories under a clear indigo sky pinpricked with the first stars. "This is definitely the place from my vision," she whispered. "I can feel it."

Gawain gave a single nod and pointed toward the back of the house. According to the plans, there was a rear door that led from the kitchen garden into the old scullery. It was the entrance with the least visibility from the grounds, but there was no telling how many people were inside. Beaumains drew his dagger and ran a few yards toward the back of the house. As Tamsin watched, he seemed to disappear, using his dark cloak to blend with the shadows. There was a tense moment of waiting, and then he signaled that it was safe to follow. Once they caught up, he set out again. After a few minutes, they were in position, the entire process smooth and efficient. The knights had obviously done this before.

The scullery sat straight across from where they hid. Now it was Tamsin's turn to take the lead. Bent nearly double, she scuttled between a series of raised beds, her feet silent on the paths strewn with straw. She had an impression of winter vegetables and cold frames, and then she was at the door. It was an ordinary door with a dead bolt, but she probed for magic. Finding none, she spelled the lock open and raised a hand to signal her success when it clicked open. A tiny voice in the back of her mind whispered this was going too well, but there was no time to listen. Gawain and Beaumains appeared at either side of her like silent wraiths. Gawain drew his sword carefully, making no sound, and Tamsin reached for the door handle.

The three of them exchanged glances. Gawain was solemn, whereas his brother's eyes danced with excitement. Tamsin reached for the door handle and turned it. The door drifted open on silent hinges, and they stepped into a darkened room.

A moment later, she understood why the house didn't have alarms. Mordred didn't need them.

Chapter 14

"No!" Gawain spun around just as the door vanished behind them. He'd been prepared for weapons, guards, hellhounds, or even just an empty house, but not this. They'd stepped through a portal and now there was no telling where they actually were. "Magic," he growled, taking a tighter grip of his sword.

A pale, ambient light seeped from the scum growing along the walls. It was just enough to make out the fact that they were underground. Tiny caves and corridors rambled in all directions, making him think of a rabbit warren. The prevailing smell, however, was of something dead.

"How did we get here?" Tamsin said in a barely audible voice.

"The doorway was a portal," Beaumains explained. "This is fae work. I've seen this kind of tunneling before."

"A portal? I didn't feel anything like that when I checked the door for spells." Tamsin shook her head. "But then I've never seen a portal. Witches don't know how to make them anymore."

Gawain used his sword to poke the wall where the door had been, but all he got was a shower of dirt. They were in deep trouble.

"What now?" Beaumains asked.

"We look for a way back," Gawain replied, trying to sound as though he did this sort of thing every day. Well, he had, up until Merlin had put them all into the stone sleep. He started down a corridor, signaling the others to follow.

Roots poked through the walls and ceilings as if a forest grew above them, but he noticed the pale, twining fingers twitch whenever someone drew near.

"Stay back," Gawain warned, but even as he said it a tendril wound around Beaumains's arm, whipping twice around for a tight hold and dragging the young knight closer to the wall. Gawain severed the root with a two-handed swipe of his blade. Beaumains sprang free, and every root in the passage recoiled, as if sucked back into the dirt.

"Binding trees!" Beaumains said it like a curse. "We're in a fae dungeon."

"Stay away from the walls," Gawain ordered. "As long as they can't reach you, it's safe enough."

Tamsin had watched and listened with wide, watchful eyes. "If Mordred has linked the house with a dungeon, then this must be where he's holding your friend."

Gawain had already reached the same conclusion. "Probably, so we might as well start looking for Angmar."

Staying well away from the grasping roots, they continued down the tunnel, Gawain in the lead and Beaumains covering the rear. Gawain was almost painfully conscious of Tamsin moving behind him. She was strong, but the quick pace of her breathing said she was afraid. That was good—that meant she'd be careful.

Everything went well for a few minutes. The foul stench in the air grew thicker and Gawain noticed the cell-like caves on either side of the corridor began to contain remains of former occupants. Mostly these were bones, but in a few he noticed the roots thrust into desiccated husks, fine shoots sucking up every last drop of nourishment.

And then he heard a sound he had hoped to forget forever. It was a sticky sound, almost a squish, but on an enormous scale, as if a thousand sucking mouths were being torn away from their prey. Despite himself, Gawain stopped short, causing Tamsin to bump into his back.

"What is it?" she asked.

"There is a beast guarding this place." He turned to glimpse his brother's pale face. Beaumains recognized the sound, too. It was plain from the horror in his eyes. "Merlin cast a spell to banish demons from the human realms, but this is fae territory. Some of the demons' pets survived."

"Pets?" Tamsin repeated. From her expression, this was something she did not want to believe. "Demons have pets?"

It was Beaumains who answered. "More scavengers looking for scraps the demons leave behind. The prisoners in this place must be protected by magic, or they would all have been supper by now."

The sound grew louder, and so did a stench that combined rot and the odor of a latrine. "Stay behind me," Gawain ordered, taking a firmer grip on his sword and stepping into a wider place where the tunnel turned.

There was no name for the beast he saw. The gray worm-like body was covered with glistening mucous that glistened in the faint phosphorescence of the underground. The head was an eyeless nub, identifiable only by a bony fanlike crest that rose along its neck. It would have been no more than an overgrown slug except for the round, questing mouth filled with needle-fine teeth. Gawain knew once it had latched onto living flesh, it would suck the blood out of a victim through skin, bone and clothing. Nothing short of death would stop its destruction.

The worm stopped, the head lifting to taste the air. Gawain could see the mouth working, the round hole gulping air. He caught a flash of those deadly teeth and went cold. Somewhere down the corridor, closer to the beast, a voice wailed in terrified despair. They had found the prisoners.

Beaumains was at his side, sword in hand. "What I wouldn't give for a nice big spear about now."

"Spears just pass through the stinking things," Gawain replied. "It's like trying to kill a pudding. The only vital organs are beneath the crest. Strike there."

"I suppose you've battled one before?"

Gawain grunted. "Back in the Orkneys. The things seem to like northern climates."

"You've fought everything," Beaumains said resentfully, and bolted toward the worm, sword raised.

Gawain bellowed in protest. A frontal attack was pure folly. The worm reared back as far as the tunnel roof would permit and struck like a snake. Skidding to a halt beneath its head, Beaumains thrust upward, driving toward the underside of the bony crest protecting the tiny brain. The brave gamble should have worked.

It didn't. The worm struck, needle-fine teeth piercing between the links of chain mail covering his brother's chest. Fingers convulsing around the hilt of his sword, Beaumains was lifted into the air as lightly as a leaf. Tamsin gasped in horror at the same moment Gawain charged, cursing his youngest sibling for a fool. Beaumains roared with pain, trying to hack with his sword but unable to do more than flail.

The worm was the size of a tree trunk, far too large to neatly slice it in two. With grim purpose, Gawain settled for chopping like a woodcutter. It was a risky move, but the thing only had one mouth, and at the moment it was full of his brother. Fury drove the blade deep. The skin split, releasing gelatinous goo that stank like a plague pit. The worm shuddered, flinging its head from side to side— and Beaumains along with it. Gawain hacked again, using the blade like a lever to hitch himself atop the worm. The thing bucked, arching the spiny crest in a gesture of self-defense, but Gawain clung on. He raised the sword and drove it deep into the head, leaning with all his weight until it was buried to the hilt.

The worm collapsed into a stinking heap. The sucking mouth let go, and Beaumains fell, landing with a bounce. Gawain braced his knees on either side of the sword hilt and pulled it free with a slurping noise that made his flesh creep.

By the time Gawain had freed himself from the worm, Tamsin was evaluating his brother's injuries. "I think the chain mail stopped it from killing him, but there are dozens of puncture wounds. I dusted them with heal-all to stop the bleeding, but they have to be cleaned."

"We need to get him home," Gawain said with forced calm. Beaumains was conscious, though clearly in pain. Gawain swore a dark curse beneath his breath. He had little idea where they were, much less how to get his brother to safety.

Tamsin looked up at him, her dark eyes wide but her mouth set in a determined line. "Tell me what to do."

"Can he walk?"

"Yes." Beaumains struggled, his boots scraping the

floor. Gawain heaved him to his feet and helped him sheathe his sword. The younger knight slumped, one hand on Gawain's shoulder, panting against the pain. "I'm fine," he said. "No bones broken. It's just a flesh wound."

Gawain schooled his face, hating what he was asking Beaumains to endure—but the only alternative was to move on. He hitched a shoulder under his brother's arm and chose a corridor that was absent of the reeking carcass of a giant worm. They forged ahead, Beaumains biting back cries of discomfort until they were no more than a soft hiss.

The next cells they found still had live prisoners—or close to living. All were fae, their beautiful features barely recognizable beneath matted hair and festering wounds. Gawain's gut grew colder with each step. He was no stranger to prisons, but this was beyond anything he had ever seen.

He almost missed the slight stir of movement in the last cell, but something caught his eye. Or maybe, buried deep in a part of himself he denied, he heard a silent cry for help. He stopped and peered into the darkness. All he could see was a pile of rags and a white smudge that might have been a faery's pale hair, but he still knew who it was. "Angmar."

"What's left of him." The voice was a dry whisper. "You said you would come, knight. I should have had more faith."

Tamsin shuddered, her healer's senses pushed to the limit. Everywhere in this place, sickness and pain howled at her to fix them, pounding at her senses at a bone-deep level. Most were too damaged to help, but Angmar of Corin still lived. She pushed forward, straining to see in the poor light. Angmar lay in a crumpled heap, one arm twisted in a way that said it was broken. His face was a bloody mass of slashes and swollen bruises. Nausea stirred in the back of her throat, but she kept her voice brisk. "He's bound with those tree roots. Help me get them off."

But Gawain was still supporting his brother. "Let me sit down," said Beaumains, his face slick with sweat. "I need to rest."

Reluctantly, Gawain lowered him to the ground. Beaumains gripped his chest, eyes closed and face drained of color. Gawain met Tamsin's eyes. She didn't blame him for the worry in his eyes. Unless they got out of there, the prognosis wasn't great.

Gawain moved to join her, mouth fixed in a grim line as he took a closer look at Angmar. "This is Mordred's handiwork. I recognize his flair."

He reached for his sword, but then stopped. "The roots are bound too tight to cut them without cutting flesh as well."

Tamsin crouched, studying the problem. She was aware of Angmar's eyes following her every move, but he didn't speak again. He probably had no strength left. The thick white tendrils were taut around Angmar's body, the tips beginning to burrow into the skin. She thought of the dead she had seen, sucked dry by the binding trees.

She pointed to the roots. "I can give these bad boys a good smack." Keeping her voice light for Angmar's sake, she looked up at Gawain. "I know how much you like magic. You might want to back away for this."

"Just do it," Gawain said.

Tamsin nodded and opened her belt pouch. She'd stored the heal-all powder in a gray silk drawstring bag. She sprinkled it lightly over the roots, careful not to let any fall on Angmar. Then she closed her eyes and chanted a scrap of forbidden magic she'd learned from her father's book.

It was one of the few dark spells she knew, and one she kept to herself. It reversed the properties of other spells, turning heal-all into a deadly, corrosive acid.

The tattoo around her wrist burned like a brand. Dark energy convulsed through her like sudden sickness, making her cry out in disgust—but the effect was instant. A hiss of foul smoke flared up from the roots, their ropy surface bubbling. Tamsin coughed, her eyes stinging from the fumes, then she signaled to Gawain to stand ready. After writhing and squirming, the roots whipped free of Angmar like snakes in retreat, coiling back to the walls with an eerie keening noise. Tamsin and Gawain grabbed Angmar and pulled him to safety, putting him down next to Beaumains.

A giddy rush of relief made Tamsin's head swim, but the next instant she was on her knees, checking the fae's injuries. His right arm was broken in two places, but thankfully the bones had not penetrated the skin. She pulled off her sweater, tying it around him to immobilize the arm. Angmar moaned in pain, bringing a rush of tears to her own eyes, but she kept working. She had no choice. This was her battleground, as surely as Gawain's was the field of war.

Gawain paced behind her, tension swirling around him like a second cloak. "This isn't getting you any closer to finding your books," he said wryly.

She checked the pulse in Angmar's broken arm. It wasn't strong, but at least circulation wasn't completely impaired. "I'm where I need to be."

"Trapped in a dungeon?" His tone was sarcastic, but the pain in his eyes said the anger was turned on himself. "There has to be a doorway here. This is where the occupied cells are, so surely Mordred has an easy way of getting in and out of this end of the prison. I am too blind to see it."

Tamsin could hear Gawain's self-reproach in every word. "Don't beat yourself up. You've kept us alive. We can't fight back if we're dead."

He gave her a half smile. "You have the spirit of a warrior, Tamsin Greene."

A warm twinge of pleasure surged through her, but she simply shrugged and went to check on Beaumains. He sat silently, slumped forward with his eyes hazed with pain. She touched his cheek, feeling the burn of a fever. The heal-all was working, but it could only do so much. It was plain he needed more help than she could provide without her full array of healer's potions. "I wish I knew how to find that portal," she said under her breath.

Angmar stirred, his eyes flickering open to bloodshot slits. He reached up and caught her wrist, his one good hand still surprisingly strong. His cracked lips moved, but no sound emerged. He cleared his throat and tried again. "I've seen it."

Chapter 15

Portals, Tamsin learned, were elegant magic—as simple as opening a door and yet hiding infinite complexities in the workings beneath. Mordred's doorway was only a few feet from where Tamsin stood, but it wasn't *actually* there—not until it was activated. The spell's energetic substructure was tied to that specific location and could be fired up with little effort by someone who knew how. Tamsin's job was to take control of the existing framework and redirect the portal to where she wanted it to go. Not that Tamsin, or any modern witch, had a clue how to do so. Thank Merlin's pointy hat Angmar was there to give her instructions.

All the fae could manage was a fading whisper, so Tamsin had to listen carefully. The first instruction was easy. If they were going to leave together, they had to be touching. Gawain took hold of his brother's shoulder in one hand and with the other grasped Tamsin's sleeve. She held Angmar's hand in hers, noticing that it was cold and clammy. She knew little about faery physiology, but he seemed to be going into shock. Tamsin clenched her teeth, feeling the weight of responsibility for all their lives. She had to get this right.

She closed her eyes, stretching out her senses to find the edges of the portal just as Angmar had described. This sort of thing wasn't Tamsin's strong suit, but she gave it her best effort. *There.* A spark of satisfaction rippled through her. Now she had to take firm hold of the door that was there—and yet wasn't.

The portal unexpectedly flung open. She experienced the same sense of surprise as when one reaches for a door handle only to be trampled by someone coming from the other side—except this was worse. This was Mordred.

His shock was the only thing that saved them. Without knowing precisely what she did, she twisted the portal away, redirecting it before the Prince of Faery stepped inside. It spun around Tamsin like a gigantic wheel, gyrating wildly as she grappled for control. She whirled like a pebble lost in a tornado, dragging Gawain and the others with her. Panic surged. She needed to find something solid, some point of reference to cling to, but her mind was reeling. Worse, she could feel Mordred's power rising to snatch the portal away.

The first image Tamsin came up with was the library where the books were, but she immediately rejected it. As much as she wanted Merlin's grimoires, the priority was getting her patients to safety. She tried for a second location and saw her car parked on the roadside blocks away. She lunged for it with utter desperation, forcing her magic through the spinning portal like a hammer blow. Light seared her, passing through her being with painful, burning intensity. The last thing she remembered was opening her mouth to scream.

The portal spit them out on the hard pavement next to her Camry. Tamsin fell from a space at least a foot above the ground, making her stumble and fall to her hands and knees. The world spun and she closed her eyes, concentrating on the sting in her palms to steady herself. Slowly, she sank forward to her elbows, not sure if she was going to throw up. She'd never used that much magic before. Ever. It felt as if she'd been turned inside out.

After what seemed like hours—or maybe seconds—later, Gawain helped her to her feet. His features were sharp with worry. "We have to go. Mordred will follow as soon as he regains control of his doorway."

Tamsin turned around with a slow shuffle to look at the car. Gawain already had the others propped up in the back-seat. Moving slowly to hide her weakness, Tamsin leaned in to get a better look at her patients, but the single street-light barely penetrated the heavy trees lining the street. She pushed away, unsure if she was fit to drive, but there was no choice. "Okay. Let's go."

She had almost made it to the driver's door when Gawain grabbed her by the shoulders and kissed her full on the mouth. There was no ceremony—it was hard, hot, desperate, and over before she quite realized what he'd done. She blinked, staggering back a step. Pins and needles swarmed up her body, every nerve on alert from that brief, bruising touch.

He smiled, a quick flash of white teeth in the darkness. "That's the fastest way I could think of to thank you for saving us."

Tamsin gulped air, hoping a lungful of the cool night would quench the flush in her cheeks. "You can take your time with the thank-yous later."

She finished on a hiccup of a laugh. The words were as inappropriate, untimely and heated as his kiss, but she couldn't help it and she didn't care. They'd nearly died. What did it matter if they yearned to celebrate life? His gaze met hers, burning with the same giddy desire. She got in the car before she surrendered to the adrenaline high. They weren't safe yet.

But as little as Tamsin expected it, the trip home went with almost eerie precision. Gawain placed Angmar carefully on the bed while Tamsin prepared a nest of pillows and a blanket on the floor for Beaumains. It made the tiny suite crowded, but she needed to keep a constant watch over her patients.

Tamsin set to work at once, pressing Gawain into service as her second set of hands. He complied willingly, cutting away Angmar's sweater and washing the wounds before she asked.

"You've done this before," Tamsin said. The fae had passed out while she'd splinted his arm, but that was probably for the best.

"I learned many things on the battleground, including what I know of healing." He looked up from washing the blood from his hands, his eyes as tired as she felt. "What I wonder is where you learned the calm of an experienced warrior."

"I don't know," she replied. "I've lived a quiet life. I never anticipated dungeons and giant monsters."

She hadn't expected anyone like Gawain, either. He was pushy and suspicious and brooding, but he was filled with a firestorm of emotions—fierce loyalty and towering courage. Beside him, the world seemed pallid and uninteresting. He was proof there were more possibilities than she had dreamed of. She could grow addicted to that heart-pounding thrill.

She fell silent as she mixed a potion for Beaumains. Some clean, simple injuries could be healed with raw magic, pressing her own life force directly into the wound. Complex injuries like Angmar's were best handled conservatively, allowing the body to do as much on its own as possible. What she'd prepared for Beaumains was a standard mixture of charmed herbal oils that would heal whatever internal damage the worm's teeth had done. As soon as he'd downed that, she'd make another to counter whatever germs the beast had been carrying. With luck, the young knight would make a full recovery.

Tamsin stopped stirring and handed the glass of medicine to Gawain. "Give this to your brother."

He hesitated before taking it from her, his fingers warm from the hot water. "Is it charmed?"

"Yes," she said, remembering his reluctance to let her use magic on his wound. "Beaumains needs the healing magic."

"I know," Gawain replied, but she saw the flicker of uncertainty—almost fear—cross his face.

The look stung. "After all I've done tonight, you're still cautious."

"I am not," he said.

But there was a tension around his mouth and eyes that said otherwise. He desired her, admired her and perhaps wanted to trust her, but the feeling hadn't made it all the way to his heart. Dislike of magic—of everything a witch was—went too deep with Gawain.

Frustration flipped Tamsin's mood, and suddenly she was angry. She'd given herself to him, but he refused to risk the most basic bond with her. "If you trust me, then why are you keeping secrets?"

His expression was confused but also wary. "What secrets do you mean?"

"Tell me what's so special about Excalibur." She wasn't sure why she cared, except that he'd avoided telling her earlier.

He lowered his eyes a moment, but then returned her regard. "It's the only blade that can kill Mordred or his mother. Not even their magic can blunt its power."

"The *only* blade? Then where is it?"

"Excalibur belongs to King Arthur. If we wish to stop Mordred, we must find Arthur's tomb."

Well, that shed new light on Gawain's determination to find his king! On top of the obvious bonds of friendship and loyalty was the very practical fact that Arthur had the one weapon they needed to destroy their greatest foes. No wonder he'd wanted her help finding the tombs.

Then another realization crept up on Tamsin. "So you went into Mordred's house knowing we couldn't kill him without the sword?"

Gawain lifted his head, looking down his nose in that arrogant way he had. "It was a risk. I could have held him off while Beaumains got you and those books to safety."

"There's no way you could have won!" And not winning meant losing in a final, permanent way.

Gawain gave another slight shrug and moved toward the couch and his sleeping brother. "Circumstances are never perfect. We couldn't wait any longer to get the books."

"But if Mordred had killed you, who would look for Arthur?" The idea of what he'd meant to do made Tamsin's scalp prickle with alarm.

Gawain turned back to her, his expression bleak. "My brother is here, and I hoped you would help him as you've helped me. I am a knight of the Round Table. We don't fight evil from an armchair."

Tamsin let out a long breath, exasperated beyond measure. "But you'll flinch at a healing potion made by a witch?"

He gave a slow shrug. "Fighting is easier for me. It's clean and simple."

"Whatever." Tamsin made a show of checking Angmar's wounds, but her pulse pounded with an aftermath of emotions. The day had been too full of unexpected blows, leaving her hurt and furious and oddly lonely.

But maybe not alone. Gawain's presence in the tiny apartment prickled along her skin. He was doing exactly what Richard had done—seeing the witch and forgetting the woman. Seeing, and flinching away in fear and disgust no matter how hard he tried to hide it.

Tears stung Tamsin's eyes, but she refused to let them fall. She mixed the second potion for Beaumains and watched while Gawain held his brother's head so that he could drink. Gawain showed such tenderness, it made her throat ache—in part because it was beautiful, and in part because she was beginning to understand that open love was something he would never show her.

In search of relief, Tamsin retreated to the balcony. The cold air slipped over her like an icy glove, but it barely penetrated her mood. She gripped the iron rail, fingers worrying the rusty patches eating through the cheap white paint. A sudden pain made her snatch her hand away as a sliver of metal drew blood. She sucked at the wound, the fresh hurt only adding more fuel to her foul temper.

Tamsin felt a wall of warmth behind her. She hadn't heard Gawain's approach but knew he was there as surely as if he'd touched her. She turned, her finger still in her mouth. Gawain's face was hidden by shadow. Still, she felt the weight of his gaze.

"You are hurt." He reached for her, but she stepped back, clenching her injured hand into a fist at her side.

"The paint hid the sharp place." Tamsin's breath escaped in sharp puffs of mist. "Is that how you see me, as an everyday face painted over creeping corrosion that eventually wounds whoever is foolish enough to touch it?"

His frown was perplexed. "I have offended you."

"Have I done anything but help you?" she said, her voice dropping to a low rasp. "I've risked my life. I've healed your wounded. I've faced your enemy for you, and you still treat me like something foul." And she'd slept with him, but she would choke before she brought that into the argument. Her pride wouldn't allow it.

"Because you are a witch?" The words were soft, almost apologetic. But not quite.

Tamsin's temper rose another notch. "Yes. You have a problem with magic, in case you hadn't noticed."

Gawain made a noise that was almost a laugh and came to stand beside her at the balcony rail. He leaned his arms on it, shaking his head. "I beg your forgiveness."

"Then I think you owe me an explanation."

He remained silent for a long moment. "Once upon a time, before she was ever Queen of the Faeries, my aunt, Morgan LaFaye, set a challenge for the Round Table. It was Christmas, and Arthur loved to have games and challenges at his revels. He boasted that, far and wide, his knights were the most chivalrous, honorable and courteous warriors there were. Within the hour, a strange knight showed up to test us. He was, of course, sent by my aunt."

"Why are you telling me a story?"

"To answer your question." He kept looking out at the city, not even turning his head. "The strange knight promised to allow one of us to chop his head off if we would allow him to return the favor in a year's time."

"And what was your first clue that this was going to end badly?" Tamsin asked, leaning her back against the rail so that she could study Gawain's face, but he kept it turned away. "And why is this in any way relevant to me?"

"The knight was green, head to toe." Gawain kept talking, his voice soft. "That should have tipped us off that there was magic involved, for green is the color of enchantment. But we were drunk at the time and more than usually stupid. I volunteered."

"To cut his head off?"

"He asked for it."

"But how…" She couldn't see what this had to do with her being a witch.

"I did the deed as requested, and then he picked up his head and rode away. By the time I sobered up, I was terrified, for I was honor-bound to face him the following Christmas. Face him and die."

Tamsin caught her breath. "Oh."

"I went. Honor demanded it. My road led to the Forest Sauvage."

"That's where the Green Knight lived?"

"Yes. Sir Bertilak—for that was his name—and his lady were most hospitable once I arrived."

"Was Lady Bertilak green, too?"

"No, but she always wore green. She was smart and beautiful and gracious. In fact, she was such a good hostess she offered to climb into my bed."

"She what?" Despite herself, Tamsin was drawn into the tale.

Gawain finally turned to her, a rueful smile playing at the corners of his mouth. "It was all part of Morgan's test, to see if Arthur's knights were truly good, or if they would abuse the hospitality of their host. If I'd accepted the good lady's offer, I would have offended her lord and lost my head, for sure. Because I respected my host's honor and did not take his wife, he let me go."

"And this Lady Bertilak still did her best to seduce you, even knowing it might kill you?"

"That was the test. She was most persuasive in those last days before the trial. After all, why not take what I wanted when I was about to perish anyhow?"

Tamsin began to see where this was going. "She used despair as a weapon."

"And she had magic and considerable beauty on her side. I am ashamed to say that I came close to the edge."

"But you didn't."

"No." Gawain straightened, folding his arms. "That's why I always wear green. It reminds me to remain humble, because even the best knight can stray from his duty. Especially when it comes to lovely witches."

Tamsin bristled. "That seems a little harsh. You came through it in one piece."

"I should have known better. I am susceptible where magic is involved."

"I'd say there was ill will involved."

Gawain's face was stony. "Perhaps, but magic always makes things worse. It can turn a game into a trap where the unwary might lose his head."

She drew herself up, temper rising again. "And it can save a life just as quickly. I won't entertain the belief magic is bad in and of itself. Not for one second."

"I believe you," he said softly, contradicting all her expectations. "But one deed leads to another. No one begins believing they will be evil, but magic allows them to take an easy path. So a gray deed leads to a black one, and soon the one wielding the magic has lost all sense of right and wrong."

Tamsin was about to deny it, but the words died on her tongue. "I can see why you say that. LaFaye is your aunt, but she didn't warn you against taking the Green Knight's challenge."

That made him laugh, and it was bitter. "Warn me? That would require a capacity for feelings she does not possess."

"But your mother was her sister. That should have made her spare you."

His expression didn't change, though the lines beside his mouth deepened. "LaFaye and my mother did not waste time on sentimentality. I watched my mother skin a man alive so that she could dupe his wife by wearing his face."

"What?" Tamsin's hand went to her stomach, afraid it would revolt. "Magic that dark has always been forbidden. Did anyone do anything about it?"

"My brother Agravaine. He killed her."

Sick with dread, Tamsin turned his words over in her mind, but her thoughts shied away from their meaning. The pictures they painted were too awful. "I don't know what to say. That's far beyond my experience."

"I would not wish it any other way."

Her hands had gone cold, as if her blood had ceased to flow. She'd come out on the balcony because she was angry with Gawain, but now she wanted to comfort him. "You can't think all witches are like LaFaye or your mother. We just aren't. Most of us are just ordinary people."

Tamsin raised her fingers to touch his face. He stiffened but didn't draw back, allowing her to trace the angles of his jaw. He was warm, his cheek rough with dark stubble. It struck her again how Gawain seemed more alive than any ordinary man. He was so full of passion and regret, it stopped her breath, as if he carried an electrical charge. Too much contact with him might stop her heart.

His hand came up to caress hers. At first, his thumb traced her palm with gentle pressure, his fingers lacing through her own. He pressed her hand to his cheek, turning into her touch so he could leave a kiss on her finger-tips. Then he pulled her hand away.

"I believe you mean well." He took a step back, leaving cold air between them. "I am sorry I wounded your feelings."

"Okay."

He hesitated, seeming momentarily uncertain. "Mordred held every advantage tonight, and it was too much like the past. I could not save people I love from harm."

She wasn't sure what past he referred to. His childhood? Or the strange game he'd played with the Green Knight? Or some other terrible scene he had lived through? "We got out together. We make a good team."

He gave her a brief, courtly bow that put even greater distance between them. "I thank you for that. I am in your debt, and will uphold our bargain."

With that, Gawain retreated inside, leaving Tamsin more confused than before.

Chapter 16

Tamsin got little sleep that night. She propped herself in a chair, refusing to do more than doze until it was time to check on her patients. But if her nursing duties kept her from true rest, so did her confusion over Gawain.

He'd held her when she'd become lost in Mordred's spell. They'd spent the night in each other's arms after finding Beaumains. She'd begun to believe Gawain would have a special place in her future—certainly as a lover, and possibly something deeper. How could she have misread the situation so badly?

Because she'd wanted to? Tamsin had to be honest— he'd made no promises. She'd taken him to her bed with her eyes wide open. The fact that he had brought up their bargain put everything back to a simple handshake deal with no strings attached.

A tight knot of bitter unhappiness cramped Tamsin's core. It wasn't fair. Being with him was like whisky after a lifetime of weak tea. But she was just a witch with a history degree, not a miracle worker. Whatever Gawain had experienced was more than she could cure with a kiss.

When Tamsin shook herself awake at dawn, her bones ached with weariness. Gawain was sitting by the wall, his sword balanced across his bent knees. He looked up, the early light showing his pallor. He said nothing as she bent over Beaumains, pressing the younger knight's wrist to check his pulse.

"The fever is down," she said, keeping her voice low. "Pulse is slow and steady. He should be fine."

Gawain exhaled in relief. "Thank you."

"Magic has its uses." Tamsin resisted the urge to give in to fatigue and frustration and say more. Instead, she crossed to the bed and touched Angmar's forehead. A sweep of her healer's magic said he was stable, but there was a long, long way to go. Mordred had done a lot of damage to the fae.

Angmar's eyes fluttered open. One was swollen and badly bloodshot, but the other was the clear, cool green of forest glades. The fae regarded her with open curiosity. "You saved me, little witch." His voice was hoarse but stronger than she'd expected.

"Hush," she replied, checking his bandages. Though the bleeding had stopped, she wanted to change the dressing on the worst of his injuries. "You need to rest."

But Angmar caught her hand, stopping her before she set to work. "Where is Sir Gawain? I have a tale he needs to hear."

"I am here." Gawain held out a glass of water to Tamsin. "I will hold him if you help him drink."

Gawain held Angmar's head as Tamsin raised the glass to his lips. The fae drank greedily and then lay back for a long moment, wearied from even that much exertion. But finally he opened his eyes again, lifting his gaze to Gawain. "I know where your king lies."

Tamsin froze where she was. The only sound was the ticking of her old-fashioned alarm clock. Gawain's jaw worked until he forced out a single word. "Where?"

Angmar seemed to drift for a moment before going on. "Mordred's dungeon is full of fae rebels. I recognized many faces, or what was left of them. Mordred hates those he cannot control. He is afraid even of what they might whisper."

Gawain shifted impatiently. "They whisper of the king?"

"Some of the prisoners have been there since LaFaye first began plotting to seize the throne of Faery. Pain and privation eventually take their toll. Their silence breaks." Angmar grimaced. "They talk among themselves, a word here, a snippet there. I put together enough of a story from these scraps to understand what has happened."

"What did you hear?" Gawain demanded, his voice urgent.

"There was a contingency plan, a safety measure to hide Arthur's tomb—and Excalibur—if need be. A decade ago, that plan was put into action. LaFaye was too close to finding the sword."

"Who were those conspirators?" Gawain asked.

"The old Queen of the Faeries, Gloriana, kept the circle small. It survives even though Gloriana lost her throne to LaFaye's treachery."

Angmar stopped to drink more water, resting again before he went on. "There was one knight of Camelot who did not go into the stone sleep, but watched over the tomb. Gloriana placed him under the protection of her magic, making him all but immortal."

Tamsin listened, but her first concern was tending to the

fae's wounds. She began unwinding the bandage around Angmar's injured forearm. The wound wasn't infected, but she would apply more healing ointment to be certain.

"This knight was a witch but loyal to a fault, for he had raised King Arthur as his own son," Angmar added, his face turning ashen with pain as she worked.

"Do you mean Sir Hector?" Gawain asked.

Tamsin's fingers froze in their work. Witchcraft. Medieval magic. A knight named Hector and a plot that had gone into action ten years ago. Shock jolted through Tamsin and she dropped the lid of the jar she was holding. It fell with a clatter, drawing everyone's attention. "A-are you talking about my father? Hector Greene?"

The moment Tamsin said it, she knew it was crazy. "Never mind. My father was no knight."

Angmar narrowed his eyes. "You are Hector's daughter? He was the very best of the Round Table."

Tamsin ducked her head, embarrassed. "I am Tamsin Greene. My father is dead."

"Sir Hector did not die," the fae said gently. "He lived in the mortal realms until it was time to resume his mission to the king."

Tamsin felt a sudden, hard rush of anger. "He left our family without telling us he was alive?" The sudden fury faded to the hurt of an abandoned child. She folded her hands to hide their trembling. *But he is alive. There is a chance I will see him again.* Joy warred with pain, leaving her utterly confused.

"It was a desperate move, if he hid his tracks so completely." Gawain had gone almost as pale as Angmar. The concern in his eyes said he understood every one of Tamsin's thoughts. "Do we know where Hector went?"

"The Forest Sauvage," Angmar replied, his voice low with tension. He turned to Tamsin. "It is a place all but forgotten, a wood beyond the mortal world that was made to beguile and confuse. It looks like our land, with the same towns and castles, but it is only a mirror image filled with hidden dangers."

"How did my father get there?" Needing something to keep her hands busy, Tamsin wrapped a fresh bandage over Angmar's wound. The familiar task steadied her. Better yet, it let her hide the depth of her distress.

"A portal, much like the one you used to escape the dungeon. The king's effigy is hidden in the forest."

"How is this even possible?" she whispered. Her fingers automatically fastened the bandage, but she had no more strength. She sank to the end of the bed, overwhelmed. "How can my father be a knight of Camelot? He was a witch, and he certainly wasn't—I mean—I would have noticed, right? He taught me to love history, but I had no idea he'd lived it."

The thought of her father—so completely loving—having lived all those years brought an ache to her throat. Who had he left behind along the way? Had he been happy in this far-flung future? Had he longed to return to Camelot the whole time?

"Gloriana was fae, but she had the good of all the races in her heart. She wanted to ensure the success of Arthur's plan to safeguard future peace." Angmar smiled at Tamsin, though his injuries made it crooked. "For that, she required a knight with impeccable character—and one with magical talents of his own."

Tamsin heard the words but barely understood their meaning. Angmar's story changed too much of her world at once. She clung to the one thing she knew. "I have to find my father."

Gawain touched Angmar's shoulder, his fingers gentle. "Do you know of any portal to the Forest Sauvage?"

Tamsin was eager. "I could open it, just as I did from the dungeon."

"That was a small portal. The one you need is much more powerful, much more difficult even for a fae. You are strong, child, but not strong enough for that." Angmar closed his eyes. "Merlin knew. The spell for the portal to the Forest Sauvage is..." He trailed off, succumbing to his body's need for rest.

Tamsin barely resisted the urge to shake him awake again. "Is what?"

Angmar was asleep. Tamsin stepped back from the bed, an idea already forming in her mind. "The secret to the portal is in Merlin's books! That's why my father had to study them."

Gawain's hand closed on her shoulder. "Mordred is on guard now. It will not be simple to return."

"I know. That was our best chance to find the library." Tamsin stopped, stricken with a sudden, desperate urge to weep—and for privacy. She'd finished with Angmar's bandages. There was nothing more she could do for her patients right then. "I'm going next door for an hour. I need some real rest." And then she would think about how to get the books. Finding them had already been vitally important, but now Merlin's tomes also held the key to a reunion with her father.

Swiftly, she picked clean clothes out of her drawers and made her way to the door of her tiny apartment. She thanked the Fates that had left the apartment next door vacant—it was her best chance to get some space. "Come get me if I'm needed."

Gawain nodded, watching her go. Perhaps it was wrong to demand time alone, but she had too much to think about. Her body ached with tension as she unlocked the suite next door and dropped her bundle of fresh clothes on the blessedly empty expanse of carpet. For the first time in hours, she had room to breathe.

And then everything crowded in. Waller. The dungeon. The portal. Her father and the fact he was a knight. For some reason, that seemed less strange than that he had left her behind. Her beloved, amazing, tender father had vanished from her life not because of a terrible accident, but of his own accord. An ache as sharp and terrible as a claw worked its way into her throat, leaving her gasping. Tamsin sank to the carpet and began to cry. She hugged herself, unable to think. Unable to do anything but give vent to the pain tearing her in two.

Tamsin didn't hear Gawain enter. She started when he slipped a blanket around her and pulled her into his warmth. He'd changed back into modern clothes, and the softness of an old sweatshirt cushioned her as she leaned into his chest. They had fought, true, but he was silently offering a truce. Instead of quieting her, though, the feel of his strong arms around her made her sobbing worse. It didn't seem to matter. Rather than pull away or try to hush her, Gawain held on, letting her weep. When she finally stopped, he said nothing, waiting until she was ready to speak.

"He was my father," Tamsin said, her voice thick and cracked from crying.

"I know." Gawain's hand cupped the back of her head, keeping her close.

"Why did he leave?" She hated the forlorn note in her voice.

"Hector wouldn't go without reasons."

"Reasons to leave his family?"

Gawain shifted, tucking her against his side. "According to Angmar, LaFaye began planning her campaign to invade the mortal realms ten years past. That would have been your father's signal to act after centuries of waiting."

"Why wait? Why not take the fight to the fae?"

"Mortals cannot cross into the realms of the fae. We had to wait for them to make the first move. It seems Hector was the lookout."

Tamsin wiped her eyes, sadness heavy in her chest. "So he was an important, mighty player in Queen Gloriana's schemes. I suppose it wouldn't matter that he had a wife and children."

"No, you are wrong. Everything he does is for you." Gawain caught a stray tear on his finger. "LaFaye spares no one. Stopping her is Hector's best chance to keep you safe."

Tamsin finally met his gaze. "Why didn't he say something to me?"

He folded her hands between his. "Don't judge your father harshly. Not until you hear his side. On these missions, many choices are made in the moment. Sometimes ones we don't expect."

"Like what?"

"You could have redirected the portal to the library when you had the chance, but you didn't. I thought about that all last night, after we spoke. Why did you abandon your own quest when it was within your grasp?"

"Maybe I should have." Tamsin gave a soft, bitter laugh, pulling her hand away and rubbing the Shadowring tattoo on her wrist. It ached with the memory of wrestling that much magic—and of the memory of her conversation with Waller. "If you can believe the Chief Elder, I'll be rewarded with a seat on the coven's council if I bring back the books. If I fail they will do with me as they please. They only sent me here to teach me humility, after all."

"You have no reason to be humble." Gawain turned her

to face him, his eyes solemn. "You took us to safety rather than securing your future."

Back in Mordred's dungeon, Tamsin hadn't stopped to consider the question. Now that she did, she just got angry. "To the abyss with the Elders. I don't make bad decisions out of fear. I'm a healer first, and I don't leave wounded behind to die."

Gawain's eyebrow cocked. "And what will that cost you, besides a seat of honor among your people?"

Tamsin looked away, unable to meet his eyes. The cost would be servitude in a thousand different ways. "It doesn't matter. It's done. We will find the books yet."

Gawain's fingers tightened on her shoulders, but then he let her go with a curt nod. "Yes, we will. And because you made the choice you did and saved Angmar, we know so much more."

That much was true. Gawain knew where his king was, and she knew where her father had gone. And the key to finding them was in the books, and that meant facing Mordred again.

Tamsin's head bowed. She was so tired, and almost protested as Gawain lifted her chin, his touch as gentle as he was strong. He kissed her, the heat of his mouth sinking deep into her spirit. There were no revelations, no simple answers in his touch, but his kindness, the simple skin-to-skin warmth of contact, soothed her heart. Knots of tension loosened inside Tamsin, allowing her to finally take a deep breath.

And yet, she had to know what was passing between them. "I thought we were back to merely keeping our bargain."

"Is that what you wish?" Gawain's fingers slid beneath the hem of her sweater, stroking the small of her back. The rough strength of his fingers alerted every nerve and sent a prickle up her spine. Tamsin rose to her knees, leaning close until their bodies met in a single, full-body caress. Her nipples ached as her breasts pressed against him, a delicious pain that grew even as she squirmed to ease it. A hot, winding tension formed in her belly.

The blanket had slipped to the floor, pooling behind her. She leaned back, allowing the soft folds of cloth to accept her as the carpet below cushioned her back. Gawain was leaning over her, his lips never far from hers as they reclined. There was no more talk, no acknowledgment of what was happening. The moment between them was too fragile.

Tamsin closed her eyes, feeling the sting of spent tears. Working by feel alone, she touched Gawain's face, pushing back the thick softness of his curling hair. His breath fanned her face as he bent close to lay kisses along her cheekbone, working his way to her temple. She dug her fingers into his shirt, pulling him closer. After all the emotional battering she'd taken, all she wanted was the forgetfulness of sensation.

His hands slid upward, pushing up her shirt. The air in the vacant apartment was bright but cool, chilling her skin. It made her want more of him touching her, and she slid her hands beneath his clothing and along the ridged muscles of his back. She loved the way they bunched and flexed as he moved, the power of his body waiting for action. As if reading her thoughts, Gawain rose up, peeling the shirt off in one easy movement.

Tamsin opened her eyes to study the play of lean muscles as he stretched and cast the garment aside. It was daylight, with nothing but the flimsy curtains to filter the light. No detail was left to her imagination. As he moved forward again, she caught his forearms, sliding her hands upward over his biceps as he came to her, finally letting her palms rest against the pads of his chest.

Tamsin could have remained there, lost in sensation, but he kept coming. Within a moment, his lips were on her bare stomach, each taste pulling desire deep from inside her core. She writhed, seeking closer contact, but he held himself back, balancing on his elbows and leaving air between them. He worked his way up the midline of her belly, pushing fabric out of the way as he went. His shoulders flexed with the effort of holding himself still, sometimes balancing on one hand, sometimes the other. It was an impressive show, driving the need inside her to a keen pitch. She felt damp and swollen, ready for him to banish every thought from her head.

She reached for his belt, preparing to take matters into her own hands. Gawain put his fingers over hers. "Not yet," he said, his voice low and husky.

Tamsin wanted to scream, but then he straddled her, knees on either side of her hips. An elusive thrum of power danced just at the edge of her perception, like a moon hidden by clouds. It had to be Gawain's—less pronounced because he was not a full-blood, repressed because he denied it, but strong enough to wake her own magic in response. Her instinct was to reach for it, wind her own power through his, but surely he would shy away. So she kept that part of her still, as cautious as if she were trying to tempt a wild beast to eat from her hand.

He helped her pull her top over her head, fanning her hair about her like a living carpet. Tamsin was so acutely aware of him, so keyed to the pitch of desire, that every movement was agony. Then he bent, taking her nipple between his full lips, the hot wetness of his mouth tantalizing through the lace of her bra. His teeth came into play, pinching her with just enough pain to make pleasure.

Tamsin arched beneath him, pulses of sensation knifing through her.

"Lie back," he murmured. "You're going to forget everything but this."

Chapter 17

Much later, Gawain slipped back to Tamsin's apartment, leaving her in a deep, exhausted slumber in the nest of blanket. He had slept, too, for a handful of hours, but those hours had been broken by nightmares of fire and screaming. Such dreams had plagued him for years. Right now the cause was obvious—there was no clear path forward when it came to Tamsin. She was a danger to him in all the best and worst ways possible—more treacherous by far than the Green Knight's wife because Gawain wanted Tamsin so much more. Besides that, Tamsin had no idea of the trap she set for him even as she'd snared his heart, and Gawain had no intention of telling her to what depths magic had led him in the past. He'd told her too much of his history already.

The antidote was action. He fully intended to be on his way to retrieve Merlin's blasted books long before Tamsin realized he was gone. After all her help, shouldering the burden of this task was the least he could do for her.

Gawain checked on the patients and found them both asleep. Unwilling to disturb them, he washed and dressed once again in battle gear. But when he stepped out of the bathroom, his brother was awake and sitting up.

"You're going somewhere," Beaumains said, rubbing his eyes. "Since you're dressed for a fight, I assume you're about to do something foolish."

"Maybe."

"Get me up. I'm not an invalid."

Gawain didn't argue, but instead helped his brother into one of Tamsin's spindly chairs. Beaumains was pale, but his eyes were clear and steady. "How are you feeling?" Gawain asked.

"Like I've been chewed on by something large and bad mannered." His brother fidgeted, casting another look over Gawain's outfit. "I'll be fine in a day or two. Your witch's skill at healing is unsurpassed."

Two impulses collided inside Gawain. "She's not my witch," he said automatically, and yet a possessive pride warmed him at the praise, proving his words false. Once again, she had him tied in knots. Was it any wonder he was having nightmares? "I need you to look after her and Angmar."

Beaumains raised his eyebrows. "Even though she is not yours?"

Gawain cursed. "Just do this for me. I owe her a debt for saving us, and I cannot let it go unpaid."

"Does this payment involve getting yourself killed?" His brother's tone grew an edge, a flush of temper darkening the scar on his cheek. "If you wait until I am at full strength, I'll leap into danger with you. There is no need to play the hothead on your own."

Gawain loved his brothers for their courage and camaraderie, and in this far and strange time that emotion flooded back with the force of a hammer blow. "I wish you could, but time is our enemy. Once Mordred discovers what he has in his library, it will be better guarded than a dragon's cave."

Beaumains sagged in resignation. "Not to mention the untold destruction Mordred will reap once he finds his new toy. Still, how are you getting into the library without a return trip to the dungeon?"

Gawain picked up the sports bag with his armor. He would put on the rest once the Henderson house was in sight. "This time, I'm not entering the house in the usual way. Not even Mordred can enchant a door that isn't there."

"What about Tamsin?" Beaumains asked, his eyes dark with worry. "She's the expert on magic."

Gawain's pulse skipped at the very notion. "Would you ask her to go back to that place?"

His brother fell silent. There was only one answer to that, and so Gawain left and started walking to Mordred's lair.

It was late enough in the afternoon that the cloudy sky had assumed the charcoal shade of twilight. The air smelled of wood smoke and coming rain. Gawain strode quickly, wanting to make good time and to burn off some nervous energy. He was about to make one of those gambles that Arthur swore would get him either sainted or dead. The fact that this immediate risk seemed the least of his problems told him a lot about the way his life was going.

Gawain reached an intersection and waited for the traffic signals to change. From there, he could see the lights on the Ferris wheel at Medievaland, spinning slowly against the darkening sky. Another few miles beyond them, Mordred was waiting. Mordred, who celebrated the same foul blood Gawain wished he could drain from his veins.

His cousin was younger, but there had been a time when their mothers had set the two boys competing against each other. Gawain, barely nine years old, had believed in his mother's love and had done everything asked of him, even learning to cast simple spells. To his shame, he had enjoyed it with a child's uncomplicated delight in the miraculous.

Gawain's specialty was fire, just as Mordred's was ice. Gawain had been proud of his flames until Mordred had dared him to set a fireball afloat. It was a trick that took control that no child possessed, but Gawain had been ever anxious to show off. Disaster fell. The older children had escaped unhurt, but their sister, just a babe of a few months, had died.

The streetlight changed, and Gawain resumed his path. Memory weighed like lead, slowing his steps. Tragic as her death was, he barely remembered his sister. But Beaumains, still crawling, had been horribly burned before Gawain had pulled him from the flames. Every time he looked at his brother's face, he was reminded of the terrible power inside him. There was no way to forget.

The months after the fire were still etched on his soul. Gawain, just a boy, had grieved until his own life had been in peril. After that, he refused to touch his power—a sacrifice as traumatic as losing a limb. The pain grew to an emptiness he suffered as just penance for his crime of murder. No one else would blame a child, so he had blamed himself.

Then came Tamsin. She was everything Gawain had ever wanted in a woman—kindness, wisdom, welcoming arms—and many things he had never expected. She was a scholar, a brave fighter, and she could make him laugh. How many had ever given him that gift?

Except that her power called to his in a way he had never felt before. At first, he hadn't been sure—it had been faint when he'd held her after the ritual, calling her back to life, but he had definitely felt it the last time they made love. If that monster was unleashed, what was to stop him from following the same vile path as his mother? As Mordred and LaFaye? Their blood was his, and Gawain was no saint. Pride and temper had always been his devils. What would stop him from indulging every desire—titles, wealth or revenge—when magic made such trifles easy to get? Gawain had seen such power break Merlin—the wisest of them all—who'd then turned around and broken the world.

Put in that context, Gawain's desire for a pretty witch seemed a small, pitiful thing. Yet from inside Gawain's heart, Tamsin was a shining treasure he longed to win. Yet how could he love someone who would be his downfall?

There was no good answer, and there wouldn't be one in his immediate future. Gawain had reached his destination. The roofline of Mordred's lair was fading into the sky and the branches shadowing its gables. Like a beast hiding among camouflage, the house waited, windows glowing gold against the dark. Gawain moved into the woods, silent as a panther, and put on his gear. In a sea of unanswered questions and moral uncertainty, retrieving Merlin's books was the kind of concrete, specific goal Gawain needed.

He'd been speaking the truth when he'd told Beaumains he would break into the library in a fashion no doorway spell would anticipate. He'd seen the opportunity on his last trip—the enormous trees that reached the roof. The roots of the one he wanted dug into the rising ground on the side opposite the kitchen garden. Gawain unbundled his sword and cloak and got down to knightly business.

The rocky, sloping ground was no challenge, and he moved noiselessly into position. Climbing the tree was harder. For one thing, it was decorated with tiny, glittering bulbs that illuminated the yard below, and it would be far too easy to draw attention to himself by joggling the lights. For another, he had a sword. The best he could do was sling the scabbard over his back and hope he didn't hang himself on a branch.

He was halfway up when fae patrols passed beneath him. Neither of the guards spoke, though Gawain felt the brush of a probing spell, as subtle as a bird's wing across his skin. He froze, suspended between one tree limb and the next, waiting for the tendrils of psychic energy to pass by. Sudden movement would trigger the roving magic and bring the patrols running. He had felt no such power the night they had landed in the dungeon. If Mordred was taking extra precautions, they'd rattled him. Gawain couldn't help a satisfied smile.

He waited until the coast was clear before making his way to the roof. Remembering the plans he'd seen, he knew the library was on the top floor with a study on one side and a bathroom on the other. The bathroom had a skylight, and someone had left it cranked slightly open. That was all Gawain needed to force his way inside. Once there, the library was only steps away.

The room was just as Tamsin had described, with stained glass and bookshelves to the ceiling. There had to be thousands of volumes, many of them old and all of them radiating the tang of magic. Gawain spun around, wondering where to begin looking. The sheer quantity of pages was overwhelming. In his day, a single shelf of books had been the most even a rich man owned.

Magic fluttered the air behind him, and he wheeled around, sword singing from its scabbard. Then he froze. It was Tamsin, dressed in dark clothing and with her backpack over her shoulder. At first glance, she looked like a burglar.

"You shouldn't be here!" he growled, but he did it softly.

There were footsteps in the hall, and sooner or later someone was going to find the broken skylight. "How did you get in?"

"Angmar gave me instructions to make a simple portal," she replied.

Gawain's gaze landed on a shimmer right behind Tamsin, bending the light like ripples in water. It made a faint hum that set his teeth on edge.

"You need an exit plan and you tried to go without me," she said, her tone accusing. "Not even spectacular sex makes up for that kind of idiocy."

Gawain knew without asking that Beaumains, in the fine tradition of little brothers, had sold him out. "Go home," he said. "I'll follow."

But Tamsin gave him a very female glare. "Don't brush me off. I don't deserve it."

He knew she was powerful, but the urge to keep her from harm's way blunted every other argument. "This is too dangerous."

Tamsin's cheeks flared a delicate pink. "Do you even know what books you're looking for?"

"If they are as powerful as you say, I should be able to detect them."

Tamsin gave him a sharp look full of questions he didn't want to answer, then began scanning the shelves. "That depends on what else is here. This place reeks of old, powerful grimoires."

It was clear he wasn't getting rid of her. Choosing the next best option, Gawain let her search while he drifted closer to the door on silent feet, sword ready. Angmar might have been well enough to give a portal-building lesson, but he obviously wasn't thinking straight. Mordred would notice a flare of magic inside his own lair. The longer the portal existed, the worse their exposure.

"Not there," Tamsin muttered, moving to the next bookcase. "In my vision, they were somewhere over this way."

He glanced over to see her reading the spines of archival slipcases that held the most ancient works. Her fingers walked across the covers, ensuring she didn't miss a single book. Gawain shifted his weight, frothing with impatience. The footfalls beyond the door had become filled with purpose. Gawain took a better grip on his sword and braced himself. "Hurry up."

He didn't need a spell book to see this could go bad in a heartbeat.

Chapter 18

The moment Tamsin's fingers brushed the fabric shoved to the back of the shelf, she knew she'd found what she sought. The worn cotton bag was her father's, a loremaster's sack spelled to keep out water, mold or anything else that could damage the contents. Here was clear evidence she was following her father's footsteps.

Heart leaping, Tamsin pulled the drawstring open to look inside. The leather-bound books she hunted were all there—each one ancient, neatly stitched and written by hand, only magic preserving them from crumbling to pieces. There were five. The smallest was barely the size of her palm and the largest little bigger than a paperback.

Tamsin set the bag on a long, polished library table and drew out the smallest book, breathing in the scent of old paper. It soothed her nerves, reminding her of winter afternoons curled up before the fireplace, her father reading to her from volumes just like these. Quickly, she riffled through the pages, savoring the feel of them.

"I found them," she said, tucking the books back inside their protective sack. "Let's go."

Three strides, and they would be back to the portal. Another second would take them safely back home.

Except the footsteps in the corridor outside had become a thunder, and the door burst open. A pale, slender man Tamsin had only seen in her vision strode through, followed by a wave of running guards. The leader—that had to be Mordred—held up a hand to stop his men.

"Cousin," said Mordred to Gawain. "How lovely of you to drop by."

Gawain stiffened, but then took a single step backward and brought up his sword. The movement was liquid, a dance step promising violence. At a signal from Mordred, he was surrounded by the fae. Then the world dissolved into a clash of steel.

Tamsin had never seen real fighting—not like this. She froze, clutching the books, for the space of a heartbeat. One beat too long.

She felt Nimueh's presence before she saw her, as cold as a sudden kiss of steel at her back. "What have you there?" the fae asked.

Tamsin wheeled around, meeting the cold appraisal in the fae's eyes. There was no point in lying. "I'm taking back what belongs to the witches."

Nimueh's eyes fell on the bag in Tamsin's hands. With one swift grab, she wrenched them away and opened the drawstring. She cocked one eyebrow as she peered inside. "I know these works. Merlin's immortal musings, blast him to the darkest abyss. I had no idea they were here."

Tamsin's fists clenched. "They belong to my people. Merlin was one of us, not a fae."

Nimueh's face went pale, a sign of emotion she wasn't

supposed to have. "He was the destroyer of my people. Think carefully about calling yourself his kin."

They were interrupted by the scream of one of the fae as steel met flesh. Nimueh looked toward the sound. Tamsin snatched for the bag, but the fae held it tight.

"I swear I will try to find a cure for what he did to you," Tamsin whispered.

The fae's lips drew back in a sneer. "Do you think me naive, little witch? Why would you help us?"

Tamsin took a gamble. "What has Mordred done for you lately?"

"Nothing. What have you done?"

"We saved Angmar. He says he was your friend."

Nimueh's lips thinned. "Mordred destroyed his prisoners last night."

"Because we took Angmar?"

"He conducted his final inquisition about Arthur's tomb. But yes, you are correct. His cruelty bears witness to the fact that he does not share well." She gave Tamsin a cool look. "Angmar was my friend, when I could still have such a thing."

Tamsin caught her breath, wondering if she had scored a point or if it was too late to matter. The tide of battle was shifting against them. Gawain leaped to the top of the library table, slashing furiously. He was heavily outnumbered despite the fact two of the guards lay bleeding.

Mordred had yet to draw a weapon. Instead, he almost strolled toward Tamsin. She backed away, but Nimueh grabbed Tamsin's arm with bone-crushing force. "Running only excites him," the fae said in a dead voice.

Mordred's ice-gray eyes were set in a face so pale it reminded her of his giant worm. Lank black hair straggled across his wide forehead. "You, Mistress Greene, have caused no end of trouble."

Nimueh pushed Tamsin to the ground. "Kneel before my Lord Mordred."

Tamsin thought she heard apprehension in the fae's voice. It was no mystery why. As Mordred's fingers brushed Tamsin's face, she felt the malevolent power in his touch. It was as cold as his eyes. Still, Tamsin didn't kneel for anyone and moved to stand. Nimueh jerked her back into place.

"Proud, aren't you?" Mordred said, amused. He took her hand, drawing her to her feet with courtly grace. "No wonder my cousin wants you for his own. Oh yes, I can see it when he looks your way, like a hound after the last slice of bacon. I wonder how good you really taste."

He made a gesture in front of her face. Pain such as Tamsin had never known wrenched through her. She gasped, rising to her toes in a vain attempt to escape the razor-sharp agony cutting her to ribbons.

"My lord," Nimueh said. "There is no need for this."

But Mordred only laughed, bending closer to inhale near Tamsin's lips. The sickening wrench grew worse, as if he was drawing her insides through her teeth. Fingers of power wriggled deep inside her, gagging her, seeking out places no physical assault could find. They tore at the private sanctuaries within—the secrets she kept, the faith that burned away night terrors, the words of love she whispered in her dreams. In a horrible flash of understanding, she realized Mordred was taking her soul.

Tears leaked from Tamsin's eyes as she shuddered, losing control of her limbs. Nimueh caught her from behind before she fell, but did nothing to stop Mordred's assault. Perhaps the fae couldn't. Fighting through her shock, Tamsin reached for her magic, but it was stunned and mute, unable to help. She started to scream.

Gawain's bellow rattled the windows as he sprang from

the table, knocking Mordred aside and delivering a vicious kick to his ribs. Mordred crashed into a shelf and collapsed under a rain of books. A guard lunged to protect his lord but fell with Gawain's sword in his chest. Unarmed, Gawain snatched up a chair and cracked it against the floor, breaking off a leg.

Mordred scrambled to his feet, but he was too late. Gawain bludgeoned him with the chair leg once, twice, and a third time. Then he tossed the leg aside with a gesture of disgust, turning aside to yank his sword from the fallen guard. Of all the warriors, Gawain was the only one still standing, and he turned to finish Mordred with the blade.

"Stop!" cried Nimueh. "Stand aside, Gawain of Lothian! Queen LaFaye bound my oath with magic, and I am sworn to protect the Prince of Faery. No mortal knight is a match for my power, and I will not let you take his life."

"How did you come to this, my lady?" Gawain asked, his eyes wild with the heat of the fight. "You were once the Lady of the Lake, as powerful a fae as ever walked the Forest Sauvage. You gave Excalibur to Arthur. You gave your name to Lancelot du Lac, the Champion of Camelot. How did you end up guarding *that*?" Gawain gave his prone cousin a scornful look.

Nimueh shook her head, her long pale hair swinging with the motion. "Mine is a long tale, and there is no time. You always showed me courtesy when I came to Camelot. For that I will spare you if you leave before reinforcements arrive."

Gawain's knuckles grew white as he gripped his sword. "Perhaps I should slay you both."

"You could try," said Nimueh. "But a battle would serve neither of us. Leave through the portal with your woman and a hope of finding Arthur. You rescued Angmar. I will give you your woman's life for his."

"Mordred has been a stone in my shoe for too long."

"As he has been a thorn in mine," said the fae. "But I cannot let you have him. In recompense, I will smooth your path to your king. That is the surest path to justice, Sir Gawain."

"How is walking away justice?"

Nimueh held up her hand, stopping his protest. "You were witch-born, and the one among the stone sleepers destined to wake first. Don't stray from your path now, Prince of Lothian. Mordred will get his reward, or I am the Lady of the Lake no more."

As the fae spoke, Tamsin slowly clambered to her feet. Her knees wobbled, but the pain had stopped. "Gawain?"

He turned, eyes widening, and sprang to her side. "Are you well?" He touched her face, as if unsure she was real.

"She lives," said Nimueh, her voice cool. "If you do not leave quickly, that will change. The fae will feel the death of their brothers and send more soldiers."

"Let us have the books," begged Tamsin.

"That is not possible," Nimueh replied. "My oath to the queen prevents it."

The bag of books lay on the floor between Tamsin and the fae. Tamsin dove for it, but Nimueh blocked her with an upraised arm. Tamsin ducked, but Nimueh was eerily fast. She snatched up the bag, chanting words of power in a clear, ringing voice. For an instant, Tamsin saw the magnificent creature she had been—a noblewoman among fae, mistress of the Lake of Enchantment.

Nimueh hurled the books toward the portal with the speed and force of an athlete. Tamsin cried out, leaping to catch the prize, but missed. A blue-white flash bleached the tiny room, bright as a flare but freezing cold. The brilliance blinded Tamsin and she curled over, sheltering her face with her arms. From where she huddled on the floor, she felt cold, fresh air on her hands as if someone had opened a door. Tamsin's first impression was of ice, as if all the heat in the world had been sucked away. There was a giddy moment of weightless nothing, where *here* and *there* were empty ideas. The white light flowed around them, so intense that Tamsin thought she was drowning in the brightness. Gawain was the only solid thing in that place, his arm hard with muscle as it tightened around her...

And then they were standing in a grassy meadow with the sun splashing down in thick golden bars through early-morning mist. Tamsin spun around. The portal was gone, but her backpack lay at her feet.

"What just happened?" she demanded. "And where are the books?"

Gawain looked around, his hands on his hips so that his dark cloak gave him a square silhouette. "At a guess, the Lady of the Lake redirected your portal to send us to the Forest Sauvage. The books are here, too, I suppose. Somewhere."

The Forest Sauvage. What had Angmar called it? *A place all but forgotten, a wood beyond the mortal world that was made to beguile and confuse.* And then there was that bit about hidden dangers. Well, wasn't that comforting?

The fact that Nimueh had the power to pull a stunt like that didn't make Tamsin feel any easier. Fortunately, the Lady of the Lake seemed to dislike Mordred enough to help them.

Tamsin shrugged her coat more closely over her shoulders and picked up her pack. The day was sunny, but there was a cool dampness in the air. Dew glittered on the long grass and picked out a spider's web in the branches of the tree above them. Apples weighed down the tree branches and perfumed the air with heady sweetness. They were in an orchard.

"Was sending us here what Nimueh meant by smoothing the path to your king?" she asked.

"I expect so," Gawain replied, then gave her a searching look. "Are you well? After what Mordred did?"

She ran a hand through her hair. It had been the most awful violation imaginable, but this was no time to dwell on it. If she did, she'd crumble—and that was the least helpful thing she could do right then. "I'll survive."

"Good." The word was simple, but his expression said a thousand things more.

"This must be someone's land," she said, changing the subject before she started to cry. "Look, there's a castle!"

Though it was hidden by a stand of oak trees, Tamsin could make out the tops of two blocky towers of stone. "Do you know who lives there?"

Gawain rubbed his jaw. It was dark with stubble. "Once it belonged to the king, but it is hard to say who dwells there now. In the Forest Sauvage, things are rarely as they seem. However, it is as good a place as any to begin our search."

They began walking toward it. Gawain moved easily, as if all the empty space of the countryside was a relief. He kept Tamsin close beside him, his fingers brushing hers and twining through them as they walked. At any other time, it would have been a delightful country stroll. Birds flitted from tree to tree in busy flocks. It was autumn, but earlier than at home.

"There are fresh hoofprints," Gawain said, indicating the grass. "A company of riders passed this way not long ago."

Shortly after, they saw a riderless horse in the distance,

but no indication of other people. Though she said nothing, that detail made Tamsin uneasy.

It did not take long before the castle emerged from behind the trees. A drawbridge led over a wide moat that reflected the towers and the sky with still perfection. Tamsin looked at the brooding gates and imagined all the monsters of the Brothers Grimm lurking inside. It was impossible to see past the thick arch of stone and the massive, iron-strapped doors that were at least three times the height of a man.

Gawain drew his sword. "Stay behind me. I'm the one wearing armor."

Tamsin didn't argue. At least he wasn't ordering her to say behind and alone in the orchard. Crossing the drawbridge didn't make the specter of the towers any better. The stone seemed to darken as they approached, as if there was a blight clinging to the gray granite. As Tamsin looked up and up, the looming spires of rock blotted out the sky. Every instinct she possessed said magic dwelt within, and it wasn't kindly.

About halfway across the drawbridge, Gawain tensed, looking up as a flock of crows swarmed from the western tower window. They spiraled and turned, a croaking, flapping mass of jet-black wings, and then dove for the drawbridge. Gawain pulled Tamsin low, shielding her with his body. Even so, she heard the hum of wind through feathers and felt the vicious stab of a beak as it plucked at her braid.

It was over in a moment, but it left her rattled. "What was that?"

"Messengers," Gawain said darkly. "The entire forest will soon know we're here."

And that meant someone had seen them. A cowardly corner of Tamsin's soul balked when they reached the massive doors of the castle gate. They were open just far enough for them to slip through one at a time. Gawain went through first, Tamsin hard on his heels. The castle walls framed the courtyard, making a large and perfect flagstone square dominated on the far side by the main castle keep.

They'd barely set foot inside when they both froze in their tracks. They'd found the riders, though none of the horses were there. Bodies littered the courtyard, sprawled in their own blood. Tamsin dragged in a breath. The gulp of air should have revived her, but the taste of slaughter washed over her tongue instead.

Gawain was on alert, sword raised and scanning every inch of the yard. "Get back out the door."

"We're giving up?"

"The blood is still wet. Whatever did this is still nearby."

That was good enough for Tamsin. She lunged for the door but stopped dead. "The doors are shut and there's no handle on this side."

There was definitely magic here, and they were trapped.

Gawain didn't falter. "Then get your back to the wall and start looking for movement. If you see something, call out."

Tamsin complied, though it took a long moment before she calmed her mind enough to look closely at the scene around her.

"There's got to be dozens of soldiers here," Tamsin murmured. "Who were they?"

Intent on searching out the enemy, Gawain didn't answer. He was looking for the living, though nothing stirred but the breeze. Tamsin shifted her weight nervously. She couldn't stay cowering by the gate. If she did, she'd freeze there like a terrified rabbit, unable to move ever again. Instead, she would answer her own question.

While Gawain prowled in ever-widening circles, Tamsin forced herself to take the dozen steps to reach the nearest of the fallen men. She crouched beside him, her healer's senses telling her he was unquestionably dead. Even so, her muscles coiled, ready to spring at the slightest twitch.

The man's features were invisible behind the bucket-like helmet. It had slits instead of a visor, making it impossible to peer inside. Gritting her teeth, she grabbed the helmet and pulled. It came off an inch at a time to reveal the honey-brown skin and white hair of a faery. The lean, beautiful face looked almost serene.

"What are you doing here?" she wondered aloud.

More to the point, who had stopped Mordred's army? Who was badder than the bad guys?

Chapter 19

Moving among the bodies, Gawain picked up a shield painted as bloodred as the massacre around them. There were a dozen things, from arms to water skins to a decent horse, that they'd need to survive in this land. He'd start with the weapons. From another corpse, he took a spear that was unbroken. He tested its balance and approved of the workmanship. With no wasted motion, he sheathed his sword. A spear was of little use in close quarters, but he wanted the reach. Whatever monster had slaughtered the faeries, it had claws and teeth, and fighting it would take all his skill. Anticipation sang in his blood.

As he continued scavenging for weapons, he checked to make sure Tamsin was close. By now, it was pure habit—he always seemed to know just where she was, as if they were joined by an invisible chain.

"Come here," he said. "I've found you a knife."

She drew nearer, but paled when he bent to clip the

leather sheath to the belt of her jeans. He looked up, reading the expression in her dark brown eyes. "Take it. I'll do my best to make sure you don't need it for anything but slicing apples."

"Thank you," she said, her skin so bloodless he could see the fine freckles across the bridge of her nose. "I don't know how to use a knife in a fight."

The simplicity of the statement wrung his heart. She was as gentle as she was courageous, a healer at heart. "It's only as a last resort."

He finished buckling on the knife and rose. Tamsin lifted her chin, following his movement with a fearful intensity. Despite her powers, despite her bravery, he was the only protector between her and this brutal reality. The thought nearly stopped his breath. He reached up, running his thumb along the clean line of her jaw and over the rose-petal softness of her lips. She sighed at his touch, the warmth of her breath almost lost to the hard, scarred flesh of his hands. All the weapons he'd handled, all the wars he'd fought had taken a toll.

"What do we do now?" she asked.

Gawain didn't have a good plan, so a bold one would have to do. "Nimueh put us here for a reason. We'll search the castle and maybe we'll find out why. Maybe we'll find Merlin's books. She couldn't give them to us, but perhaps a scavenger hunt isn't against the rules."

"She attacked me before in the church," said Tamsin. "Why is she helping us now?"

Gawain frowned as the fae's words came back to him: *Mordred will get his reward, or I am the Lady of the Lake no more.* "Mordred crossed her. He never knew how to keep allies, much less friends."

Wisps of hair had escaped Tamsin's long braid and blew like threads of sunlight across her face. He brushed them back, his hand feeling too large and coarse for the delicate job. Gawain couldn't help a smile. "You may have studied castles, but I've lived in them. We should begin our search with the room where such books would be kept."

"And where is that?" Tamsin smiled. "Since you're an expert and all."

"These are valuable books of magic. If the lord of this place has found them, then they will be with his other treasures, close at hand." He bent and kissed her temple, where the skin was so fine he could see tiny blue veins. "Follow me and stay close. Someone sent those crows to greet us. This place is not deserted."

She gripped his hand a moment, her long, fine fingers folding over his, and then released him, as if she'd taken what courage she needed. "Then let's go."

Gawain looked around the courtyard. He could pick out the granary, bake house, chapel and kitchen. But what he wanted was in the tall keep that overlooked it all. He picked up his salvaged weapons and led the way.

The keep was a square tower with a central stairway. They ascended slowly, stopping often to listen for footsteps or voices, but heard nothing. There were rooms on each floor, and all seemed deserted. A scatter of leaves and dirt had blown in through the narrow windows.

He paused again. Another crow burst from an open window in a flap of wings. The sound startled Tamsin, who clutched his elbow before she could stop herself. She snatched her hand back with a look of apology and nervously wiped her hands on her pant leg. She knew better than to get in the way of his sword arm, but her instinct was to look to him for protection. That felt right to Gawain, and he held on to the notion as he climbed the stairs to the top of the tower, the spear raised to thrust at the first sign of claw or tentacle.

What they found instead was a private room with large
windows and comfortable furniture. In contrast to the rest
of the castle, it looked as if someone had been there minutes before. A pewter plate and tankard sat on the table.
The plate was scattered with crumbs of bread and cheese,
the tankard still half-full of dark amber ale. Gawain suddenly felt thirsty though he knew better than to eat or drink
anything where magic was present. The room looked rest-
ful, even pleasant, but he could feel the thrum of dark energy just under the sunny surface, like a fruit gone rotten
beneath an unblemished skin.

Tamsin had fastened on the shelf of books behind the
table. There were about twenty—a generous collection
when everything was written by hand. She had opened
the cover of one and was scanning the Latin text with an
ease Gawain admired. "This is a book on demonology,"
she said with a mix of wonder and revulsion. "I thought
demons were banished."

Gawain winced. "Merlin banished them from the realms
of humans and faeries. The Forest Sauvage belongs to no
one but itself. It's possible one or two might linger here."

She let the cover of the book fall closed and backed
away from the lectern where it sat. "Were the demons
truly that bad?"

"Yes," Gawain said, leaning the spear against the table
so he could begin his search. "For all the destruction Merlin caused, I do not blame his instinct to scour them from
the world."

His thoughts were interrupted by the sight of a drawstring bag sitting on the window ledge, half-buried by a
jumble of other items—a hat, a hunting horn and a wadded-
up cloak. He lunged across the room and snatched it up.

"I have them." He passed the bag to Tamsin. "We were
right. Nimueh did want us to find them."

Tamsin's face lit up with relief as she reached inside to touch the covers, the gesture almost tender. "You're brilliant." She reached up, winding her arms around his neck and pressing her lips to his.

The warm taste of woman went straight to his core as her tongue slid against his, firing needs there was no time to assuage. Still, he pulled her closer, taking her weight against his chest. The green, rich scent of the woods still clung to her hair. He could feel her magic, but in this dark place it felt pure as virgin snow. He stroked down the graceful curve of her back, thinking all the mysteries of the world could be reduced to the geometry of that shape. Everything he needed to know in that moment was here, in his arms, and her name was Tamsin.

Gawain broke the kiss reluctantly, leaving a few of its smaller siblings behind. Finding the books would mean nothing if they couldn't discover a means of escape. He brushed Tamsin's cheek with the backs of his fingers. "Now let's find a way out of this place."

"Absolutely." Tamsin unzipped her backpack and rearranged the contents, adding her own spell book to the cloth bag and zipping it all up again. Gawain idly wondered if the pack had magical properties that allowed it to hold far more than it should, but then he'd seen women do amazing things with their purses, medieval or modern. Finally, Tamsin stood, shouldering the pack. "Let's go."

A sixth sense buried deep in Gawain's core raised a warning flag moments before he heard the smooth, light baritone.

"Not so fast."

The voice made Gawain's skin crawl. He followed the sound but could see no speaker. He reached instantly for Tamsin, pulling her close to his side as he turned for the doorway. He'd barely made it three steps before he stopped dead. Tamsin's gasp said it all.

"It's bad luck to speak of demons," said the figure. "It has a way of making us notice you."

The demon was—at the moment—wearing the face of a man. He was tall, bald but for a tightly clipped black beard, and dressed in robes the shade of drying blood. What gave him away were his pale yellow eyes slitted like a goat's.

Gawain stepped in front of Tamsin, making his body her shield. "What do you want, hellspawn?"

"The same thing as you. The books. Which you are stealing from my study, by the way." He stepped aside to peer at Tamsin over Gawain's shoulder. "That's not only unwise, it's downright rude."

"Those aren't your books!" Tamsin protested. "The Lady of the Lake sent them here for us to find."

"That might be true, and then again it might not," said the demon. "They appeared right in the middle of my courtyard. How am I to know they weren't meant for me?"

"The books appeared in the courtyard? Along with Mordred's fae armies?" Gawain scoffed.

"Oh, them." The demon's mouth curled in a way that boded no good. "They were seeking the castle's former master. Apparently the gentleman had something they want."

"What was that?" asked Tamsin.

"I don't know. I never had a chance to speak to the previous occupant of the castle. He had the wits to move out when he heard me coming."

Gawain tried to guess when that might have been. Long enough for the dirt and dead leaves to make drifts in the empty rooms.

"Now leave me the books and go," the demon ordered.

"Or try to go. I have a hard time making up my mind about uninvited guests. They can be such a crashing bore."

The demon pointedly glanced out the window at the carnage below. "On the other hand, every so often they keep things interesting."

Gawain's mind raced. Their odds of survival were low enough that there was little to lose in a gamble. He picked up the spear. "I like interesting." He jabbed the tip at the demon's face. It might be a magical being, but as long as it wore flesh, it could be hurt.

It flinched back far enough that Gawain could push Tamsin toward the door. She scrambled forward, starting down the stairs with lightning speed. Gawain followed, dropping his guard in his haste to get Tamsin out of harm's way. That was a mistake—the demon caught him with a backhand that sent him sprawling against the wall. He'd slung the heavy wooden shield across his back and it took the brunt of the blow, but the iron rim dug into the backs of his thighs. He staggered upright, pain surging up his body, and slashed with his weapon. The demon kept its distance, a slight smile on its lips.

Gawain really didn't like that smile. Rather than pressing the attack, he edged toward the door and the sound of Tamsin's steps clattering down the stairs. The demon feinted, and Gawain parried, drawing a thin line of blood from its palm. The demon's blood turned black the moment the air touched it.

Finally, Gawain reached the doorway. The demon rushed him then, but Gawain had the spear ready, hovering just before the demon's eyes as he descended the stairs backward two at a time. With a disgusted look, the demon slammed the door in his face. Not stopping to argue, Gawain turned and bounded down the steps to catch up to Tamsin.

She'd just about reached the bottom of the tower when he found her. A half-dozen steps separated her from the floor. A dozen more would take her to the courtyard. But she wasn't moving another inch. The fae were on their feet again, though they were still unquestionably dead. Gawain halted on the step behind Tamsin, fighting the urge to simply stand and stare.

"Zombies," she said in a cracked voice. "Faery zombies. That's just—wrong."

Chapter 20

Gawain wished he'd had a gold piece for every time he'd heard "wrong" when demons were involved. He'd have gilded armor for himself *and* his horse.

The fae were starting to drift toward them with slow, deliberate steps, effectively blocking the main door of the keep. They were eerily silent, the only sound the clink of armor or squish of ruined flesh. Worse, they looked hungry. Panic rose like a gibbering imp inside Gawain, but he slammed it down hard. Tamsin was counting on him, and surrender was not an option.

He slipped the shield off his back and slid his forearm through the grips. "Stay with me," he said. "We're going down the stairs and out the back of the keep. Keep running no matter what and look for a water gate. There should be another entrance to the castle grounds used to bring in supplies by boat."

Tamsin gave a spastic nod and clutched her backpack

more securely. The dead were close enough now to see their eyes. Already, the film of death was turning them to opaque, grayish marbles. Gawain's stomach rolled. This kind of nonsense was exactly why everyone hated demons.

"Go!" he ordered.

Tamsin dashed. The zombies lurched forward, but not before Gawain vaulted from the last steps and stuck his spear through the throat of the first one. It barely slowed the thing down until he gave a savage twist that severed its spine. By then, three others had rushed to fill the gap. Gawain shoved the body, spear and all, into their path and drew his sword. Baring their teeth, the next wave trampled the fallen. Gawain slammed the shield into his closest foe and slashed the sword, aiming for heads. Two fell, but the third dropped to its knees and fastened its jaws on his calf. Gawain glanced down in disbelief. The fae was trying to gnaw through the leather of his high boot. With a cry of disgust, Gawain chopped off its head, shook away the remains and ran after Tamsin.

She had reached what looked like a guardroom. Gawain followed, slammed the door and pushed a heavy table against it.

"What now?" Tamsin asked. Her eyes were round with shock.

"Through the window," Gawain replied, boosting her over the wide stone sill. A body hurled itself against the door, making the table squeak on the floor. "Then run for your life."

He had exactly enough time to crawl after her before the walking dead smashed their way through the door. It seemed like miles across the grass to the stone wall that rimmed the edge of the moat. More faeries streamed from the courtyard in pursuit. Gawain saw a small gate in the distance but despaired of reaching it in time. The fae were gaining on them too fast.

They had gone halfway when Tamsin fell to her knees, gasping. Mordred had sucked away too much of her strength. "Let me carry you," he said.

"Then how are you supposed to fight?" she panted, sitting back on her heels. Her eyes were fixed on the approaching enemy, her expression a mask of horror. "I'll slow you down. It's my turn to do something."

"What?" Gawain gauged the number of seconds they had before the dead faeries were upon them. Not many.

"Help me up," Tamsin said, struggling to her feet.

As he did, he saw a pale blue light pool in her hand. A fireball. He flinched, recognizing the same spell he'd learned as a child. The one he'd used to burn down the nursery. Memory burned in his blood.

"Stand back," she ordered. "If I get this right, you owe me a glass of wine."

Tamsin concentrated, digging the magic from deep inside her. Exhaustion made her power slow to come until, at what seemed like the last possible moment, she sent a ball of pale blue light hurtling into the pack of hungry dead. She squeezed her eyes shut, but her ears heard the impact like a cracking egg.

Tamsin opened her eyes to see something red raining from the air. Bile burned the back of her throat.

"Tamsin!" Gawain bellowed.

She jerked around to see one of the dead rushing at her, eyes blank as marbles. She shrieked from pure reflex and danced out of its way. Gawain stepped in its path, jabbing with the metal edge of the shield and following with a downward slice of his sword. Another zombie struck, shattering his shield. At that point, she lost every inhibition she'd ever had about using offensive magic. By the time Gawain had downed his new opponent, pieces of dead fae scattered the field.

Tamsin waited for the next assault, but it didn't come. Instead, the remaining fae stood still as scarecrows. "What's wrong?"

Gawain wiped his forehead on his sleeve. His eyes were wild. "They're dead, not stupid." He was backing quickly toward the water gate, never turning away from their attackers. Tamsin followed suit, a primitive voice screaming at her to *run, run, run away!* but knowing that would just remind the zombies to chase them.

The tactic worked until they were almost at their goal, when a raven swooped down, croaking. As if the call woke up the dead, the fae sprang forward once more. But by that time, Gawain had the small gate open and they were scrambling down to a tiny boat. Gawain pushed it into the moat at a run.

"Get in!" he ordered, splashing into the water.

Tamsin balked when her boots hit the water. She'd never learned how to swim.

"Hurry!" Gawain ordered, sheathing his sword. "Their bowmen are arriving!"

Tamsin gave up trying to keep anything but her backpack dry. After a determined bound through the water, she crawled into the boat and landed in a heap of soggy fabric. She'd made it just in time—the current caught the vessel and sent the boat drifting into a spin, carrying it away from shore. "Help!" she cried.

Gawain was right. A fresh contingent of fae were taking up position beside their fellows. There was a thrum and a sound like giant bees. Arrows splashed into the water mere inches from the boat.

"Gawain!" Tamsin peered over the side. He was nowhere in sight. For a panicked instant, she blinked against the brilliance of the sun on the water, and then ducked again as another flight of arrows spattered around her. This time two thumped into the light frame of the spinning boat.

To her enormous relief, Gawain's hand appeared over the edge, followed shortly by the rest of him. He'd ducked underwater, and the mail shirt he wore glittered like scales as he climbed aboard. He made a muffled hiss of pain as he landed, and clawed his sodden cloak out of the way. A feathered shaft stuck out of his thigh.

"Oh, no." Tamsin stared at the arrow. Gawain's pain was her first thought, but underneath that was primal fear for them both.

"I've had worse."

Gawain grabbed the oars from the bottom of the boat and locked them in place. Then he paused, clearly gathering himself. He was drained of color and his mouth was clamped in a tight line, as if holding the truth inside. Tamsin's blood went icy. He was hurt.

"I can stabilize that," she said. "That should help until we get to shore."

"There's no time." Gawain plunged the oars into the water and turned the vessel toward the opposite shore. Tamsin twisted to look at the castle. The dead faeries were crowding around the water gate as if they were unsure what to do next.

"Can fae swim?" she asked tightly.

"Of course," Gawain replied, his expression grim. "They'll come after us soon enough."

Tamsin summoned her power one last time. She had enough juice for one more fireball, so she made it big. She loaded it with all the confusion, annoyance, fear and frustration she had in her. It sailed, a falling star of power that flared with cleansing heat as it struck. Tamsin and

Gawain ducked, shading their eyes. When she looked up, the bank by the castle moat was empty. She wondered if their foes were dead or merely hiding.

A long minute passed as Gawain rowed, but nothing moved. Her thoughts skittered away as she tried to focus on what she'd just done. Assault magic teetered on the edge of darkness. It was something her father had taught her but nothing that the Shadowring Elders condoned. It smacked of black spell casting, the very thing that Gawain feared.

A dark, hollow place opened up inside her, and she shivered.

Silence followed, broken only by the splash of the oars and the murmur of the water against the side of the boat. Gawain's movements were jerky with pain. She didn't attempt conversation, instead drying their clothes with what little magic she had left. The fabric went stiff and scratchy, but Gawain's cloak—along with a sliver of magic—worked well enough as padding to keep the arrow in Gawain's leg immobilized and the bleeding minimal. She offered to try the oars, but Gawain just gave her a very male look.

Rather than rowing them back to the orchard, he found the stream that fed the moat. They didn't get far before they passed the carcass of a horse. By the color of its trappings, it had belonged to the army that had invaded the castle. "It bolted from whatever killed its masters," said Gawain in a grim voice. "But it didn't get away."

Tamsin turned away. Injured animals upset her deeply. "Do we know what attacked it?"

"It takes something large to bring down a warhorse."

Later, they came across a piece of a saddle floating downstream, but no other signs of carnage. They followed the stream until the water grew too shallow to navigate. By then, the sun was past its peak. Tamsin helped Gawain ashore and pulled the little boat under the cover of some low bushes. With Gawain leaning on her shoulder, they climbed up the bank to see where they were. The land looked wilder here, with rolling moors and the silver slash of a river fading into the distance.

"The sea is that way," Gawain pointed.

"Do you know where we are?" Tamsin asked in surprise.

"Perhaps. I know where we would be if this were Camelot. If the Forest Sauvage holds true, my castle lies ahead. It will be the best choice for us to find safety and shelter."

His voice held a note of cautious hope. Tamsin hitched her pack higher on her shoulder. "How far is it?"

"We should reach it by nightfall if we make good time."

"You're not going another step on that leg."

"It's only a flesh wound." But even his brave words couldn't cover the lie.

Tamsin helped him to the ground. He did no more than grunt a protest, which meant the injury had to be bad. Tamsin knelt and examined the wound, refusing to let her fingers tremble. The arrow had buried itself in the muscle of his thigh. She guessed a stubborn temper and buckets of adrenaline were all that had kept Gawain going that far.

"There is good news and bad news," she ventured. "The good news is that the arrow didn't sever any major blood vessels."

"How do you know that?" He closed his eyes. A sheen of sweat covered his face.

"You're not dead yet." She swallowed. Her throat felt thick and swollen with panic. "The bad news is I don't have my medicines here. I'll have to improvise."

His lids cracked open. "You improvised fine with those dead fae."

A knot twisted in Tamsin's gut. "I've never used my power that way before."

She expected something from Gawain—either congratulations or revulsion, since he hated magic so completely—but he remained impassive. Whatever his thoughts, he meant to keep them to himself. After a long moment he asked, "Did Hector teach you to do that?"

"Yes." She unfastened the knife from her belt. The first thing was to cut away the clothing from around the wound and get a better look. Nervous energy was fizzing inside her, but her mind was curiously blank. Probably the result of shock.

She began slicing at his clothes, wincing inside as he flinched. "I'm not sure if I should be proud or terrified of blowing them all up."

"We lived."

She nearly snapped at him. She wanted more than two words. Needed his response. But then Gawain clenched his fist, giving the ground a thump as she fully exposed the wound. Apparently, the moment of fight or flight was over and his pain receptors had caught up with events.

"I hate witch fire," he finally said. "Gives me nightmares."

"I'm sorry it bothered you," Tamsin replied, keeping her voice neutral. She was being an idiot, thinking of her own needs at a moment like this.

Gawain's mouth flattened to a line as she prodded the wound. "The walking dead bothered me more."

She didn't reply. Images replayed in her mind of the spell striking, exploding and tearing the enemy to pieces. She shuddered, revolted all over again. She hadn't killed anyone—the fae had already been dead—but it felt as if she had. The experience had changed her—she knew that much—but she still wasn't sure how.

She pushed that aside. Her problems were for later. "I'm going to have to get the arrow out, and then I'm going to have to use raw magic to heal you. The backpack got in the water and while the books are fine, my herbs and powders are spoiled. I'm sorry. I don't have any other way. Even if you could walk, there's too much chance of infection."

She met his gaze, bracing for an argument, but his blue eyes were dull.

"Do what you must," he said. "I trust you."

Chapter 21

Tamsin caught her breath. She'd feared he would refuse her, just as he had when she'd bound his arm. This was a hard-won privilege. "Okay."

Gawain gave a curt nod. Before she could react, he reached down, grabbed the arrow shaft and tore the point out of his flesh. His bellow of pain chilled Tamsin through, but she clamped her hands over the spurt of blood and pushed her healing energy into the wound. The flesh under her palms was hot and wet, a gaping tear sucking at his life. The last of her energy pounded into him with every beat of her pulse. Red rivulets of blood escaped through her fingers, soaking the ground where she knelt.

Tamsin's shoulders ached as she pressed down, her muscles protesting the abuse they'd suffered that day, but she also was inside him, knitting together each nerve and fiber, putting him back together as methodically as a mason laying bricks. Time slowed and lost meaning as she worked, her mind diving deep until she experienced Gawain almost on a cellular level.

There, she found out so much more about him. Power coiled deep inside him, strong and wild from long neglect. Tamsin felt his magic stir as her energy brushed against it, but she resisted the impulse to explore. At the same moment, she saw the ruins where his boyhood trust had been shattered, and felt the healing energy of the deep friendships that had put him back together again. From those friendships came an unexpected, stubborn hope. Tamsin breathed on that flicker of light, coaxing it brighter. Hope was a healer's greatest weapon.

When Tamsin withdrew, she did so slowly, letting go a tiny bit at a time until she was sure her repairs would hold. When she finally opened her eyes, she swayed with exhaustion. A pink scar on Gawain's heavily muscled thigh showed where the arrow had been, puckered and deep, but the muscle beneath it was sound.

Tamsin collapsed on the grass. With a last wisp of magic, she repaired his leggings. All that buff male was distracting.

Experimentally, Gawain rose, putting weight on his leg with a look of intense concentration. "It doesn't even hurt."

"It has no reason to," Tamsin said.

The wind tossed his dark hair as he looked down on her, his eyes searching her face. "Thank you."

"You're welcome." Her magic was spent, and so was her ordinary strength. Waves of exhaustion reminded her it had been hours since she'd eaten dinner, and they hadn't brought food with them. In fact, they had lost everything but her backpack and Gawain's sword.

"Are quests always this wearing?" Tamsin leaned back on her elbows, tipping her face up to the afternoon sun.

"Generally," Gawain said, putting his hands on his hips

and squinting at the horizon. "Worse if it involves something with nasty, big, pointy teeth."

"What now?" she asked. "We have the books. If my father was looking for them to get to the Forest Sauvage, presumably they should be able to help us get home, but we have to find him and your king first."

"Agreed." He sank to the grass beside her, then leaned over and brushed her lips with his.

"What's that for?" She hadn't expected affection so soon after using her magic on him. Even now, she could see the turmoil behind his blue gaze, but he gave a slow smile.

"I'm expressing my gratitude. A simple thank-you seemed inadequate after you conquered an army of the walking dead and then healed me." Gawain kissed Tamsin again, this time with more passion. Despite her fatigue, desire ached within her, as languid as the afternoon warmth. She raked her fingers over his shoulders, rejoicing in the raw male force that coiled there. Her body began to ache with need.

"You should rest," he murmured as he ran his hands down her form, but the stroking did nothing to settle her down. His shirt was unlaced at the neck and showed the strong muscles of his neck and throat. Tamsin put her mouth there, tasting the salt of his skin. Gawain's breath sucked in. "I want you in my bed," he murmured.

"In your castle?" She sank back on the grass, looking up at him.

"Yes. It's a good, strong bed with a feather mattress, and I am lord and master there."

She smiled, but it came with a tinge of sadness. Though he wanted her now, would he remember eventually what she was? There was a big difference between letting her fix his leg and keeping her forever. "Are you trying to seduce me, Sir Gawain?"

"I am." He pulled away with an expression that said how much that restraint hurt. "But we have a long road ahead and I'd rather finish my conquest with you safe under my roof."

His look was regretful but also possessive, as if he was bargaining as much with himself as with her. "I want you in my arms, in my bed and on my lands. And I want you safe when night falls. This is the Forest Sauvage, and not a good place to be in the woods after dark."

The deep rumble of his words and the sentiments they expressed were as sexy as hell. Nevertheless, her exhausted body yearned to stay here in the soft grass, basking in sunlight and Gawain's good mood. She gave a moan of protest, wishing with every fiber of her soul for a hot meal or a shower or a decent all-terrain vehicle that would get them to the castle without walking until her feet were covered in blisters.

It was there, with her ear to the ground, that she heard the clop of hooves. Tamsin rolled over, shading her eyes. A horse stood at the edge of the brush that lined the stream bank, mouthing its bit nervously. By the color of its trappings, the glossy bay stallion was another of the fae's horses, still with its saddle and bridle. Tamsin sat up slowly, caution seeping through her. The beast was huge, breathing hard and flecked with sweat.

"Look!" she whispered.

Gawain was sitting cross-legged beside her. When he saw the mount, he rose in one smooth motion. The horse skittered backward.

"He's terrified," Tamsin said softly. The horse's ears twitched at her voice.

Gawain nodded, but he was smiling as if he had finally won a roll of the dice. "This is an excellent piece of good fortune. He is scared now, but he is used to a master. He will come around."

Tamsin remembered her wish of a moment ago and wondered if their need had drawn the horse their way, or if the beast had been drawn to her healing power. Could Gawain have unconsciously called it to them? She couldn't begin to guess, and she certainly wasn't going to suggest it. He'd probably send the horse away if he thought it had been summoned.

And it looked as if the horse and Gawain were coming to an understanding. With exquisite patience, he drifted toward the beast, every motion deliberate and slow. He didn't approach directly, but wandered over to the beast's left. All the while, he murmured to it in soft, low tones. The horse stamped, snorting and swishing its tail. Gawain turned and made his way to the right, closing the distance between them by degrees. The moment he got too close, the moment the horse made a low, unhappy sound, Gawain backed away.

Tamsin watched, fascinated. Gawain wasn't a patient man, but here he showed a leniency she hadn't seen before. Then again, he was capable of relentless persistence bundled in a layer of charm. How else had he dragged her into an unlikely quest for a stone king?

Eventually, the horse began to follow Gawain's movements, coming ever closer. He caught the horse's bridle, whispering in its ear and patting its neck. The horse whickered, bobbing its head as if agreeing to the situation. Then it nuzzled Gawain's ear.

A minute later, Gawain was in the saddle, Tamsin perched behind him with her arms wrapped around his waist. She'd stowed her pack with the saddlebags, securing it tight to the saddle. She'd never had enough practice to be a good rider, but Gawain more than made up for her shortcomings. All at once, getting to spend the night in a real bed was becoming possible.

By the time the sun was fading, they had almost reached the river that reflected the pinks and reds unfurling in the sky. Clouds had been gathering as they rode, filling the air with a clammy promise of rain. Tamsin rested her cheek against Gawain's back, fatigue lapping at her like warm water. She snapped her eyelids open and blinked, realizing she was drifting. Then she squinted. There were birds circling in the sky. Crows, surely, but they were behaving oddly. The black forms were flying in an odd spiral pattern, making a whirlpool of silent black wings. Then she remembered the crows on the drawbridge. Suddenly, she was wide-awake again. "Gawain!"

He stiffened when his gaze followed her pointing finger. "By the saints!"

The sky, which had seemed so beautiful a moment ago, filled with threat. There was no cover of trees this close to the river, leaving them completely exposed.

"The demon isn't done with us yet," Gawain growled.

The flock of crows was picking up speed, the shapes blurring into a single slash of black that was approaching faster than any bird should fly.

"I thought those were messenger birds," she said uneasily.

"They are." Gawain's profile was sharp with tension. "There's more than one way to communicate."

Sensing something wrong, the horse tossed its head and snorted. When Gawain urged it into a canter, the stallion bounded forward eagerly. Tamsin clung on for dear life, the wind swallowing her cry of surprise. Gawain aimed straight for the water.

"Where are we going?" she yelled.

"The river. Demons won't cross a natural body of water."

"But there's no bridge!" Tamsin pointed out.

Gawain didn't reply, but looked over his shoulder. Whatever he saw made him frown.

Then she registered what he said. "That's a demon?" Not just a demon, *the* demon. The creature in the castle had taken possession of the crows.

A deep shadow blotted what light was left in the sky. Tamsin couldn't summon the courage to look. All those claws and sharp beaks had to be what had devastated the fae host in the courtyard and then torn their steeds to pieces. Now it was diving toward them.

A cry like rending metal shredded the air. Gawain bent low over the horse's neck, but their double weight was taking its toll. The horse was exhausted and afraid, sweat lathering its sides. Nevertheless, its hooves pounded in a steady, determined rhythm, eating up the ground. But the valiant effort wasn't enough. The river was still a minute's ride away.

A steady thunder of wings sounded just behind them. Tamsin gulped air and tried to ready a defensive spell, but her strength had been spent. Tears of frustration wet her cheeks as the horse strained onward.

Then she saw the slash of a claw through the air, and all thought froze in pure terror. The talons—sharp, black and glossy—were as large as a pitchfork. She managed to blink once before the claw slashed again and she was dragged from the horse by her coat. Tamsin felt herself lurch into the air, saw Gawain twist in the saddle to catch her, heard the stallion's scream of fright. The fabric of her coat tore beneath her weight and she fell free, landing hard in the sandy mud of the riverbank.

Gawain wheeled the horse and it reared, hooves slashing. Tamsin scrambled to her feet despite the stabbing pain where she'd landed on her hip. Then she got a look at what the crows had become. They had melted together into one enormous entity. The creature was huge and black and winged, but there its resemblance to a true crow ended. It looked like a bundle of rags in flight, if rags had a slashing beak and eyes of burning scarlet.

"Run!" Gawain roared. He drew his sword, standing in the stirrups to deliver a flashing cut. The creature shrieked in pain, a sound so terrible Tamsin covered her ears. It was too much for the horse, who bucked violently, throwing Gawain to the ground. He was on his feet in a moment, snatching up his sword, but the stallion was tearing for the water. "Run!" he cried again, dashing toward her. "I'll get you home, I promise!"

Tamsin fled, tears stinging her eyes. She felt like a rank coward, but she had no more magic to help him. She caught at the horse's stirrup as it splashed into the ice-cold waters. Tamsin grabbed the saddle with her other hand, hanging on as the river dragged at her legs. Her feet lost contact with the earth, a reminder she couldn't swim—but the horse could. It plunged ahead, intent on the opposite bank. With the last of her strength, she heaved herself up until she had a firm grip on the saddle. Desperate to escape, the stallion barely seemed to notice.

Tamsin glanced back at Gawain, and her heart stopped. The creature had blocked his path to the river and now it hovered just above his head. Gawain thrust upward with his blade. The thing screamed as feathers fluttered down like deadly petals, dissolving before they reached the earth. A moment later, the monster shot upward, flapping furiously, and Gawain darted for the water, though not fast enough. Like a hawk, it stooped and struck. The wings closed around the knight until he was crushed to the ground.

Tamsin shrieked in dismay, an explosion of grief breaking her apart. Seconds passed in stunned disbelief, the sound of the rushing river the only touchstone of reality. Nothing else made sense. The thing's beak tore at something, now too much like a crow with its meal.

Then it winged back furiously, lifting from the ground with Gawain in its claws. His chain mail hung in shreds, ripped through by his opponent's savage beak. He struggled, legs flailing in the air, but he still had his sword. He drew it back, and with a mighty blow stabbed the point through the creature's belly. The night-black talons released and Gawain fell.

Whatever spell held the monster together snapped, and its scream of rage was all that was unholy. The creature exploded into a thousand cawing, flapping crows that scattered in all directions. The noise was too much for the horse. It had borne Tamsin to the middle of the river, swimming her safely past rocky rapids and treacherous currents, but the explosion of dark energies shattered its will. It plunged and twisted, and Tamsin lost her grip.

She slid away, flailing for something, anything to grip. Her waterlogged clothes dragged her down, down as the force of the river sent her tumbling into the rush of white water. Tamsin gasped a lungful of water, choked and began to panic. A jutting rock struck her in the ribs with the force of a fist, making her flip and tangle in a tree limb that had caught in the boulders. At least that gave her something to hang on to while she coughed until it hurt. Her teeth began to chatter from the cold.

It didn't take long for her strength to fade, her sense of the world shrinking inward on herself and the branch and the cold. She didn't see Gawain come for her until he was there, his strong arm winding around her so that he could swim them both to the safety of the shore. Her body floated against his, sheltered, protected and borne away by his unflagging strength.

Chapter 22

"The Forest Sauvage mocks travelers." Gawain slid off the horse, then turned to help Tamsin down. They had finally reached Gawain's castle, shivering cold and with their clothes half-dried by Tamsin's flickering magic. "It presents images of what we hope to find, but they are never the same. Just as the land appears to be Camelot, this is a shadow of my home. I know my way through this forest, but many unwary travelers have been fooled by these reflections and lost their way."

It was hard to see what Gawain's home looked like in the heavy dusk, but it was around the same size as the castle they'd just left. Gawain took her inside to a tower room and lit a fire. There was plenty of wood, clean blankets, and even a bowl of fresh apples and pears, but no people. It was as if all the servants had suddenly been spirited away, but in the capricious forest they might never have existed.

They found dry clothes, Gawain producing a soft gown

for her from one of the private chambers. The fabric was light but warm, edged in fine embroidery. "It's green," he said with a self-mocking smile. "I thought you might like it."

After that, Gawain left to care for the horse, who more than deserved oats and a good rubdown. Tamsin found the books, which were still dry from the magic of the lorekeeper's bag, and sought for the portal spell Angmar had mentioned. She found it and read it through several times—she definitely wanted to have an emergency exit in place—but the firelight made the words dance on the page, and her eyelids drooped.

As the evening grew darker and Gawain didn't return, Tamsin began to fret over every noise and creak. It was one thing to have studied ancient times, to have visited castles as a tourist with guidebooks and camera in hand. It was another to be alone in one after tangling with a demon. The orange light of the fire did little more than deepen the shadows crawling up the stone walls. Tapestries stirred in the draft, the movement bringing their woven figures to life. Tamsin wrapped her arms around her middle, huddling closer to the hearth even though the heat and smoke brought tears to her eyes. Wood snapped and popped, sending up a shower of sparks.

She tried to remain calm, to rest, but it was hopeless. Every time she closed her eyes, she could feel the swirling sensation of the river. Gawain had saved her more than once that day, shown her exactly what it meant to be a knight of the Round Table. What he could do, what he was forced to do to survive—there weren't words enough in all the libraries in the world to capture it. If her magic gave him pause, his reality did the same to her.

Wind whistled through a chink somewhere in the ceiling, mimicking the mournful cry of a bird. Uneasiness lapped at Tamsin until she finally rose and paced the room. There was little furniture—just a table and chairs and some iron-bound chests against the wall. Nothing to distract her from the fact that Gawain was nowhere in sight.

Eventually, she couldn't stand his absence any longer. She lit one of the candles that sat near the hearth and, shielding the flame with her hand, went back down the twisting stairwell of the tower. The candlelight barely made a difference in the darkness. She moved carefully, feeling the edges of the narrow steps with her toes and praying no random gust left her stranded in pitch-dark. Once she reached the main floor, the high arched windows let in the light of the full moon. Tamsin left the candle on a sheltered ledge and went outside.

The wind was clammy with the moist ocean air. Shivering, she took a few steps along the rocky path, listening for Gawain's footsteps. There was nothing but the rustle of the tall, sweet-scented pines and the rhythmic rolling of the water. Tamsin craned her neck, taking in the overwhelming brightness of the stars. Witch or not, she was a city girl and often forgot just how dazzling nature could be.

The path from the castle ran past the pines and down a rocky beach to the ocean. Tamsin only had to stand at the head of the path to see Gawain's tall form looking out at the moonlit water, a silhouette against the stars. She set out, her head bowed against the wind. As she approached, she could see he had a fresh cloak around him, this one lined with fur.

He caught sight of her and straightened. "What are you doing out here in the cold?"

Tamsin stopped, her teeth chattering. "I missed you."

He made a sound deep in his throat that might have been a chuckle. "You'll catch your death." He drew her close and wrapped the edges of the cloak around her. The thick, soft fur was already warmed by the heat of his body. Tamsin snuggled close, resting her head against his chest.

"I did not think I'd ever see this place again," he said. "Even if this is just the forest's reflection of it, I wanted a last look."

Waves slipped and slid in an endless shimmer. Tamsin let the play of moonlight fill her consciousness. "Did you live here long?"

"Ever since I won my spurs and became a knight. Arthur gave it to me."

He said it simply, and yet she heard the longing in his voice for a life he had lost. Tamsin touched his cheek. "You walked away from all this to come to my time."

"I had a duty to my king."

There was nothing to say to that. The utter certainty in his tone left no room to argue. Tamsin turned her face into the fabric of his tunic. He smelled of smoke and woodlands. "I'm glad you came to me."

His lips brushed her hair, his big hand cupping the back of her head. "So am I. Sometimes duty is rewarded."

Tamsin took a breath to ask the questions burning in her mind: how he felt about her magic now, and what would happen once he'd found his king. Did they have any kind of a future together? And then she let her questions go. There were too many unknowns. Asking wouldn't do a bit of good.

They both fell silent while the ocean lapped and splashed at the rocks in an endless conversation of its own. Tamsin had stopped shivering, but the sharp cold of the air and Gawain's delicious heat led her thoughts toward the night ahead. She tipped her head up in an invitation for another kiss. Gawain pressed his mouth against hers, his breath a warm flame.

He made a pleased sound, as if he had discovered hidden treasure. "I believe I'm done patrolling for the night."

After that, they returned to the castle. The bedchamber was in the tower, above the room where Tamsin had been reading. Gawain lit the fire, feeding it until a merry blaze chased the damp. He went in search of something to drink while Tamsin warmed her hands and looked around her. In the middle of the room was a bed framed by heavy woven curtains hung from the ceiling. Furs were piled on it for warmth. It was elegant and primitive at once—a bit like Gawain himself.

He returned with a jug of wine and a basket of dried fruit and nut meats. "There are some stores in the kitchen but not much ready to eat. If this can tide us till daylight, we can put together a decent meal in the morning."

He poured the wine into a heavy metal goblet and then picked up the poker he'd left warming in the fire. He thrust the poker into the wine with a bubbling hiss and then passed the goblet to Tamsin. The steaming brew was spiced with cloves and cinnamon and sweetened with honey.

"Oh, that's good," she said. The warmth hit her stomach and spread like a miniature sun. She passed the goblet back and watched him drink, the muscles of his throat working as he swallowed.

He returned the goblet to her, brushing her fingers with his, trailing his palm over her waist as she took another sip. Tamsin swallowed as much from nerves as from thirst. They had been together before, but in this place Gawain's manner was subtly different. This was his home, his world, and here he was lord. He leaned closer, his breath fanning the side of her neck. Before she realized what he was doing, he'd slipped the tie from the end of her braid and was loosening the strands. They shone pale in the firelight, crimped to waviness from the tight binding. Gawain arranged her hair over her shoulders, stopping now and again to dig his fingers into the mass, his strong fingers caressing.

"That's better," he said, his voice dropped low in his chest. "You should wear it loose more often."

Never had she felt so owned by a man, so much his to pet and enjoy. It left her unsteady. "It gets in the way."

"But I like it, and you're my woman."

"I'm *your* woman?" It was so Neanderthal—and yet a thrill of excitement sparked in her belly.

Gawain took the wine from her and set the goblet on top of a chest. "I don't mind my tongue here within these walls, and tonight you are mine."

And he took her in a scorching kiss that demonstrated how unruly his tongue could be. Tamsin gripped his biceps, needing to steady herself. When they finally pulled apart, she knew Gawain was right—he was done holding back. It struck her that she had no game plan, no way of dealing with Gawain unleashed.

He took both of Tamsin's hands in his. "It will be warmer in bed."

The bald statement nearly made her laugh, but the look in his eyes stole her breath. Their bright blue was shadowed in this light, turning them to a wicked, smoky darkness. Her stomach flipped. "I don't know," she said, her words just above a whisper. She'd meant to sound coy, to tease, but the words came out with almost stammering sincerity. She suddenly felt awkward. "It's too cold to take off my clothes."

Gawain rubbed the dark stubble along his jaw. "I have some ideas that may help with that."

She gave a slight smile, regaining her footing. "Perhaps you'll go warm up the sheets for me?"

"Oh, yes." Gawain laughed, the sound low and deep.

"I'll play lady's maid, as well, and help you with your garments."

He scooped her up so quickly she had no time to waver. Instinctively, she clutched at his shoulders, bringing herself yet closer into his embrace. She searched again for a snappy comeback, but none came. They were past banter and into far less predictable waters. "Gawain?"

He kissed her forehead—a soft, light benediction. "There is nothing to worry about here. This is my fortress."

"How do you know we're safe?" She'd set wards around the castle's perimeter, but they were no more than alarms. They would warn, not defend.

Gawain didn't reply at once. Instead, he carried her to the bed and set her down on the soft, luxurious mound of furs. Then he drew his sword with a long rasp of steel and set the naked blade on the floor beside them. "This is my world, and I know my business here," he said quietly.

Tamsin's mouth went dry. "I'm sure you do."

His smile said that he'd intended every innuendo. "Are you still convinced you'll be cold this far from the fire?"

Her heart pounded as he leaned down, the waves of his dark hair glinting auburn in the firelight. He picked up one of her feet. He drew the boot off slowly and let it fall to the floor with a soft thump. His hand closed over her stockinged foot, gently kneading her toes. Even through the fabric, she could feel the heat of his hands. She hadn't realized how tired her feet were until that moment, and she fell back with a blissful groan. The other boot came off the next moment.

"That feels wonderful." She surrendered her other foot. "You have a future as a love slave. Or maybe a cabana boy."

The bed shifted with his weight as he knelt beside her. "A true knight knows many weapons beyond a simple blade."

His fingers dove beneath her skirts and found the top of her right stocking. He'd given her undergarments, as well as the dress, and now she wondered why he had bothered, since they were coming off so soon. He undid the bow of the garter and began sliding it down, fingers trailing against her skin. As he uncovered her ankle, he bent to kiss its hollow, his hair brushing like silk along her calf. Tamsin flinched, heat flaring from her core.

Gawain looked up, a glint in his eye. "Do you like that?"

"I never realized ankles could feel so good."

"Every inch of a woman's skin deserves respect." He eased down the other stocking. "Dare I say worship?"

"You dare," Tamsin murmured. "There isn't much you wouldn't dare."

"It seems you're coming to know me very well."

So it went on, one article of clothing after another. Eventually, she wore no more than her shift while Gawain still had his shirt and leggings. "That's not fair," she complained.

He closed his mouth over hers, stopping her complaint as he cupped her breasts through the fine linen. His thumbs circled her nipples, bringing them to aching points. When he finally broke the kiss, he left behind the taste of wine and spice. Tamsin sucked in a ragged breath of air, her concentration splintering. "Not fair."

He nipped her ear, making her gasp. "If I touched you skin to skin, my control would not last."

"And mine?"

His teeth brushed her neck. "You will surrender yours to me, over and over."

"Is your control so weak you need to steal?"

Gawain pushed her back on the furs. "Then have it your way, Mistress Greene."

He shed his leggings, his shirt barely veiling the jut-

ting length of his erection. Tamsin's skin heated in a delicious flush of anticipation—and then it flared to electric
life when the shirt came off in one impatient tug. The firelight loved him, showing the strength in his limbs with
unabashed celebration, as if he was art come to life. She
rose up on her elbows, meeting him halfway as he rejoined
her. Their lips touched, his forward movement slowing
so that their collapse into the soft sea of fur was gradual
and luxuriant. They rolled so that Tamsin was on top. She
stroked the silky length of him, bending down to taste
the salt of his smooth skin. Every cell of her wanted him
inside her, but she needed to anchor this moment of sen-
suality in her memory. That meant taking her time to experience everything.

"If a woman deserves careful admiration," she whispered, "so does a man."

His eyes drooped with lazy pleasure, reminding her of
some huge cat. His hands crept under the hem of the chemise and glided up her thighs, kneading her flesh. She
leaned forward to grant him better access, and his rough,
strong palms curved over her buttocks. Bracing her hands
on either side of Gawain's head, Tamsin bent to taste his
lips. He took the opportunity to slide the chemise upward
until she caught it and slipped it over her head. With her
arms raised, she was fully displayed for his pleasure.

She caught the flare of his eyes, the parting of his lips.
His hands immediately caressed her breasts, a possessive,
greedy gesture that told her far more than any words. Tamsin pressed her hands over his, holding him close, feeling
her heartbeat and his pulse in the same moment. Feeling
their magic rise and twine together for an instant, as inti-
mate a communion as a kiss.

They were so different, sprung from two utterly different times and cultures. And yet—something more impor-

tant ran beneath all those divisions. Something that made their hearts beat as one.

Tamsin bent over her knight, her hair pooling around them like a golden curtain as she pressed her lips to his. The taste of wine and spice had faded, and all that was left was heat, desire and man. It was more than enough.

Chapter 23

Tamsin woke as the dawn chorus of birds raised their voices. There were birds in the city, but never so many or at such volume. She opened her eyes slowly, aware of the furs tickling her ears. The air in the room was cool, but the nest beneath the covers was toasty warm. She snuggled closer to Gawain, aware every muscle in her body had been worked hard the day before. He was still snoring lightly, for once completely relaxed. As Tamsin curled against him, his arm tightened around her waist. Even in sleep, he was aware of her.

She allowed herself a moment of cautious hope. Gawain had proved his attraction to her more than once last night. Perhaps he had come to her because he needed help to find his king, but releasing Arthur from his stone sleep did not have to mean the end of their story. Despite everything, hadn't they come too far to pretend there was no bond between them?

Gawain came awake with a snuffle and an enormous yawn. Tamsin took advantage of the moment to straddle him, folding her arms on his thick chest. She lowered herself until they were nose to nose. "Good morning," she said.

"Good morning, fair lady." Unshaven and tousled, he looked utterly wicked. He gave her a roguish grin. "I trust you rested well."

Tamsin reached under the covers. "I find at least part of you thoroughly rested and ready for more action."

He reached up, lacing his fingers through her hair and drawing her down for a kiss. "I always sleep best in my own bed."

Tamsin sank into the kiss, nibbling on his lower lip and teasing with her tongue. As she kept his mouth busy, she rocked forward and brushed against his jutting member. Gawain groaned, arching his head back. "Temptress."

Tamsin broke the kiss and carefully sat back on her heels. The motion pushed the covers down, leaving Gawain bare. She ran her hands down his torso, touching all of him, possessing every beautiful, masculine plane and hollow. In the pale morning light, she could admire each detail, each flex as he moved. Tamsin tried to pretend it was medical interest—to ensure yesterday's wound was still healed. In truth, her inspection was just greed. She enjoyed ogling him.

Now that she was out from under the blankets, she was conscious of the cool air. Gawain's heat was like a beacon. She ran an encouraging hand up his member and then followed it with her lips, tasting salt and musk and man. His expletives spurred her on as she discovered just what he liked and where. Once she had him twisting on the feather bed, she scraped her teeth along his skin, drawing a shudder through him. "Shall I keep going?" she asked sweetly.

He caught her with lightning speed, pinning her on her stomach. It happened so fast, the room swam around her. He drew a deep breath, his lips grazing the skin of her shoulder. "You nearly made me beg for mercy," he murmured, nibbling at her ear.

"Nearly?"

"That's a hard admission for a man of the sword."

"As long as it's hard, I'm good with that."

Gawain nipped her skin, a light pinch that sent a shock of pleasure-pain through her core. "Now it's my turn."

He was behind her, pulling her up to her hands and knees and positioning her hips to his liking. He was gentle, but there was no mistaking who was in charge. Tamsin closed her eyes, happy to let him have his way. She felt him part her and leaned into his touch, letting the sensation fill her. She felt her own wetness on his fingers like an eager invitation.

Then his weight shifted, and he pushed inside her from behind. She sucked in air, as if filling her lungs would somehow equalize the pressure. She seemed too full, too sensitized to possibly take all of him inside. His hands grasped her hips more firmly, adjusting the angle as he withdrew and plunged again. Tamsin's muscles tightened, trying to hold him, trying to control the yearning that spiked through her with every twist and pull. Her aching breasts swung with each thrust, with every jerk of her hips as she braced to meet him. She had been cold, but now sweat trickled down her spine as their rhythm peaked. Air came in gasping cries. She couldn't hold on to her sanity any longer.

Finally, Tamsin let go, allowing the maddening fullness to take her. She shuddered around him, hungry pulses of exquisite need. Gawain thrust deep with a triumphant moan, his pleasure frank and lusty. When they finally sank back beneath the covers, they stayed wound together long after the sun streamed through the high windows. Finally, they both fell back into the profound sleep of utter surrender.

When Gawain finally convinced himself to rise, he left Tamsin sleeping and went to explore in daylight. His first stop was to tend to the stallion, the next a quick bath in the icy-cold pond outside. Once dressed in fresh clothes, he went to find breakfast. Now that it was daylight, he could see more precisely what the storerooms held. He gathered an armful of provisions and set to work on breakfast. His cooking skills were basic, but he knew how to make a pot of boiled oats.

Keeping busy helped Gawain think. As Tamsin said, they'd found the books. Now it was time to find Hector and Arthur and escape back to the real world—preferably before the demon found a way to cross the river. They'd been lucky to escape it yesterday, but there was no reason to believe it would give up.

But if—when—they made it back safely? Gawain paused, a sack of oats in one hand. The black iron pot hung over the fire was bubbling, waiting for the grain. He dropped a few handfuls in, measuring by eye. He cooked like he did most things, by instinct. Most of the time it worked out.

But now, he had no idea how the future would unfold. He would be at Arthur's side, living in a strange future. Their purpose was to fight a foe bereft of any compassion and to rally the rest of their brotherhood—who were all no doubt equally bewildered. Once, he would have said duty and companionship were enough to fill his life.

He desperately wanted to say they still were, but Gawain's traitorous heart was reluctant to answer. Against all odds, against everything he'd experienced in his life, he was deeply attracted to a witch who stirred his own despised magic. Sooner or later, his blood would fully waken and then what? His mind shied away from the implications.

Decisions—when they really mattered—came slowly for Gawain. He was reluctant to trust because his loyalty once given was iron. He swore few oaths because they always bound him for life. His heart—well, beyond his brothers and his king, he'd never given it to anyone.

Tamsin had done everything to earn his faith, but believing in his own goodness was harder. He was afraid of what she might unleash in him. He was afraid of trusting himself.

Working by habit, he added a pinch of salt to the oats and set about slicing thick slabs of cured ham. If this had been his real castle, there would be dogs under his feet, a bustle of cooks and potboys and stablemen yelling in the courtyard. There would have been a large, bright life he knew and loved all around him. Now there was silence, the castle an empty tomb. He could feel the Forest Sauvage watching him, testing his resolve. Making sure he felt vulnerable.

"Bugger that," he muttered under his breath. He could hear Tamsin's feet on the stairs, and his spirits lifted. As long as she was there, he was anything but alone.

She came pattering into the kitchen, wearing the clothes Gawain had given her. She was a vision, her long golden hair combed and braided and her cheeks pink from the fresh air. "Is that food? I could eat a horse."

"I wouldn't advise it. We've only got one." He motioned her to a stool at the big kitchen table and set a wooden bowl of porridge in front of her. There were honey, walnuts and dried apples to add to the breakfast, as well as the sliced ham. He kissed her ear. "This is plain fare, but—"

"It's delicious," Tamsin said, waving away his apology. "Hot and filling is what I need right now."

Gawain sat down with his own bowl. "Then I am delighted to supply your needs."

She tilted her head and pointed with her wooden spoon. "You are the master of double meaning."

"I have been called Gawain of the Silver Tongue."

"Was that by your publicist or your stylist?" She nibbled at a dried apple.

"The court at Camelot prizes chivalry in all its forms. I'm more than just a big sword, you know."

A crease formed between her brows. He could tell she was trying not to laugh. "So you've given me your opinion of Merlin. How about your king? Arthur sounds like such a paragon, but was that what he was really like? The way you talk about him, he sounds barely human."

Gawain was taken aback, and he chewed a mouthful of ham to give himself time to frame an answer. "Your world does not understand kings. The concept has lost most of its meaning."

"A lot of kings went bad," said Tamsin. "We made other choices."

So Gawain had heard. He tried to put it in simple terms. "Kings are responsible for every single person they rule—those who go hungry, those who die, and those who need justice. Kings swear to shed their blood for their people, and that oath binds them until death. Arthur never goes to war lightly, and when he does he leads from the front lines of his men."

That was all true, but Gawain knew he had barely captured a tenth of who Arthur was. He tried again. "He welcomes everyone alike to his court. He is fair and a good listener. He makes sure every maid has a partner when it is time to dance. No concern is too small."

"Sure, but does he have any bad habits?" Tamsin asked.

Gawain smiled. "He laughs at his own jokes. It's best to pretend he's actually witty, or he sulks."

That made Tamsin grin. "Good to know."

But a kernel of doubt was forming in Gawain's heart. He had never seen it as a flaw in his king, but Arthur was no lover of magic. Merlin had been the exception, but then Merlin had failed the way he did everything else—with over-the-top spectacle. When they had gone into the stone sleep, Arthur had ordered Merlin to stay behind. There would be no more magic at Camelot. So where did that leave Gawain's relationship with Tamsin?

A clatter of hooves broke through his thoughts.

"Who's that?" said Tamsin, clearly wary.

"Let me see." Gawain grabbed his sword from where he'd leaned it by the door and strode into the courtyard. What he saw made him whoop with joy.

"Sir Hector!" he called. "I thought I was going to have to search the length and breadth of the forest to find you!"

The old knight swung down from a tall gray gelding. Hector was of average height, squarely built, with a mane of iron-gray hair that stuck up in spikes when he pulled off his helmet. "No need, Gawain, my lad. Thanks to that blasted demon, the forest is abuzz with your arrival, and there's no time to waste."

Gawain gripped the man's forearm in greeting. "Even so, we have much to speak of. Angmar of Corin told me you have kept watch over Arthur's tomb."

"Ah, yes." Hector harrumphed uneasily. "There's a tale to tell. I fell in with the fae resistance after Arthur banished me."

Gawain was stunned. "Banished you?" And then he remembered—-Hector was witch-born, and Arthur had scoured all magic from his court. Hadn't he just been thinking about that? "But if he sent you away, why are you looking after him?"

The old knight gave a mighty snort as he tied up his horse. "Arthur is my foster son. I can't very well leave him to Mordred. Never you mind, when we thaw him out, I'll knock some sense into him. King or no king, he's never too old for a slap to the head."

Gawain squeezed Hector's shoulder. He'd never been close to the man—or to any of the court who dealt with magic—but he had always respected Hector's level head. "I am glad you are here, and there is much I have to tell you. I have met your daughter Tamsin."

"Have you, now?" Hector asked quickly, with a lift of his shaggy gray brows.

Then Tamsin was in the kitchen doorway, and Gawain's worlds collided. In his reality, he'd seen Hector only months before, whereas she hadn't seen her father for ten long years. The stunned look on both their faces made his chest ache.

Tamsin's face crumpled. "Dad?"

A long moment passed while Hector studied his daughter, recognition dawning on his face. The last time he'd seen her, Tamsin would have been little more than a child with one foot on the path to womanhood. Now she was fully mature, a poised, graceful beauty in full flower.

Hector wheeled on Gawain, the color draining from his cheeks. "Why did you bring my daughter here, to this dangerous place?"

Gawain's ears burned. Unbidden, a vision of what he and Tamsin had been doing in his bed that morning exploded in his brain. "It is a long and colorful tale."

"I don't doubt it," Hector growled. "You had better start explaining yourself, boy."

Gawain didn't get a chance to reply. Tamsin flung herself at her father, thumping him once on his breastplate with the flat of her hand. She was crying, her face mottled with tears. "Why did you leave me? Why did you lie about who you are?"

"I didn't leave you," said Hector. "Benjamin Waller trapped me in the Forest Sauvage and locked the portal tight."

Chapter 24

"Explain everything," said Tamsin once she had steered her father into the kitchen. She couldn't seem to let go of his arm, and clung there as if he might vanish without her touch. He looked sunburned and shaggier, but every feature was exactly as she remembered it. He hadn't aged a day, which matched what Angmar had said about the old faery queen making her father an immortal guardian of the knights.

He put his hand over hers. It was broad and capable, just as she remembered it. "Surely you understand why I never told you who I am?"

His voice was kind, but the words rankled. She didn't understand—not at all. Hot, sour disappointment pounded through her, bringing heat to her cheeks as she met her father's brown eyes—so like her own. Tamsin dropped her hand from his sleeve, not wanting the contact now. "I suppose it's like the old wartime saying that loose lips sink ships. No one can accidentally tell what they don't know."

"That's it exactly," Hector replied gently. "Arthur's safety has always been paramount."

And trust between father and daughter came second. Tamsin looked away, hiding her hurt. "Did you tell the Elders?"

Gawain had been occupied with tending Hector's horse. Now he set out more food and ale, pushing a tankard into her father's hands. Hector drank deeply, wiping foam from his mustache and beard and then heaving a satisfied sigh. "No, never. But after centuries of drifting from coven to coven, covering my tracks as best I could, I slipped and Waller figured it out."

"And?" Tamsin asked.

"Things became complicated, but let me launch this story at the beginning. When Morgan LaFaye took the crown from the old faery queen, it took a long time to consolidate her power." Hector took another long swallow of ale. "It was only in the last fifty years that LaFaye gathered enough strength to mount her campaign on the mortal world, and her first order of business became finding and destroying the tombs. That was my signal to act. To keep our scent covered or at least confused, I was instrumental in arranging the move of the old church to America. In time, I also scattered the tombs across the States. I reasoned that if I split up the tombs, Mordred or his mother might find some of the knights, but not all."

"So you're the culprit who put me in a museum basement," grumbled Gawain.

Hector chuckled. "I thought Los Angeles would suit you. Somewhere there is an action-adventure movie in want of a barbarian."

Gawain raised his eyebrows as if about to utter a scathing comment, but Hector went on. "You were just a girl, Tamsin, when I went to Carlyle. Not long before that, Angmar's friends had whisked Arthur's tomb to the Forest Sauvage for safekeeping. This was not my choice of hiding place, particularly since the rebel fae closed the portal when they left and promptly went into hiding. I had no means of getting here."

"Why did they do that?" Gawain asked.

"LaFaye was hot on their heels and they weren't thinking about my problems. I understand many ended up in a dungeon after that."

That detail fit with what Angmar had said. Tamsin wondered how many of the bones in Mordred's dungeon had belonged to those fae. It was the stuff of nightmares.

Hector continued. "I knew the church in Carlyle had Merlin's old books and the spell for the forest portal was in those pages. He learned it from the Lady of the Lake and recorded it there."

Tamsin had been sitting with her head bowed, unable to look up at her father. Finally, she met his eyes. "There's one thing I don't understand. You're talking about something that happened ten years ago. Why didn't the fae mount a full-on attack then?"

"The fae are immortal and have time on their side," Hector answered. "They do not march an army into the human lands, but they come in twos and threes, set up lives among the population, and bide their time. When they rise up and conquer the human world, there will be no place of safety left to hide in. Excalibur is the only weapon that will defeat LaFaye and her son. Failing that, the only spells strong enough to combat fae magic were in Merlin's library, and he is gone."

"Not quite. We found his books in the house of a man named Henderson," said Tamsin.

"Henderson bought those books from the church," said Hector. "I approached him as the loremaster of Shadowring. When I asked to use them, he agreed. However, he kept very close watch on everything I did, and that is where I made my mistake. He determined I wanted to build a portal to the Forest Sauvage. Not a common desire, to say the least."

Hector sighed, as if the events still depressed him. "It turns out Henderson was a close friend of Waller and told him everything I did. Unknown to me, Waller had a diplomatic understanding with LaFaye and my cover, as they say, was blown. Fortunately, I'd told Waller I was researching demons. They had no idea I was trying to reach Arthur's tomb. All they saw was a way to get rid of a pesky guardian."

"So Waller convinced Henderson to trick you?" asked Gawain.

"Indeed. Thus I ended up trapped here without the spell to get myself home."

"Why not simply kill you?"

Hector laughed, the sound like an amused bear. "It is one thing to trick me, but I am not so easy to kill, either by sword or by spell. Not by the likes of Henderson, at least."

Gawain swore. "What Waller doesn't understand is that LaFaye will destroy or enslave the witches. Mordred already killed Henderson."

"Pity," said Hector with genuine regret. "He was foolish, not evil."

Tamsin studied her father, everything he'd said churning in her mind. As a child, she'd seen him as a bulwark against the world, protecting her from every possible harm. He'd been the center of her love and admiration as only a father can be to his girl. She'd given him everything and yet he'd only shared a sliver of himself. Did she really know him at all?

Hurt hardened to resentment inside her. It would have

been so much easier to live with these revelations if she didn't love him so much. Then she wouldn't have been so disappointed. Her fingers curled in her lap, crushing handfuls of her dress.

The men were still talking. "You have Merlin's books!" Hector exclaimed. "That was well done. We can make good use of them to locate Arthur's tomb."

"Haven't you found it?" Gawain asked in confusion.

"Oh, I know where it is, more or less," Hector replied with a grimace. "But we'll need the spells to get it back. In the meantime, we can build a portal and get Tamsin home to where it's safe. This is no place for my daughter."

That was it. Tamsin sprang to her feet and met her father's eyes, letting her anger show. "That's not up to you anymore."

Shock spread across Hector's features. His mouth dropped open as he clearly struggled for words. She didn't wait for his reply as she stormed into the courtyard to let her temper cool—but it didn't. Since hearing Hector was alive, Tamsin had dreamed of meeting her father again. She'd wanted him to respect the person she'd grown to be. That wasn't at all what was happening.

Tears of frustration leaked down her face, hot in the cool autumn air. She wasn't a child, to be ordered to bed early. Most of all, she deserved more than lies and secrets from the father she loved so very much.

Tamsin wasn't sure how much time passed before she heard Hector's footfall behind her. Her stomach tightened, as if bracing herself. Every instinct said the conversation they were about to have wouldn't be easy.

"What would you have had me do?" her father asked from behind her. "I swore an oath of silence. Gawain just told me of your visit to the dungeon. You saw what was there. If Mordred had caught wind that someone in the coven knew about Arthur, he would have cheerfully filled every cell with Shadowring witches. How could I risk our family that way?"

Tamsin closed her eyes, the cold wind fanning her cheeks. She was shivering, but refused to turn around and go inside. "I get it. But think how I feel. You're not the father I knew. You're standing there in a chain mail shirt with an ax strapped to your saddle and a mission that doesn't include me in the slightest. Children always have a moment when they realize their parents have their own lives, but this is a little extreme."

"I understand it's a shock."

"Really? I don't even know how many families you had all this time. Am I your first daughter? Your hundredth? Do I rank among your favorites? After all these centuries, I could share DNA with a lot of people. Don't you think I have a right to know?"

Hector cleared his throat. Even so, his voice cracked as he spoke. "You'd be surprised how few times I've sought the comfort of a family. Living forever is a more frightening prospect than you would think. I've watched everyone I loved die."

Tamsin's heart lurched, and she turned around. Her father's expression made him look oddly naked, as if a barrier she'd never even noticed had been stripped away. "At the very least, you could have warned me that the fae weren't gone from the earth."

He nodded, looking at his feet. "You're right about that much. I'm sorry."

"I'm not going home," she said. Her chest ached, wanting to end this and take her father in her arms, but she needed to make this one last point. "I've held up my end on this mission. Ask Gawain."

"He's told me in glowing terms." Hector looked up. "He is the reason you have to go. He's not for you, Tamsin."

"What?" His words hit her like a slap. "Don't even start. I've had enough talk about suitable matches from Mom and Stacy. I choose who I'm with."

"That's not what I'm saying," Hector took a step closer, his eyes dark with sadness. "I see the way Gawain looks at you."

Tamsin shivered, but this time it wasn't from the cold. It was the thrill of hearing her private hopes aloud. "But?"

"It's bad enough his view of the world is centuries out-of-date, but in the end he will turn on you because you are a witch."

"No," she said quickly. "He has no reason to. He knows what I can do already."

Hector shook his head. "If you say that, then you don't understand the true nature of his struggle. You're better off far away. It will save you a great deal of pain."

Tamsin pressed her lips together, breathing deep before she answered. In truth, she wanted to scream with frustration. After Richard, she hadn't cared much about marriage. That relationship hadn't been a selling point for romance of any kind, but with Gawain, she'd known what it was to feel cherished. To be in a partnership. She would rather be alone than settle for less, pain or no pain.

"I'm not going back," she said. "For a lot of reasons, including Gawain, but also because that's what Waller wants. He'd rather I ended up an obedient servant of Shadowring."

"Who asked his opinion?" Hector growled.

Tamsin rubbed the vine tattoo around her wrist. "We had a long conversation during which he tried to shame me and threaten me, and when that didn't work he said he'd make me an Elder if I gave him Merlin's books."

"He did what?" Hector demanded in a rising roar.

"He faked your funeral, you know, just so nobody would wonder where you'd gone. I think I'm safer here with the demons."

With a huff of disgust, Hector folded his daughter in his thick, strong arms. "Hush, lass. We'll knock his head in later." He rocked her gently, rumbling words of comfort like a great bear cradling his cub.

That was when Tamsin knew for certain that she had her father back.

An hour later, they were on the road to Camelot.

As a historian, Tamsin had read stories of the place—the name seemed to refer to a castle, a town, or a kingdom, depending on who was telling the tale—but serious human scholars treated it as a legend more than a fact. Witches knew it had been real, but most of their records were lost during centuries of persecution. Now Tamsin would see Camelot Castle—or a reasonable facsimile thereof—as no one had for centuries. A thrill of anticipation washed away the strain of the morning.

She clung to Hector as they rode through the forest. On horseback, a war ax hanging from his saddle, he seemed utterly at home. It would take some time to work through her feelings, but she was beginning to enjoy this version of her father.

Gawain had ridden ahead on his great bay stallion. Now he returned along the track through the forest. "The path looks clear."

"Good," said Hector, and he urged the gray to go faster.

After another few minutes, they emerged from the edge of the trees, and there it was—Arthur's castle. It stood on a rise overlooking the surrounding land, the round, pale towers gleaming in the sunlight. Tamsin craned her neck to get a better view over her father's shoulder. The crenellated walls and pointy towers were straight out of a story-book. Hundreds of colored pennons snapped in the brisk wind, as if the place had donned its party clothes. But like Gawain's home, it seemed deserted.

"It's beautiful," she said.

"It represents all the Round Table stood for," said Hector. "Arthur brought peace to the land from this place. Camelot was a promise he kept for a good long time."

Gawain moved his horse beside them. "What next? I am curious to know how you have been here so long and yet have not located the tomb."

Hector shifted uneasily. "Oh, I kept Arthur's tomb in a stronghold not far from here until a demon drove us out. I had gathered a library of grimoires and he must have smelled them all the way to whatever unholy haunt he hid in. Some demons fancy themselves scholars and can't resist a decent collection. At any rate, he moved in and took the place for himself. I fled with the tomb and little else."

"We met that demon," said Tamsin.

"It killed Mordred's fae army when they attacked the place yesterday," said Gawain. "Did they come expecting to find Arthur's tomb?"

Tamsin answered. "Nimueh said Mordred questioned the rest of his prisoners to death."

Hector bowed his head. "A few knew I intended to come here. No doubt that's how he tracked me."

They were silent a long moment before Hector spoke again. "With a demon in the neighborhood, I took extra care. I hid the tomb in Camelot using the strongest spell I knew. The tomb's not just invisible, it's completely unde-tectable. I need a good seeking spell to find it."

"If you were the one who hid it, why don't you know where it is?" Tamsin asked.

"It's the nature of the spell. When it hides something, it hides it."

Gawain squinted at the castle on the hill. "Camelot is a big place. Will the spell lead us directly to Arthur?"

Hector nodded slowly. "Yes, the time a spell saves makes up for the risk."

"What risk?" Gawain asked sharply.

Hector gave a rueful smile. "Magic attracts the attention of others. When you cast a seeking spell, you never know who else might be watching."

Despite his caution, they were decided. The party dismounted and stretched their limbs after the long ride while Hector sorted through the spell books Tamsin took from her backpack.

Tamsin felt the pull of the surrounding beauty—the cool forest and sun-drenched meadows. If this was anything like the real Camelot of old, she understood why Gawain spoke of it with such feeling. The fact that he'd given it all up to save the future—her world—struck her more deeply than ever. The next few hours would decide if his sacrifice had been in vain.

Sobered, Tamsin turned to watch her father. She'd seen her father do magic before, but now she felt a twinge of anxious anticipation.

Hector had selected the book with a dark blue cover tooled with gold leaf. He found the spell he wanted, read it through and then handed the book back to Tamsin to stow away again.

"You will see the thread of the spell," he said. "Follow it as soon as it's visible and send me a signal along the thread when you've found its destination. I'll dismiss the spell and catch up to you."

Tamsin didn't like the idea of separating, but Gawain nodded his agreement. They mounted his bay and waited while Hector got to work. It took about five minutes before she glimpsed a pale blue ribbon of light snaking toward the castle, the air around it shimmering like a heat wave.

"There!" Tamsin pointed. "I can see it."

Gawain followed her gesture, frowning. "So can I." He urged the bay forward, and they cantered toward the castle. Already familiar with the twists and turns that led them up the hill and through the gate, Gawain rode with confidence, eagerness in every line of his body. Tamsin held on tight. At that speed, all her focus had to be on staying in the saddle.

They thundered into Camelot's courtyard, the bay's horseshoes ringing on the stones. The blue thread of magic had thinned the farther they'd traveled from Hector, but Tamsin could see where it snaked into one corner of the yard, where a heavily carved door stood open.

"That's the Great Hall," said Gawain. He dismounted and lifted her down from the bay. "Let me have a look around before coming in."

"I could provide a light."

"The less magic the better, if spies are watching." He drew his sword and marched toward the door.

Tamsin cursed inwardly as Gawain disappeared inside. He was right about the magic, but it was hard to accept. She was too much a twenty-first-century woman to stay behind while a man did the fighting, especially when she had effective weapons of her own. The horse snorted, as if agreeing with her thoughts, and began cropping the grass that sprouted between the cobblestones. Time passed. Tamsin looked at her watch impatiently, realized she wasn't wearing one and then took her backpack from the horse's saddle and started for the door.

Her stomach churned with impatience. This was Camelot—home of a king who'd led armies, battled demons and convinced the Round Table to travel through time. Gawain spoke of King Arthur with affection and reverence. Her father guarded Arthur even though the king had banished him. Tamsin hadn't known it, but Arthur and his deeds were a magnetic force around which much of her life had revolved. It felt as if he had the power to make or break her happiness.

She wasn't waiting a moment longer to clap her eyes on this man.

Chapter 25

Gawain lingered in the gloom of the Great Hall. Before him stood the Round Table and the hundred and fifty tall chairs that surrounded it, each hung with the shield of the knight who had won the right to sit there. Tapestries lined the walls in brilliant hues, showing the exploits of Arthur and his knights. Above, there was a gallery for onlookers and another for musicians. The feasts in the glory days had been something to behold.

The polished wood table was not, as some imagined, a solid circle. Instead, it was made in sections that fit together in a ring. Speakers could address the Round Table from the center, essentially giving each member a front row seat. That was where the Green Knight had issued his challenge, and where Lancelot had publicly taken Beaumains to be his squire. For many, many years Gawain's life had been tied to the events that took place in this room. He stole a glance at his own seat at Arthur's side, and for once was filled with hope instead of loss. They could build this all again, couldn't they?

They would have to build it better. Mordred had been a master of half-truths, pitting friend against friend until the company of knights fell to pieces. That couldn't happen again. This time, they couldn't swerve in their loyalty to king and cause. This time, they had to hold Arthur's word above their own petty concerns. This time, the stakes were even higher than before. If they faltered, Mordred and La-Faye would crush the mortal world.

"Gawain?" Tamsin stood in the doorway. "Is everything all right?"

"Come in," he said, and wasn't surprised when she stopped in her tracks to stare. With the doors wide open, there was just enough light to glimpse the splendor of the room. He tried to see the place with a stranger's eyes, but it was too close to his heart.

"Everything is fine," he said. "Or it will be, once we find the king. Look, the seeking spell stops right there." Gawain pointed to a spot in the middle of the Round Table's circle, where the pale blue thread shimmered to nothing.

"I see that," Tamsin replied, still turning in place to see all of the room. "This is amazing."

"Of course it is," he said. "It's Camelot."

They slipped through the aisle between sections of the table, following the spell to its end. Tamsin seemed to wind the thread of light around her wrist and give it a sharp tug. The signal for Hector to join them, Gawain supposed.

He swept a foot through the empty air where the seeking spell stopped. "I don't feel anything."

"You won't," Tamsin said. "If the tomb is truly obscured, it's more than just invisible."

"Then how do we move it through the portal?"

"We don't," said Tamsin. Then she reached inside her pocket and retrieved the tiny volume she'd used the night she'd awakened Beaumains. "There's a much faster way. I don't see why we should drag the tomb with us when all we need is your king. If I bring him back from the stone sleep, the cloaking spell will dissolve on its own."

Gawain laughed, drawing a surprised look from her beautiful dark eyes. He dropped a kiss on her sun-bright head. "Have I ever told you how truly magnificent you are?"

"Not nearly often enough."

Tamsin began reading from the spell book, her light, sweet voice rising and falling in a language Gawain didn't understand. His first impulse was to stand and stare at the space where the tomb should have been, hungry for the first glimpse of his king and friend, but that would help nothing. Instead, he went to the door and looked out, sword in hand and alert to any danger.

The wash of magic behind him raised the hair along his arms, but he was growing accustomed to being around a witch's power again. It stirred the dormant magic in his veins, heating it the way her beauty heated other parts of him. For the first time in many, many years, he yearned to reclaim that lost part of himself—and yet the very idea disturbed him in the extreme. Gawain had learned not to play with fire, literally or in metaphor.

This time, though, the tingling power signaled that the quest for Arthur was nearly done. Gawain and Tamsin had kept their bargain, to the betterment of everyone. Did that not make this alliance with magic worthwhile? Was there not something here to learn? Gawain pushed the question away, but not as far as he might have done once upon a time.

He felt rather than heard trouble arrive. A tapestry fluttered with a draft that shouldn't have been there. Gawain spun, sword raised.

"Hello, cousin," said Mordred, his face puffy and bruised from the beating Gawain had given him. Tamsin cried out in shock. Gawain's sword twitched, but he checked his blow. There was no way he could strike, for Hector was on his knees before Mordred, his head bloody and back arched in pain. It wasn't hard to see why—Mordred's fingers were wound in the older knight's gray-streaked hair. As Gawain watched, his cousin gave the hair a twist, bringing a grunt from his prisoner.

"Let my father go!" Tamsin cried.

Mordred didn't even look her way. He wore armor, the same blue-black steel Gawain remembered from so long ago. He was expecting a fight, and Gawain was happy to give him one.

Mordred gave a serpent's smile. Frost began to form on the weapons hanging in the room as Mordred's power sucked the heat from the air. He was getting ready for more mischief. "I think we have a few things to discuss."

"Did you enjoy my beating so much that you came back for more?" Gawain lowered his arm. Any blow that would kill Mordred would hurt Hector. That was fine—Gawain could wait. "I honestly thought Nimueh might finish the job."

"She's gone, the slippery fox." Mordred fixed him with a bloodshot eye. "Bolted. Vanished. When I hunt her down, she'll pay for letting you go."

Nimueh on the run? That was interesting news, but it could wait. "Tamsin," Gawain said. "Keep reading the spell." They needed Excalibur if he was going to finish Mordred once and for all.

The room had filled with the golden brilliance of Tamsin's magic, though the tomb was still invisible. Her eyes were wide with distress and fixed on her father. "But—"

"But I say you don't read the spell, or I slit the old man's throat." Mordred's bruised smile was a leering mockery. "However, I do thank you so much for leading me to Arthur's tomb. Hunting for it has been such a tedious business."

Relying on speed, Gawain slapped Mordred's arm with the flat of his blade, praying surprise would be on his side. It worked. Mordred let go of Hector, who slumped to the floor without a word. Gawain glanced down just long enough to see the old knight was not bleeding, but in that split second he lost his advantage.

Mordred lunged and snatched the spell book from Tamsin's hands. Mordred laughed as she lashed out with a fireball. "Concentrate, little witch," he sneered, batting it aside. "Gawain did better than that when he could barely reach the table."

The gibe made Gawain flinch, but he let it pass. The golden light from the spell was beginning to soften, a sure sign that Tamsin's magic was unraveling. Mordred had used Hector to distract her, and it had worked all too well. Gawain adjusted his grip on his sword, calculating his odds.

Gawain lunged, aiming not for Mordred's heart, as his cousin would expect. Instead, he pricked the hand holding the spell book. The book fell, but the motion left Gawain's defenses open. In a flash, Mordred's sword—a black blade he called Viper—was in his cousin's hand.

"You want to do this?" Mordred snarled, his lean face mottling with rage. "Man to man?"

"Gawain!" Despair filled Tamsin's cry.

The purity of it pulled at Gawain's core, pleading that he come back safe. No one had ever called for him like

that before, but there was nothing he could do to offer re-
assurance. Grabbing his shield from the back of his seat at
the Round Table, Gawain rounded on Mordred, smashing
the shield hard into Mordred's half-prepared sword thrust.
It wasn't a regulation move, but it forced Mordred a step
toward the door—and away from Tamsin.

Gawain rained blows on Mordred, keeping him too dis-
tracted to throw a spell Gawain had no hope of blocking.
He followed with a blow to Mordred's breastplate that sent
his cousin staggering back. Mordred's heel slipped, making him stumble. For a moment, Gawain thought the fight
was won, but Mordred was quick, whipping his sword
around to parry Gawain's next blow. Gawain kicked him
in the stomach hard enough to send him skittering into the
courtyard, away from Tamsin and her father.

Gawain grinned. He fought for her now, this woman
who had called his name.

The moment the coast was clear, Tamsin dove for Hector, only to discover he was conscious and had pulled the
spell book under the protective shield of his body.

"You were faking it!" she cried.

"Here," he said, pushing the book toward her. "Not faking it. Securing the prize so that worm of a faery prince
didn't remember what he came for. I'm not as young as I
used to be. I've come to appreciate guile."

Tamsin met Hector's eyes. Whatever distance had been
left between them was gone. "How badly are you hurt?"

"He knocked me out and threw me on my horse," Hector said gruffly. "I'll be fine."

She took his arm, helping him to his feet. He moved
stiffly, grabbing the Round Table for support. "Get on with
the spell. Gawain will need Arthur's sword if he is going
to survive this fight."

"Then help me," she said, taking up the book. "Two of us will make it go faster."

Hector gave a smile she remembered from childhood—warm and filled with mischief. He grasped her hand in his, kissing it. "Delighted to."

They began reading, their voices weaving together in a web of magic. Tamsin fell back through the years. It had been far too long since they had done this, father and daughter. It was like coming home and remembering who she really was all at the same time.

The dome of gold had faded to a mist, but now it came back stronger, glittering like a fine rain. Hector's voice rang low and firm while Tamsin's made a softer invitation. The rain became a fall of diamond-bright sparks that began to cling and slide down a solid form. Tamsin's words nearly faltered as she saw what the brilliant light outlined—a sleeping man, tall and broad shouldered, with a gleaming, wicked sword that reached from his chest to his heavy-booted feet. She made out a neat beard and fall of waving hair, a strong, handsome face and pointed crown. Just as it had with Beaumains, color seeped into the sleeping form, painting him in reds and golds, with the lions on his surcoat a brilliant yellow. Tamsin stared and stared, unable to take in what was before her. Every illustration, every painting of Arthur Pendragon had looked just like this man.

She glanced up at her father, noticing the tears tracking into his beard. With a sudden ache in her throat, she realized her father had raised this king from the time he was a boy. Arthur was his foster son. In a strange way, he was almost her brother.

The vine tattoo on her wrist warmed, channeling her strength as it had when she'd raised Beaumains. But even with Hector's help, this awakening was harder. Maybe it was because they were breaking the cloaking spell, too, but the harder she pushed her magic, the more it seemed to resist her urging. Her head began to throb in a way that made her stomach queasy. Tamsin closed her eyes.

And snapped them open again when she heard her father's indrawn breath. At once she saw the tomb was nothing but a piece of stone. This time, she knew enough to look around. Arthur of Britain stood at the door, staring out at the courtyard. Although she could see only his back, she had no trouble taking his measure. He stood with confidence, a man surveying all that was his. With her inner sight, Tamsin perceived the golden aura of majesty around him, the power that was his birthright and his burden. It wasn't witchcraft—she could tell at a glance that the king was fully human—but something just as old.

"Your Majesty," said her father.

Arthur spun to face Hector, his ice-blue eyes snapping. He drew his sword, wielding its enormous size as if it were no more than a fork. "Sir Hector," boomed King Arthur in a voice clearly used to command. "What, by all the devils, is going on?"

Hector grabbed Tamsin's arm, pulling her down so that they knelt before the king. Tamsin bowed her head, noting the supple leather of the king's boots just before the tip of Excalibur swung into view. It caught Hector's chin, forcing him to look up.

"I exiled you. How dare you return to my castle?"

Finally free to move in the courtyard, Gawain launched into a furious attack. Mordred blocked every blow with easy expertise that spoke of magic more than practice— a dangerous shortcut. It was a fast way to burn through power only to have it fail at a crucial moment—but Mordred was the Prince of Faery. He had reserves most could only dream of. All Gawain could do was buy time, and it was clear Mordred was confident enough to play along.

Mordred's next blow shuddered against Gawain's sword with inhuman force. Gawain staggered back, barely able to raise his shield in time to meet the next blow. He cursed as his vambrace bit into his arm.

"What's the matter, Mordred, trying to compensate for squandering your army on a demon's breakfast?" Gawain taunted.

Mordred cursed. "More where they came from. I have the whole of Faery at my beck and call."

"But will your mama let you have them? You always did break your toys."

Mordred countered with an upward thrust. Gawain moved to block it, but Mordred snarled and dropped the point of his sword just before it struck. Gawain didn't have time to adjust, only twist to avoid it. The edge missed his breastplate but drove in behind. Gawain felt Viper tear through the mail of his shirt and score his ribs in a searing, white-hot bite that went down to the bone. His mind blanked with the agony as he spun and drove his shield into Mordred's shoulder. They flung apart, reflexes alone keeping Gawain on his feet.

The light in the Great Hall was almost blinding now, spilling golden rays into the courtyard like a wandering sun. The spell was nearly complete. Gawain only had to keep fighting for a little longer.

And then he heard the raucous clamor of crows. Both opponents looked up at the sound, for both knew what it meant. A swirl of black birds was diving out of the sky, melding into one horrific raptor with a beak like a scythe.

The demon had found them.

Chapter 26

The bird wheeled low overhead, opening wings that spanned at least twelve feet. The horses reared, screaming in terror. One by one, they broke free and bolted from the courtyard to the woods beyond. The bird's great beak opened and spoke in the demon's measured tones.

"I see the thieves who stole my books, I see the wretch who sent an army to my doors and I smell deep magic. I see many, many nights of dark entertainment ahead."

Fast as lightning, it stooped like a hawk, diving straight for them. Gawain had fought the monster once before and he braced himself now, prepared to sell his life dearly. But Mordred was ready, too, blasting frozen fire right in the demon's feathered face. The demon shrieked and flapped away only to dive again, the slashing claws inches away from Mordred's flesh.

Gawain leaped in, chopping at the demon between Mordred's attacks. Together, they gave the creature no rest. His breath rasped as the battle went on, skirmish after skirmish. The two cousins worked in tandem, as equal partners as they had always been relentless foes.

Sweat stood out on Mordred's cheeks, yet he was in his element, turning the bright afternoon into a swirling mass of inky clouds. Fork after fork of lightning crashed into the demon, setting it alight in a corona of blue fire. The demon stretched its beak wide and belched down a blast of greenish flame. Mordred raised his hand, fingers spread wide, and forced the fire back. The collision of their wills shook the earth. Mortar rained down from Camelot's walls.

Gawain's skin crawled from the after-burn of magic as the demon circled away, shrieking in pain. Mordred fell to one knee, his magic seemingly exhausted. His sword dangled from one limp hand.

"Well, that was unexpected." He gave a sharp grin. "This forest never was the best neighborhood."

Gawain braced his hands on his knees, breathing hard. For a fleeting instant, he saw what might have been—not Gawain and three brothers, but four, if only fellowship with Mordred had been possible. "We made a good team."

"Indeed," said Mordred. His chin jerked up. "Damn and blast, here it comes again."

Gawain straightened, looking skyward. That instant of distraction gave Mordred what he needed. He drove Viper through Gawain's mail, magic parting the steel like paper. If the slash to Gawain's ribs had hurt, this was beyond pain. This was a white-hot forge inside his chest.

Gawain fell to his knees.

"Do you think I would ever *willingly* fight at your side?" Mordred murmured in his ear. "I would rather feed myself to my pet worms."

The king held Tamsin and Hector at sword point, demanding answers. "Tell me again. What do you mean the knights have not awakened from the stone sleep?"

Arthur seemed disoriented, as if his mind hadn't caught up yet. Maybe the concealment spell on top of the stone sleep had been too much.

"Only Gawain and his brother have awakened," said Tamsin, still on her knees at Arthur's feet. She'd answered the question at least twice before. "Something has gone wrong with the magic."

She cast a sideways glance at her father. He didn't look well, and she worried about the blow he'd taken to his head.

"Only two of my knights?" Arthur pulled her attention back his way. He was pale, his eyes filling with a mix of fury and panic. "Is there no end to the treachery of magic?"

Arthur also seemed just a wee bit paranoid.

Swords clashed outside, but he was oblivious. Maybe swordplay was a normal sound at Camelot, or maybe he was one of those people with amazing focus. But, unlike Arthur, Tamsin couldn't tune out the noise of combat. She heard the horses whinny—they were frantic about something—but Excalibur's tip did not waver from her father's throat.

"Maybe you want to check on Gawain and Mordred?" she suggested, but the king didn't seem to hear her.

"Why is it that every time something goes awry, there is a witch standing nearby?" Arthur's jaw worked, his eyes sparking with temper. "I wake up from my sleep in the wrong place, centuries out of my own time, with LaFaye set to destroy the world and my army vanished, and what do I find but witches at my elbow?"

"Maybe witches who want to fix the problem," Tamsin said, earning a warning glare from Hector—but she was getting frustrated. "Maybe you should consider my father did his best to keep Mordred and his mother from smashing you to bits while you slept."

The king's cheeks flushed, turning a mottled shade that

didn't agree with his red-gold hair. Nevertheless, this time he listened. "Is this true, Sir Hector?"

"Yes. LaFaye's predecessor granted me immortality to carry out the task."

"What happens to you now?" Arthur asked, anxiety creeping into his tone. Was it a good sign that he was asking after her father?

"I've found my king. My mission is over, and my immortality gone," said Hector, taking Tamsin's hand in his. "I am relieved to be an ordinary man with a loving family once more."

Tamsin caught her breath, shaken by her father's words. "Isn't that enough proof of loyalty, even for a king?"

The sword tip inched in her direction. "You are bold, Mistress Greene. An unbridled tongue is a dangerous attribute when speaking to a crowned head."

Another clash of swords outside set Tamsin's nerves on edge. "Maybe I am bold, sire, but we all went through a lot to find you and bring you back to life. I'm really hoping you're everything I've been told you are, because we're going to need some five-star leadership to get us out of this jam."

Arthur held her gaze, meeting her challenge and matching it with his own. There was wariness in his eyes, but also sharp, intelligent curiosity that hadn't been there a few minutes ago. Tamsin exhaled, feeling the first twinges of relief. She had no doubt waking from an enchantment was hard, but she needed the king to come around, and fast.

"You have known me from the cradle, Arthur," said Hector, gruff with emotion. "Do not doubt me." Tamsin's heart twisted on behalf of her father. She folded both her hands around his.

Arthur saw the gesture, and his face softened, but his words did not. "After Merlin and Mordred and LaFaye, I cannot grant magic users the trust I once did. You woke me from the stone sleep, but that does not guarantee your intentions."

"What kind of a guarantee do you want, sire?" Tamsin asked, almost pleading. "Mordred tried to kill me. Then he tried to take my soul. I went to his dungeon and I hope never to see another worm as long as I live. Gawain and Beaumains shed buckets of blood for you, as well as Angmar and his friends. Witches, fae or mortal, we've all been there for the cause. Gawain is out there fighting for you right now!"

Arthur's brows rose, and finally he turned his head toward the racket outside. "Gawain knows his business and his loyalty is above reproach. If he fights, it is in my name."

"Then don't question our commitment, because his cause is ours," Tamsin said, getting desperate. "If what Gawain says about you is true, you're better than this."

It was a foolhardy thing to say to a king, especially one holding a huge sword, but she was tired and too much a woman of the modern day to coddle a king. He was going to have to earn her respect. Seconds ticked by, the air so tense it might have smashed like glass.

Then she saw a glint of something that might have been reluctant amusement in the king's eyes. Excalibur's point drifted to the floor. Arthur blinked, seeming to fully come back to himself, as if the last shreds of the sleeping spell had finally lifted.

"I can see you are Sir Hector's daughter. You have no fear of putting me in my place." He smiled, and it was like the sun coming out from behind a cloud. Tamsin suddenly understood why strong men swore to serve this king. "I don't recommend you do it often, but, once in a very long while, I appreciate correction."

Hector released a huge breath. Arthur bent down, clapping him on the shoulder. "Rise, old friend, and accept my apologies." They got to their feet, Arthur enfolding Hector in a warm embrace.

"Who did you say Gawain is fighting?" Arthur asked, once he let Hector go. He asked the question casually, as if it were no more than a tennis match. Knowing Gawain, maybe he had daily bouts back in the day.

"Mordred," she said, as Arthur took her hand and kissed it. She gave the curtsy she'd learned in ballet class, hoping it would do.

Arthur's head snapped up from the kiss. Suddenly, he seemed to grasp the situation. "Mordred? He needs my sword!"

Before she could speak an unholy shriek split the air.

"The demon!" Hector exclaimed.

"Demon?" Arthur spun toward the door, Excalibur leaping to the ready. Tamsin's breath caught as Arthur's energy rose bright and hot. He was human, but all at once he was every inch a charismatic warrior king.

All three of them crowded into the doorway of the Great Hall just in time to see the monster flapping into the sky in a trail of smoke. "What in all the hells?" Hector demanded.

And then Tamsin saw Mordred drive his black sword into Gawain's side. She sprinted from the door, ignoring her father's bellowed order to stay where she was.

King Arthur was a pace behind.

"Gawain!" Tamsin screamed from somewhere that sounded very far away.

Gawain swayed toward her voice, but he could not raise himself. A chill was stealing inward, robbing his hands and feet of sensation. He cried out, a groan robbed of breath. No more than a rattle.

Figures bolted from the Great Hall into the courtyard,

gray shapes that surged in and out of focus. If he could only see Tamsin's face—but a veil had come down, turning everything dark.

Mordred turned toward the figures. Shocked recognition twisted his face into a snarl. "You!"

The single word, uttered with such hate, snapped Gawain's world back into focus. He was a warrior, sworn to protect, and his duty was not done. Almost of its own accord, his hand grabbed the hilt of his fallen sword. It felt heavy as lead, but he stabbed the point into the earth between the flagstones and levered himself up. One foot at a time, he forced himself to stand. Mordred paid him no heed, his face turned toward the hall. If Gawain had been able to lift his sword right then, he could have cut him down—but he simply didn't have the strength.

He turned to see what transfixed his treacherous cousin. A glimpse of familiar blue eyes and a blade-sharp nose was enough. Arthur, his king and friend. Fierce joy flamed through Gawain, straightening his spine despite the pain. Tamsin had done her work. Now there was hope and a way forward.

Tamsin! His eyes found her just yards away, running fleet as a deer toward him. She looked more beautiful than Gawain had ever seen her—her lips parted and eyes wide, all her attention bent his way. She was utterly exposed, a step ahead of Arthur. Gawain's instincts flared a warning.

Mordred's power rose and shaped itself to attack—not at Arthur, not yet. He meant to bat Tamsin out of his path, ridding a troublesome obstacle to get to the king. Powerful though she was, Tamsin wouldn't easily survive another direct attack from the Prince of Faery.

In that instant, all Gawain's confusion faded. The only thing that mattered was the fact that he loved her. Gawain slashed his sword upward, willing all his forgotten power into the strike. The blade sang with the release of magical energy, a high, clear note that pierced deep into Gawain's bones. Far above in the sky, the demon replied with a harsh scream of hungry rage.

For a moment all was purity—the autumn sun flashing on steel, the sharp, breathless agony of one final push. Gawain roared his defiance as the edge of his blade connected with flesh and bone. Mordred lifted into the air, howling in surprise. The spray of blood sizzled as it fell, dissolving in the heat of Gawain's rage made manifest.

Time unwound, suddenly slowed to a dreamlike pace marked by the drum of Gawain's heart. Mordred fell, eyes wide and staring at the sky. Tamsin ducked away, Arthur pulling her aside to cover her with his body. At first Gawain assumed it was from all that blood, but the sky blackened as the demon swooped again. Gawain fell to his knees, stones hard against the heels of his hands. The jolt shot through him in rainbow shards of pain.

The demon circled overhead, screaming with the sound of a thousand agonies. Time surged forward again. Tamsin was there, her slender arms around his shoulders. "Gawain?"

He put a hand to her arm, feeling the life in her. It was sweet and wild, like a berry bursting on his tongue. His magic lunged forward, craving her touch.

Gawain snatched his hand away. His power was free, running wild. He could feel it throbbing in him like a limb coming awake.

Tamsin's eyes widened. "What? You're hurt. You need to get inside."

Her hand immediately went to his wound, but he flinched away, not wanting to soil her with his black, bloody magic. Not wanting to stir that vile power one bit more.

Her lips pressed together in a stubborn line, but she

looked as if she was about to cry. "Don't fight me now. You need help."

She didn't understand. He'd tried to kill his power. Instead, it had just killed for him—again. He hadn't even needed Excalibur or Arthur to do the job.

Gawain cursed his foolishness. He thought he'd escaped what he truly was, beaten the vile taint of his mother's blood, but no. He'd just confirmed his own worst fears. He retched, and the pain in his side made the world go black.

Tamsin's face crumpled as she turned away to speak to someone else. "He's not cooperating!"

"Let me go, Tamsin," he whispered.

"Don't tell me what to do," she snapped. "You're in no condition to get stubborn on me."

She was right. The strength he'd found to save her was fading fast. Shock was setting in, his limbs starting to tremble. He clenched his fists, trying to hide it. "You kept your part of the bargain. Take the books. You earned them."

Shock scattered his thoughts, making it hard to reason. All he knew was that he could not be with her. He loved her too much to burden her with the anguish that consumed him.

"Is that it?" she cried. "The bargain's over and now you don't need me? You got what you want?"

For a heartbeat, the words barely penetrated. He was too caught by fury and disappointment at his own failure. But then Gawain drew a mighty breath as reality crashed through his heartbreak. He was hurting her. Tears were coursing down her face. That wasn't what Gawain meant to do at all, but his body and mind were both failing him. "No, Tamsin. Not what I want. It's all I can give you."

"Don't do this!" she said in a low voice. "I deserve more from you."

And he yearned to say more, to take her in his arms, but parts of him were going numb again. One limb, then another. Mordred's wound was taking pieces of him away.

"Leave him to me." Another set of hands, hard ones this time, dragged him to his feet. "I've got you, old friend."

The demon screamed above them as Gawain brought Arthur's face in to focus. The monster was signaling another attack. "My lord." He tried to swallow the blood in his mouth, but his tongue felt thick and dry. "Run."

"Agreed." Arthur hauled him forward as the sky filled with the thunder of the demon's wings. Tamsin sprinted ahead, seeming to grow more and more distant with every step. It was an illusion bred by Gawain's mounting fever, but it was also truth. She was slipping away. He wanted to call her back, but he was losing consciousness.

Gawain's vision narrowed to a pinpoint. The last thing he remembered was the demon flapping upward, Mordred dangling limply from its claws. The Prince of Faery had become dinner.

Chapter 27

"I'm a killer," Gawain said to Beaumains.

"You are a knight," Beaumains replied, sounding kindly if somewhat impatient. "Cousin or not, Mordred had it coming."

They were sitting on the top row of benches that formed the spectator stands at Medievaland. Below were the tourney grounds, but no bouts were on and the stands were empty.

They'd returned just hours ago, after Hector and Tamsin had opened the portal back to Carlyle, landing just outside the theme park. About twenty-four hours had passed since Gawain and Tamsin had set foot in the Forest Sauvage.

But to Gawain, it seemed like months since Hector had left him at Medievaland and taken his daughter home. Both witches had been exhausted after reviving Arthur, healing Gawain and opening the path back to the mortal realms. The knights had elected to come here instead of crowding into Tamsin's tiny home. The king was off roaming the grounds, looking more or less like one more costumed player.

Beaumains leaned back on the bench. "When I got the call from Tamsin to come here and find you, Mordred's death was all I could think about—but in a good way. Praise the saints and devils, he's finally gone. Call me bloodthirsty if you like. I don't care how you did it."

"I do," said Gawain, his stomach like lead. "Not that I regret ending the threat of our cousin, but because of how it was done. Being a soldier, a knight is one thing. I understand honest steel and know when and how to use it."

"But magic is different?"

"I don't need to remind you that it was my magic that killed our sister. I nearly killed you."

Beaumains made a noise of understanding. "That was a tragic accident when you were a boy. Mordred goaded you into it. He was a menace even then."

"But I fell into his trap out of pride." Gawain studied his brother's ruined face. "I hurt you."

"I know." A sad smile softened the words. "But I also remember you pulling me from the fire. You were the greatest of heroes to me then, this warrior who walked through flames to rescue me. We all stumble, brother, sometimes terribly, but it is how we make amends that matters. And don't forget you were a child. You didn't have the wisdom of a man."

Gawain bowed his head. "I tried to atone. I thought I had cut the rot of our mother's magic from my soul, but here it is again."

"Does it need to be rot? I have to confess, I'd sooner have inherited mother's magic than her singing voice, but children don't get to pick."

Bitterness twisted Gawain's lips. "You don't think I've been tempted by the glitter of untold power?"

Beaumains sat up and punched Gawain's arm hard enough to hurt. "You're worried that you'll turn bad. I'm not. No sooner would you come up with a wicked plot than you'd start apologizing for it. You think too much to enjoy the life of an evil witch."

"I'm not a witch," Gawain said automatically, but the words held no conviction. He had no more choice in the matter than in the color of his eyes or the curl of his hair. There was nothing he could do. Nothing.

Gawain leaned forward, bracing his elbows on his knees. He had fought for years to deny the truth, but that had availed him not at all. After all this time, he'd finally surrendered to his nature. Shame came like a blow to the gut.

But it *wasn't* surrender, not in the sense of giving up. Frustration clawed at Gawain, pulling apart all his assumptions. He'd used the talents he had to save the woman he loved, and he refused to believe that was wrong.

Beaumains had a point. With magic came responsibility. Merlin had forgotten that, but Gawain would not. He'd seen the consequences of misused power, from the temptations of Lady Bertilak to the tragedy of Angmar's people. Gawain was not perfect, but he knew deep in his soul that there were lines no one should ever cross.

He let out his breath. All at once the cold afternoon crowded in, clean and sharp and filled with the distant clamor of fairgoers. There was a purity to accepting what he was, much like the song of his magic flashing down his sword. That had been a perfect moment, intent and action in utter harmony. All he'd cared about was keeping Tamsin safe.

That act of love had forced Gawain to destroy his hard-won belief in who he was. He'd always been the boy who had transformed himself from killer to champion with the force of self-denial. He'd masked his magic, crushed it, but that had been a lie. His love had made him face the truth—and then he'd pushed her away.

"What are you thinking?" Beaumains asked uneasily. "There are no suicidal heroics in the works, right?"

"No. Nothing that simple, I'm afraid." Gawain straightened as Arthur mounted the steps of the stands, a perplexed look on his face. Gawain knew the expression. It was the look of a medieval warrior seeing Medievaland for the first time. Forcing his pain deep out of sight, he gave a sympathetic smile as Arthur reached their bench.

"This place is very," the king began, turning back for another look, "um, cheerful."

"It grows on you," Beaumains offered. "You should try the corn dogs."

But Arthur turned back, serious now. "We have a future to plan. I understand from Hector that Angmar of Corin has been taken into hiding by his allies."

Beaumains nodded. "They came and got him yesterday."

Arthur gripped Excalibur's hilt. "The rebel fae have offered to provide for our needs until we gather our brothers. We must act quickly. Mordred may be gone, but Queen LaFaye will demand vengeance for his death."

Gawain had barely finished one mission, and Arthur was already looking ahead. But that forward push was part of what made the king a great general. No one caught him napping.

"What about the witches?" Beaumains asked. "Should we not be winning them to our side? They could be powerful friends in this war."

Arthur appeared to consider, and then shook his head. "Not after Merlin."

"Sire," said Gawain, opting for the formal title this time, "you saw what happened with Mordred? I used my power to kill him. I did not even need Excalibur."

Arthur cast him an assessing glance. "Those were extreme circumstances."

"I can't guarantee I won't do it again," Gawain replied. "I carry witch's blood in my veins."

Arthur folded his arms, his brows knit in concern. "Is this the effect of keeping company with Hector and his daughter?"

Gawain hid a flinch at the mention of Tamsin. "Consider what they've done for you."

"I have. I'm certain that Hector has shown me more grace than I deserve, and we have repaired our friendship. I was a fool when I sent him from my side."

Gawain seized that concession. Despite his own private struggles, he understood now that magic was a weapon the new Camelot would require. Arthur had to keep the witches safe in the coming war—and realize how badly he needed them. "Hector's daughter sacrificed her own interests to save us from Mordred's dungeon. She has healed our wounds, taken us to find you and shown more courage than half your knights. Hector and Tamsin are proof that with a good heart, magic can be turned to good ends."

Beaumains gave him a look filled with curiosity, but said nothing.

Gawain was arguing for a better Camelot. He was saying what should have been said centuries ago, opening Arthur's mind even as he struggled to adapt to this new view himself. "We can't afford to divide ourselves because of our differences. We should unite because of what binds us together—friendship, justice and a safe place to love and raise children free of the horrors of conflict."

The king shook his head. "Merlin believed all that, and yet he still failed us."

"He proved that one man can't solve the world's problems by himself. He refused to allow anyone to point out the flaws in his thinking. If he'd taken the advice of the fae sorcerers, he would never have made the mistakes he did. Blame his pride, not what he was."

For a long moment, Arthur turned away to survey the bright madness of Medievaland. "I suppose this is all because you're in love with the witch?"

Gawain rose and came to stand beside him, shoulder to shoulder as he had done on a hundred battlefields. "I love her, but no. I'm saying this because I'm your friend as well as your loyal servant. I'm saying it for the fae, who need a cure for Merlin's blunder, and for the witches, who need to break free of their fear. You need new allies with a variety of strengths, including magic."

Arthur's face creased in disbelief. "But you hate magic. You've hated it since the first time you came to my court."

"That's the part you can blame Tamsin for. She made me rethink what I assumed to be true." Gawain turned and nodded to Beaumains. "Though it took a wise brother to help me apply the same logic to myself."

With a weary snort, Arthur clapped a hand to Gawain's shoulder. "They call you Silver Tongue for good cause."

The three knights stood together, pondering the beginnings of the new Camelot. It would work, Gawain decided, because Arthur was willing to grow. In the end, the king wouldn't turn away valuable alliances, and he certainly wouldn't turn his back on his friends. He would lead them the way he had in that long-ago campaign to unite the petty kingdoms of Albion—by the hearts. That was why they would win again.

Gawain nodded. "I have always been your man, old world or new."

"I know," said the king. "I thank the saints and devils that you are at my side. Now go to your witch and thank her properly for healing you."

"Healing me," said Gawain. "Indeed, sire, truer words were never spoken."

Hector slammed Waller into the wall of Tamsin's apartment. "Start explaining."

The Chief Elder had arrived at Tamsin's door just hours after they'd arrived home. When Tamsin had opened the door, Waller's first words had been something about Tamsin's lack of good judgment and obedience. Word had reached him about the fight at the Henderson house.

That was before he'd noticed Hector in the room.

Now Waller was dangling from Hector's grip. He waved his hands as if to weave a spell, but then gave up and started clawing at the iron fist pinning him by the throat. The knight might have been barefoot and wearing Gawain's too-tall clothes, but he was clearly in control.

Tamsin viewed her erstwhile tormentor dangling against the wall. She couldn't summon much sympathy.

Waller gurgled, his lips turning blue.

Hector released his grip a fraction. "Talk."

"Whatever you want, it's yours. Money. A better house. You can have your old job back," Waller said between gasps. "I can make that happen."

Hector made an incredulous noise. "Employment is the least of my concerns, you lickspittle weasel. Besides, my daughter seems to be doing just fine in her position. Unlike you.

"What do you want?" Waller cried, but his eyes shifted, as if seeking a weapon.

Tamsin shifted closer, readying a spell just in case. Waller wasn't known as an expert in fighting magic, but she didn't trust him one bit.

Hector tapped the tip of Waller's nose with his free hand. "I haven't been home long, but I've made a few calls to some old friends from the other covens. They were very interested to hear that you were aligning yourself with LaFaye's interests. They don't approve. They think Shadowring's council deserves a housecleaning."

"Then they're fools," Waller shot back. "The witches are too weak to battle the fae. Too much was lost after Merlin gave us a black name."

"Ah, yes, it's Merlin's fault you're such a coward," Hector mused. "A dead sorcerer is so easy to blame. Tell me, has LaFaye promised you a special treat if you deliver the covens to her control?"

At that, Waller began a frantic struggle. Hector put a hand on the man's chest. "Stop, unless you want me to crush you like the spider you are."

Tamsin felt power building in the room and knew the Elder was summoning his magic. She moved in quickly, calling a fireball to her hand. A small one—she had her damage deposit to think of.

"He said stop!" She held up the coruscating ball of blue fire. "I've fought zombies. Fast ones. You don't want to mess with me."

"Don't give yourself airs, girl," he sneered, proving exactly how stupid he was.

Tamsin held the ball close enough for Waller to feel the heat. "Just try it."

Waller stilled as quickly as if someone had flipped a switch. Fear glazed his eyes, but so did a vicious anger.

He deliberately turned his attention to Hector. "What do you mean to do with me?"

"The Court of Covens has some questions for you," her father said, serious now. "They've had an eye on you for some time. They knew you were coming this way and asked me to escort you to them once you arrived. Some fae friends of ours set up a portal to take you there."

The look on Waller's face was too delicious to waste. Tamsin kept the ball of fire in one hand while she fished in her pocket with the other. She pulled out her smartphone and snapped a photo of the two men. Hector raised his eyebrows in question.

Tamsin texted the picture before she hit speed dial and put the phone to her ear. "Stacy would never believe any of this without evidence. Want to say hi before you go, Mr. Waller? Something tells me our paths may never cross again."

Chapter 28

An hour later Tamsin was alone. Hector had left through the portal with his prisoner, and her call to Stacy was done. Tamsin sank onto the edge of her bed, exhausted. Someone—perhaps one of the rebel fae who had come for Angmar—had made the bed with fresh sheets and washed the dishes. It was a polite gesture, but it made Tamsin feel forlorn. It reminded her that her home had been alive, filled with people, and now every last one was gone. Solitude pressed in with almost physical force.

Tamsin closed her eyes. Stacy had been ecstatic, shocked and outraged in turn by Tamsin's story. There would be a real Thanksgiving dinner now that their father had returned. It was something to look forward to—and Tamsin did. Really.

Except she wasn't sure she could resume the old patterns of her life again. She'd glimpsed another world filled with danger, one where she fought as an equal and the history she'd studied had come to life. One filled with larger-than-life warriors who believed what she had to offer wasn't merely important, but critical to success. For a while, she'd mattered.

Until she hadn't. She'd given Gawain what he'd asked for, and then he'd asked her to go.

In a fit of temper, Tamsin hurled a pillow at the wall. It bounced harmlessly away, making just about as much impact as Tamsin apparently had on Gawain's heart. Tears hovered behind her eyes, but she refused to cry anymore. She was tougher than that. She'd proved as much lately.

A knock came at the door. She rose to answer it, but instinct made her hesitate. She sensed something—danger passing by like shadow over moonlight. Silently, Tamsin approached the door on tiptoe. She'd had her share of battle experience in the past few days, but she still played it safe and checked the peephole. No one was there.

Readying another fireball, Tamsin opened the door and looked into the corridor. It was empty. Irritated now, she stepped into the hallway to find a large blue sticky note on the outside of her door. The bottom was folded up to hide the writing. Tamsin reached up, then stood there with her hand poised, wondering if she was going to like what it said.

Summoning her courage, she pulled the note down and flattened it in her hand. The writing was in old-fashioned copperplate script.

Did I not promise you he would get his reward?
I am in your debt for my freedom, but I am gone. Do not look for me.

PS Tell your knights their horses are at the theme park.

Also, the demon sends his thanks for the snack.

- N

Tamsin stared at the note. Nimueh? Since when did fae leave drive-by sticky notes? Yet her mood lightened. The Lady of the Lake had helped them. It felt good to know they'd been able to help her in return.

She looked up to see Gawain getting off the elevator. Someone must have let him in the front door. At the sight of his tall frame, still dressed in full battle array, her heart leaped and sank at once, leaving her feeling queasy. Tamsin drew herself up, standing her ground until he drew near.

"My father's not here," she said.

Gawain stopped. "I did not come to speak to Hector. I came to see you."

A sudden surge of panic flooded Tamsin. She had no idea what to say since he had ended their—whatever it was they had. Too much had happened for anything to feel casual.

So she thrust the note at him. "Look at this. If I'm reading it right, Nimueh has skipped town. Plus, you're up some horses." She stopped, realizing that she was babbling.

"So it seems." Gawain crumpled the note. He'd barely looked at it, only at her. "May I come in?"

Tamsin stepped back, her mouth going dry. "Okay."

She followed Gawain inside, locking the door behind her in case any other roaming fae decided to drop by. Gawain paced her small living space like a caged lion. Not that long ago, they'd been naked in her bed. Not that long ago, they'd been naked in *his* bed, too. She'd thought there was a chance of a relationship, but she'd been so wrong.

They'd had a bargain, and it was over.

Her throat constricted painfully, as if she were imploding inside. "Let me guess. You're sorry, but you're not that into a witch. It's not my fault, it's just you. Plus, it's hard to maintain a relationship when you're always out on a quest."

Gawain frowned. "Don't assume you know what I'm thinking."

"You have your king. I have my books. That's what you said."

He turned to her, folding his arms. "Don't hold those words against me. I was bleeding when I said them."

"And you wouldn't even let me stop it." Tamsin was on a roll. "You got a taste of your own magic out there, and it scared you. You think I'm responsible for that."

"Yes." The one simple word hung in the air, seeming to fill the room.

"That's it?" Fury pushed Tamsin's voice higher. "That's all you've got to say?"

Gawain drew near, putting a finger over her lips. "Let me talk."

No, don't! It was one thing for her to throw bitter words at him, but she couldn't bear the reverse. Angry as Tamsin was, she wanted to stop his mouth with hers so that he would not speak. That way, he couldn't say the words that would break them apart forever. Even a minute's reprieve was something. Whoever preached ripping the bandage off had never been in love with an impossible man.

Panic clawed inside her. There was still a retreat, still a path back to something good for them. Back to the place where they simply *had* to touch each other and where every glance was a heated invitation. They'd been there for such a short time—surely it was worth giving such happiness a fighting chance?

But, reluctantly, Tamsin nodded.

Gawain took her hand in his. "I've told you about some of the things I saw my mother do when I was growing up. I told you about how Lady Bertilak tried to tempt me even though it might mean my death. And you've heard plenty of times about how Merlin's mistakes caused so much damage."

"Yes," Tamsin said in a small voice.

"Well, I've got one more story to tell you about magic in my family. It didn't happen to me, but to Gaheris, one of my middle brothers."

Tamsin braced herself. "Is this going to be awful like the other stories?"

"I don't think so," he said. "But that's for you to judge."

Tamsin looked down, unable to meet his intense blue eyes. "Get on with it, then."

Gawain smiled, his expression touched with nerves. "Early on in his time at the Round Table, Gaheris was tricked by magic into marrying the ugliest crone in the world."

"This story sucks." Tamsin tried to pull away, but Gawain held on fast.

"Have patience. There is a point to this tale."

Tamsin fidgeted, but let him continue.

"The bride's name was Dame Ragnall, and she was witch-born. She was not just unpleasant to look at, she smelled like a dead cat left in the sun for weeks. She was rude and coarse of speech and manner so that no one wished to be in the same room, much less sit with her at a meal. But Gaheris was a man of honor and would not go back on his word. So, he made the witch his one true wife and he swore he would take no other women to his bed. Thus he went to his wedding night anticipating no pleasure."

"Are you saying that's what he got for marrying a witch?"

"I'm saying that he would have been a fool to break his word." Gawain gave her a quelling look. "The tale does not end at the wedding. When Gaheris shut the bedchamber door that night, he was astonished to find his ghastly wife had turned into the most beautiful—not to mention sweet-smelling—woman he had ever encountered. Not only that, her entire manner had changed. She was soft voiced and courteous, full of wit and as much wisdom as the craftiest counselors of the realm. Needless to say, Gaheris was overjoyed by this change and asked his bride what had happened."

"A magic curse," Tamsin said in flat tones.

"Which had been partially lifted because Gaheris had kept his word and taken her to wife. Dame Ragnall told him that because the curse was only half-broken he had a choice—he could have her beautiful at night and ugly during the day, or the other way around. It was a choice between his pride—for what man did not wish everyone to know his lady is the finest above all others?—or his pleasure."

Despite herself, Tamsin was curious. "What did your brother do?"

"The wisest thing in the world," said Gawain. "He trusted her. He told his wife the decision was hers to make."

That wasn't what Tamsin had expected to hear. "And?"

He met her eyes. "That broke the curse entirely, for a woman cannot be her true self if she is subject to another's choices. The fact that he trusted her allowed her beauty to shine."

Tamsin's heart beat fast as she turned the meaning of the story over and over, but she wasn't sure what he meant by it. Gawain reached up, brushing his thumb over her lips.

"I've held on to the terrible things magic has done. When I discovered it was still inside me, I dreaded what it might make me do. I thought it a curse."

"It's not. It's like the bride in the story." Tamsin suddenly understood his meaning. "Act with honor and trust yourself enough to make the right choices, and what is fearful can become our joy. We are the magic we make."

"That's what Ragnall said many, many years ago. I should have listened to her then."

"What happened to them?" Tamsin asked. "Dame Ragnall and your brother?"

"They were the one bright oasis in my family. Ragnall was a beautiful soul and given freedom of choice, she was her true self every hour of the day. My brother Gaheris lived a long and happy life with her. Their love was founded on trust and respect and they spread happiness to all who met them. You won't find his tomb among the stone sleepers. He would not leave her to follow us into the future."

Tamsin felt tears sting her eyes. "That's both beautiful and sad."

"Not sad. Their love was a blessing. That is the kind of magic I want with you. I love you, Tamsin Greene. I will be your true knight as long as you will have me."

She ducked her head, biting her lip to keep it from trembling. He wanted her, magic and all. She'd yearned for that kind of love from him, and he had just laid it at her feet.

A slow smile spread over her lips. "Did you truly think me a wicked witch?"

"Your magic called to mine from the first moment we met. You terrified me."

"Ah," she teased. "You don't think you're too black hearted for me? Corrupting magic could go either way, you know."

"I believe you are my anchor, Tamsin Greene. As long as you're at my side, no evil will ever have power over me." Though he said it with a teasing smile, there was sincerity in his words. He truly needed and loved her.

Tamsin felt the weight of his trust. She slid her arms around him, laying her head against his chest. "I love you, too, Gawain."

Their conversation unraveled after that, but in the best way possible. It deteriorated in the shower, where Tamsin took great pleasure in getting soapy for the second time that afternoon, and crumbled still further as they rumpled the crisp, clean sheets of her bed.

He kissed her slowly, letting his lips linger over hers so that their breath commingled, warmth against warmth. "What sort of magic do you think we can make together?" she asked.

His grin was suddenly sharp with mischief. It was an expression Tamsin hadn't seen before, and it made her insides tighten with anticipation. He took her hand, kissing the tip of each finger in a way that made her squirm with pleasure. Who knew such a simple sensation could travel so deep into her core? Then his lips found her wrist, his tongue darting to mark the fine veins beneath her skin. The brush of his cheek was rough as he worked his way upward, nibbling the crease of her elbow, then the curve of her shoulder. Gawain had a way of devouring every inch of her, leaving nothing without savoring its delights. He understood what it was to claim a woman.

Tamsin shifted, leaving a kiss on his chest as she rolled him onto his back. Indulgent, Gawain complied, even lifting her so that she straddled him more easily.

"Let me," she said, brushing his sex with hers. Already stiff, it hardened yet more at her touch, weeping as she swept across the engorged tip. Gawain grabbed her hips, holding her still. Tamsin settled, positioning herself to sink, inch by languorous inch, until she was stretched wide and full.

Gawain reached up, cupping her breasts. His eyes were slits, the blue veiled by thick lashes until the color was lost in smoky shadow. Tamsin rocked slowly so she could lean into his touch. His neck muscles corded, throat working as he controlled his response. From above, she could trace the angles of his face with her gaze. She felt a lost, desperate tenderness for him then, a longing to be with him in every sense of the word.

His fingers brushed the tips of her breasts, bringing her nipples erect. The sensation made her shiver, and that translated from her body to his. She rocked again, finding a rhythm that matched his kneading hands. The feel of his rough palms was too exquisite, too much, but he gave no quarter, driving her further into madness.

"More," she said.

"Always."

He was thrusting, drawing her into a riptide she couldn't resist. She was caught on a knife's edge, wanting more, wanting less, rocking deeper to end the driving need for relief. She burned, her skin slick with sweat and the need to have him touch it all. Tamsin grabbed his strong, thick arms, using him to steady her movements. The first pulses of release shot through her, ripping a moan from her throat. Gawain pushed hard, driving her higher until she shuddered, every nerve igniting with pleasure. A moment of blind wonder took her.

And yet it didn't end there. They rolled in a tangle with her arms locked around his shoulders. Before the pleasure had even faded, Gawain was moving again, thrusting deeper, faster, returning her to ecstasy. She gripped hard, nails scraping skin as she arched against him. One last, strong stroke, and they fell into bliss together.

"Tamsin," Gawain murmured softly. "Tamsin."

She couldn't move for the longest time. Didn't want to. Her head was cushioned on Gawain's shoulder. His arm curled around her, pulling her close.

She laced her fingers through his. "That's the sort of magic we'll make together."

"That was just the first line of the spell," he murmured, and caught her mouth with his. "Every word, every line, every verse will be a declaration of my desire."

"I heard they call you Silver Tongue."

"As long as they also call my words true. I am yours to command, Tamsin Greene. Whatever you desire, you shall have it."

She laced her fingers through his, utterly content. "I want this."

"Then on my honor, I am yours," Gawain promised. "Forever."

* * * * *

Afterword

The legends about Arthur, Merlin and the knights of Camelot come down to us from a variety of times and places. Not surprisingly, various versions of the stories don't always agree on who did what or why. The only thing that's certain is that the folks in Arthur's court led extremely complicated lives.

I have simplified a few things and tweaked others to fit my story. The character of Gawain—hotheaded and proud, but unfailingly loyal—is fundamentally as I found him in legend. I'm glad I was able to give him a good home in our time with someone able to match his generous spirit.

REQUEST YOUR FREE BOOKS!
2 FREE NOVELS PLUS 2 FREE GIFTS!

H HARLEQUIN®

INTRIGUE

BREATHTAKING ROMANTIC SUSPENSE

HI15